～ JOURNEY TO ～
MARTA'S FAITH
A STORY OF DETERMINATION AND RESOLUTION

BETH TORRES JOHNSON

WESTBOW
PRESS®
A DIVISION OF THOMAS NELSON
& ZONDERVAN

This is a work of fiction. All of the characters, names, incidents,
organizations, and dialogue in this novel are either the products
of the author's imagination or are used fictitiously.

WestBow Press books may be ordered through
booksellers or by contacting:

WestBow Press
A Division of Thomas Nelson & Zondervan
1663 Liberty Drive
Bloomington, IN 47403
www.westbowpress.com
844-714-3454

Scripture taken from the New King James Version® Copyright ©
1982 by Thomas Nelson. Used by permission. All rights reserved.

ISBN: 978-1-6642-2570-1 (sc)
ISBN: 978-1-6642-2571-8 (hc)
ISBN: 978-1-6642-2569-5 (e)

Library of Congress Control Number: 2021904128

Print information available on the last page.

WestBow Press rev. date: 3/19/2021

This book is dedicated to the good Lord, who walked beside me in all my endeavors. To Audie May, a wonderful and loving mother-in-law who taught me so much about God's Word. To my husband of forty-four years, Reese, who has been patient and supportive of my many ventures. And to my children, Lisa, Crystal, and Jere, for their patience and support of my work for the Lord.

Special thanks to Gunnery Sgt. A. Johnson, United States Marine Corps (retired), for sharing his invaluable knowledge of military life in time of war.

Contents

Chapter 1

Beginning of Sorrows

July 1952

Marta protested, flipping her raven-black braid off her shoulder and wiping the sweat off her forehead with the back of her hand. Alice, her mother, couldn't understand why Marta had to be so stubborn. The summer heat exhausted both of them. Across the street next to Aunt Ellen's house, someone was playing honky-tonk music, "Don't Stay Away," a Lefty Frizzell tune. The amplified melody added to the laziness summer produced. Even the farm animals stayed under the shade of the trees, not wanting to eat, though their hunger pangs told them it was dinnertime.

Marta looked out the kitchen window. No longer could she see miners driving to the mines or hear the copper ore mine explosions or trucks carrying heavy loads out of the Arizona mountains. The road in front of their parsonage was empty and lifeless, a ghost town in the making. The only sounds she heard were those of buzzing flies and her own sobbing noises. She turned around and took a seat at the large kitchen table.

The frenzied flies flew through the parsonage's open windows; the screens had been removed long ago. Earlier, Alice had ordered her seventeen-year-old daughter, Marta, to air out the house, hoping to remove the summer heat out of the fanless home. The parsonage contained no cooling system of any kind because it had no electricity.

"I won't go. I won't." Marta continued arguing with her mother as hot tears flowed down her rosy cheeks. "Someone needs to be here waiting for Phil. The Korean War could end at any day; they'll be sending him home, and he's going to find it abandoned."

"That's no problem. We'll arrange for Aunt Ellen to watch for him." Alice spoke calmly through her daughter's hysteria.

"What if he gets lost trying to locate us and can't find us? And what about Grandmother? I can stay and care for her while she's recovering from her stroke. There's no need for her to stay with Aunt Ellen. Please, Mom, let me stay," Marta said stubbornly, her rebellion showing she cared for her family.

"Since you turned seventeen, you've become disobedient and doubtful, especially of your religious belief. Have faith in God, girl; it'll be all right. Aunt Ellen will look after Grandmother and wait for Phil. We shouldn't be gone forever, I don't think. You need to stop acting childish!" Alice reprimanded with a heavy heart.

"What? You don't know either!" Marta whined.

John, Marta's dad, stood on the parsonage's front porch with the younger children: Julian, age fifteen; Daniel, age twelve; and Linda, age five. He didn't want to meddle in this female affair, though he felt guilty for causing it. Even with the shut door, they could hear the argument through the parlor's open window.

Alice paced the kitchen floor. "Marta, I'm telling you, things will work out. We'll get through this, but as of now, money is tight. Since the copper mine closed, most everyone in the church has left. There won't be any more tithes. How are we supposed to survive? There aren't any jobs in this small town—not for Dad's skills, anyway." Alice worried she'd not be able to calm her daughter's fears.

"Why did Dad have to be a pastor? So he'd be poor the rest of his life? Couldn't he have found a different line of work?" Marta sobbed hysterically, wiping her tears on her sleeves.

"Shame on you! God called your dad into the ministry. When He calls, we must answer and do His bidding." Alice wondered about her daughter's rebellious state. She turned to the kitchen window. The flower and herb gardens leading down to the front drive way were drying up due to the lack of water. The road down from it was empty. A small shed stood off to the right of the gardens, and the bright, late-afternoon sunshine beating off its aluminum roof stung her weary eyes. They were drained from her crying earlier that morning. She too was sick to her stomach at having to leave their home of seventeen years. There was no guarantee they'd be returning.

"So what you're telling me is that God has called Dad to go to California! That's why we're moving?" Marta fingered the table's wooden top, pressing hard to keep her trembling from showing. The grave news of their sudden move pounded in her head. Since Dad had met with the family last night, notifying them of the move, she'd not slept well. She was tired and irritable.

"I can tell you that we're being pushed out of the parsonage, the church, and the town by God's loving plans. He's allowing what has happened with our finances to move us out. Otherwise we'll die here. We don't see the reason why this is happening, but someday we'll have the answer." Alice spoke softly, trying to keep any alarm out of her voice.

"No, no, y'all taught us to have faith and believe God's meeting our needs. I don't understand. Can't we stay here and have faith God will bring people back? It's not fair to do this to Phil and Grandmother."

John, inundated with the angry words he was hearing, went inside. "Alice, you and Marta need to stop this bickering. Marta, we can't change what happened to the copper mine. But I hoped you'd trust us to do the right thing for the family. As our finances dwindled, I sought God's will for us."

"Dad, it's not fair. Why did this have to happen during my senior year? Worst is having it happen while Phil is gone and Grandmother isn't well enough to travel."

"Listen, Marta. This is God's will. I was in my prayer closet praying for wisdom and God's plans for us, and I was impressed to go to California. I went to the mountains and sought solitude with the Lord, to ask confirmation for His will. Well, a week ago, I was in the store, and posted on the window was a help-wanted poster advertising work in California. The San Joaquin Valley contains work of every variety. The farmers need laborers in the fields. I sought such an answer." His expression was one of gratitude.

"But, Dad, you always said your calling was here in Organ Pipe Cactus Wilderness. Arizona isn't such a terrible place. We have our friends, relatives, and school, and our little library at the store—everything we need is here. One more thing," Marta blubbered, breathing erratically as she tried to pull herself together. "Every time you've been on the mountain chopping firewood these last few weeks, we were scouting for cypress trees. We were thinking of Christmas here at the parsonage with our family and friends. How can we walk away from our traditions and lifestyle so suddenly?"

"Marta, you're working yourself up for nothing. God has us in His care. You need to stop this arguing right now!" Her dad had had enough of her teary-eyed debate and her insensitivity to their problem.

In the meantime, outside on the porch, Julian had his ear pinned to the window. "What a big crybaby!" he declared to Daniel and Linda. "Can't she get it? It'll be fun and adventurous. That sissy!" Julian was sullen. Before returning to listen, he pulled Linda's braids. "Scoot over. I was here first." After pushing her away, he scowled, freckles gathering tightly around his broad nose.

"We might walk into the enemy's camp!" Marta could barely speak as the pain in her chest choked her words. She crossed her arms on the table, placed her head on them, and sobbed out loud. The sudden news of moving from her home of seventeen years was devastating.

Her mother hugged her, holding her until her bawling stopped. "Dear, one more thing—you don't have to fear the unknown. Whatever trials we go through will strengthen and grow our faith. Trust me, Daughter. Your frustration will ease as blessings come our way in the new home. You'll see God's love as you've never experienced." Alice didn't understand Marta's rebellion and prayed silently. *It has to be so. Please, dear Lord, send us Your blessings.*

"Yes, Marta. I've taught you and everyone in my congregation that no matter our predicament, God is always there. Surely you know that by now." Dad kissed the top of her head.

"I have faith, but that's exactly it. Would God move us out so suddenly in the middle of family trials? It's not fair! My faith lies in this home with all of us being together; I wouldn't know how to use my faith anywhere else. I can't understand this change. I'm worried I won't be able to adjust, keep my faith, and believe in blessings for our family's well-being."

"Quit being so lurid. I've heard enough," Dad admonished, hoping if he showed his anger, she'd stop her tantrum.

"I'm sorry, Dad, but I can't. It's too much to bear with my conscience. Good times with my family give me strength, hope, and joy! I can't see any future in this valley. It sounds like a bowl of dust, and come winter, you say it'll fill with something you call fog." Marta stopped her whimpering and starred at the empty table. Alice began pulling out a loaf of bread and meatloaf from the cold box.

Heavenly Father, help me not to lose my faith in You. Give me a vision filled with hope to carry me during this change. Amen. Marta thought to herself. It was God's will for her to receive a dream, but would it be as she'd requested, or would it be as God desired for her? She felt her methods for meeting goals would encourage and strengthen her ideals to create a brighter future. She had yet to learn of God's faithfulness.

Chapter 2

The Move

Marta stared at Aunt Ellen's house across the street as they packed their belongings. It was August 1, and the dry air pulled moisture from her eyes, causing them to itch. What they couldn't take with them was piled in the shed. Breakable items, like the kerosene lamps, were carefully packed with old rags and placed in wooden boxes, which sat in the back of the seven-foot trailer the old station wagon would be pulling.

There was enough space in the trailer to pack a few pieces of furniture, some dishes, a small round table used to hold an oil lamp, mattresses, and frame rails. Also added were four used tires to change flats during the trip.

"Alice, we can't haul any more. We've gotta cross the steep Tehachapi Mountains before we hit the valley," John said worriedly, noticing the kitchen chair Alice had brought out. "If we're overloaded, we might not make the climb. I can't risk that."

Alice winced and stopped as if to think about his remark. "Well," Alice said after sighing, "God has to provide a dining set for us." She stomped back into the house with the chair in her arms.

With Julian's help, John wrapped a canvas tarp over the trailer and tied it down with rope. It was secured enough so the wind wouldn't blow it off and cause an accident. They finished near midnight. John hoped his family might sleep for a few hours before they'd be up and traveling the long journey.

"John, let me clean the parsonage before we leave. It won't take but a few minutes with it being most empty." Alice handed Julian the duster and Marta the broom. "Daniel, here's a pail and wash rags. You'll scrub the windows. I'll scrub inside the cupboards and the wood stove. It won't take but a few minutes if we work together."

John finished pulling out tools from the toolshed and loading them into the back of the station wagon. After finishing late into the night, he walked tiredly into the house. "Let's get some rest," he told his weary family. "Are you all finish doing what you needed to do?"

"Yes. I even made some quick sandwiches and some tea for the trip," Alice said proudly, placing the bag of sandwiches and jar of tea in the empty icebox.

"I'll wake everybody at three. We're leaving at four in the morning. I hope to travel through most of the desert in the cool morning hours before it gets scorching hot. Once the sun comes up, the heat might cause problems for the vehicle. Let's say our prayers and get to bed." John prayed humbly, not knowing what to expect in the journey ahead. The hot morning would arrive quickly. He didn't know how many desert miles the wagon would make before the heat made trouble for the engine and tires.

The inside of the cab was quiet except for the churning of tires and the rumbling of the station wagon's engine.

JOURNEY TO MARTA'S FAITH

Marta couldn't sleep and cried softly in the morning darkness; tears of hopelessness filled her eyes. No one could see her in the back passenger seat leaning against the window, sorrow filling her heart. She placed her Bible in a cotton bag next to her legs and sensed calamity in the family's move to California. The move to the San Joaquin Valley, where plenty of farm work existed for the migrant worker, wasn't her idea of hope.

Fear and dread gripped her nerves. *Lord, Christmas is a few months away; the family might be ill prepared for it this year.* She questioned their destiny. *Could it be that happy times together are gone forever*? These and many more fear-based questions haunted her. *Perhaps we'll return home later and reunite once again.* She didn't know what awaited them and tried thinking of their old place and the things she loved. She'd find comfort in these memories.

She thought back to their parsonage. She pictured the small barn behind the home that housed a few chickens, a couple of cows, and goats. The animals had provided eggs and fresh milk. The garden pots filled with store-bought soil contained vegetables and flowers, and they were her favorite. The cacti in the backyard provided them with fresh cacti palms, a plant they used as a vegetable side dish. Its fruit, the prickly pear, was a favorite for fruit salads. A few olive trees provided berries for canning, and they pressed the seeds for cooking oil.

There, Marta felt secured from the infringements of the world. The familiar desert and mountains seemed to offer hope for their future. They were a hill-country family satisfied with their simple lifestyle.

Marta loved her small community and appreciated

the townspeople's friendliness and their faith in God. No other town could replace the security and contentment she felt there with the people she saw as family. Their morals, ideas, and traditions were also her beliefs and customs. The love she felt for them, grounded in their unity and respect for each other, couldn't be shaken.

They celebrated the Christmas holiday together when, on Christmas Eve, they visited homes and dropped off gifts of food. All wrongdoings committed against one another were forgiven, especially Julian's manipulations against his family and the business owners.

She thought of the cypresses in Arizona, an evergreen harvested yearly for their Christmas celebrations. She remembered their delicate, short blue-gray needles and stems with resin glands, which produced a long-lasting fragrance that always reminded her of joyful family gatherings. No other conifer ignited such passions as did this tree.

The family was torn apart. The closing of the mine had disrupted their lives. Everything seemed to be coming to a close for Marta. The Korean War had begun last June with thousands of young American men drafted, including Phil. He'd been gone for over a year, and only a few of his letters reached them. One took several months to travel across the oceans, where it then made its way into the family's isolated town. She missed hearing from him and couldn't bear losing him forever.

She and Phil, as the eldest of the children, helped their mother carry the burden of raising the three younger kids and assisting with many other chores. Phil's main concern was Julian; he could handle him when Julian became mean and spiteful. He always worried Marta wouldn't be able to control him when he and his dad ran errands. Leaving Julian with her was like leaving her with a cask of lit powder, ready to explode.

Marta attempted to influence him with moral behavior, even at the expense of suffering his brimstone and fire. She felt it was essential for her to stop his pranks before he destroyed their reputation in town. He'd caused many of the town's people to lose faith in their father's work. A few townsfolk respected their family, but only by the grace of God. Their dad, the local minister, had warned his children not to bring ill repute upon their name or the Lord. Marta could see that Julian didn't care. He hoped only to please his narcissistic personality.

Marta sat quietly, reflecting on their move. She glanced out her car window and saw darkness. There was a new concern for her. *Will our old rig make it to California's San Joaquin Valley with its heavy load?* Darkness hid the scenery around the vehicle. The road was empty except for a few rabbits running through the beam of the headlights. *There might be no one to help us if the vehicle breaks down along the way.* It was the long, isolated stretch of loneliness that worried her.

The move had caused Marta to retain as many memories as her mind was able. She remembered her grandmother's paralyzing stroke and was glad the woman had stayed with Aunt Ellen. She hated how Julian had deliberately announced the news of Phil's leaving to Grandmother when everyone else in the family was keeping it a secret, so as not to hurt her. In his deceptive, uncivil manner, Julian wanted to deliberately hurt her, telling her that her favorite grandson was overseas and that she wouldn't be seeing him soon, and perhaps never again. How cruel was that? *Perhaps it was out of jealousy for Phil,* Marta speculated.

Aunt Ellen, who'd been in the hallway, had heard his conversation with Grandmother but wasn't alarmed until she'd heard a loud, thumping sound. She ran into her room and found her sprawled on the floor. "Children, come help me! Something has happened to Grandmother," she'd hollered. After they'd helped her to bed, Ellen had pulled Marta aside and explained what Julian had said. "I think he meant it as a callous joke, but it's terrible what happened to her." Ellen had seen many of Julian's mean deeds against Marta and her siblings and understood his abusive behavior. But had he crossed the line on that day when he'd caused Grandmother's stroke?

Trying to understand his attitude wasn't easy. Ellen felt pity for the kids. He could be such a likable boy around their parents and be pure evil behind their backs. And why had he mentioned Phil's absence to Grandmother? Ellen hoped he'd behave with Marta, Daniel, and Linda after she returned home. John and Alice would soon be back from their missionary work and would be sorry they hadn't been there for Grandmother.

Ellen hated seeing how cruel Julian could be, yet like the other children, she never told Alice or John of his bullying conduct. Since Phil had left, she and Marta had noticed how deceitful and meaner he'd become. Ellen hoped his parents would find out and discipline him. She preferred the children tell their parents about his conduct; she figured it would have more meaning that way.

Marta continued to recall that dreadful day of her grandmother's stroke. She could still see the pain on Linda's face. "Grandma, take my doll; she'll be your friend.

You gotta get well!" Linda had cried at seeing her unable to respond. A year later, Grandmother still suffered from the effects of the stroke, though there was movement in her limbs, and she was mumbling brief sentences. Marta remembered the child's words and her tear-filled eyes. *She hurts as I do.* Marta wondered and worried about her young sister, whom she loved dearly.

The words of malice toward Grandmother, in Marta's opinion, had been the worst prank Julian had ever pulled. She remembered how Aunt Ellen had taken him outside and given him a scolding about his uncaring attitude. He had laughed and run off up a hill, behind the church. Fierce indignation was revealing a rebellious and irresponsible person in the fifteen-year-old boy. Things were to get worse between Julian and Marta. She prayed she could withstand him until God changed his attitude. *But will he listen to God?*

With so much loss behind her, Marta's grief was profound. She was torn with doubt and uncertainty. There was a slight relief for her in that Aunt Ellen would keep the family posted on any letters arriving from Phil, plus she would assist Grandmother. Still, the pain she felt in her heart and the nagging thoughts of the move penetrated her conscience and were too difficult to erase.

She thought back to her argument with her parents the week before they'd left Arizona. "Mom, settling in before Christmas is tough. We can't suddenly change and adopt a new lifestyle. It'll be hard picking up our traditions and daily routines. Will we have our family gathered in time for the holiday?" While fixing her eyes on the darkness around the rig, she spoke loudly for her mother to hear her. "Ma, do you think we'll find a conifer tree in the valley?"

Marta sat forward, waiting for her mother's response. "Mom, did you hear me?"

"Marta, get your mind off those thoughts. We have enough on our minds without having to worry about the future." Alice leaned her head back against the seat and peered out her window. The darkness was intimidating, yet she spoke with confidence so that Marta might not sense her fears.

"We gotta have a cypress tree. It's the reminder of everything we believe: hope through God, peace, joy, and family good times," Marta stated adamantly.

Alice tried to appease her daughter's concerns. "Look, Marta, the mountains near the valley are filled with conifer trees of every variety. I'm sure we'll find pine, juniper, fir, Douglas, or most any kind. When it's time, God will provide. Quit worrying," she said exhaustedly, considering it an inappropriate conversation for the time and place.

Though impressed with her mother's scope of knowledge of such trees, Marta wished she understood her reasons for wanting a cypress. *My faith lies in this tree. What type of conifer will we use for our first Christmas in the valley? This move has turned our lives upside down.*

The anxiety of having a cypress or conifer tree for Christmas didn't end. She resigned herself to solve this mystery before Christmas Eve, the night of their traditional celebration. Hopefully it would be with family and friends.

Chapter 3

Remembering Phil

A new thought occurred to Marta as the station wagon rumbled its way across the dark, lonely desert road. *Will Phil find us when he returns——if he returns?* "Dad, you said they drafted Phil. What does 'draft' mean? We studied it in class, but I'm still not sure what it means." She spoke calmly, hoping her parents wouldn't detect her grief. She wished that whatever the word meant, it hadn't applied to Phil. But it had.

The sun's absence did little to ward off the warmth already infiltrating the vehicle on this stifling August day, and Marta's thoughts and conversations kept her from boredom and feeling the agony from the heat.

"The draft is a way of filling the military ranks when the government requires soldiers. Young men like your brother are called upon to serve their country. Unfortunately, the Korean War came unexpectedly, and none of us were ready for the draft to happen." Dad spoke in a solemn, deep voice.

Marta wished this recruitment had never occurred so that Phil could've come with them.

"I know what it means another way. Our teacher

explained it," Julian remarked, intruding on their conversation. He gave his explanation without being asked to do so. "The American armed forces needed replacement soldiers, so our government started this system of recruitment." He turned and grinned at Marta, his high eyebrows arched with pride.

Noticing his grin, she wondered whether he meant it out of kindness, vanity, or spite. She could only guess. One thing she understood about this ordeal of the draft was that she couldn't blame Phil for registering with the army and receiving orders to go.

"Dad, do you think Phil's mail will continue being late because of poor weather over there in Korea? Remember, he mentioned in his last letter a monsoon season they were expecting." Marta remembered the words she'd read.

She also remembered their joy upon getting a letter. "We got a letter from Phil!" They'd all jumped with glee at seeing the envelope. They had been glad he was all right. It stated his unit would move somewhere toward northern Korea as they pushed the intruders away from the south before the New Year. Despite fighting heavy scrimmages, they were hoping for a victory. Hopefully, they could move before thick snows fell.

John and his family wrote one last letter upon leaving. They had notified Phil of their move to California. Even so, they had no way of knowing whether he'd received their mail. John had his doubts but didn't express them.

Marta prayed that they would hear from him again before December. "Mom, do you think Phil will join us in California in time for Christmas?" she asked over the humming of the old rig, hoping her mother would give her an assuring answer, refilling her with hope for her family's unification.

"I don't know. We can only trust God to help him come home as soon as possible," Alice replied, trying to sound hopeful.

"Surely they have to allow the soldiers furlough, don't they, Dad?"

"I'm sure they'll give him leave soon. Marta, quit worrying so much. Now, go to sleep; it'll be daylight soon." Her dad concentrated on the road ahead, hiding fears that also raged inside his mind.

The children's soft snores kept Marta awake, allowing her to listen to the soft music playing over the radio Alice had turned on. Every tune reminded her of Phil. He loved listening to secular music. She was glad the station wagon's engine sounded healthy. But how healthy was it? *Blazing heat could hinder the engine's operation. God has us in His care. Gotta stop fretting.* She'd try enjoying crossing the desert and finding the beauty within it.

Chapter 4

The Journey

"John, are you sure the radiator and tires will hold up on this trip?" Alice whispered, hoping the children wouldn't hear the doubt in her voice.

"Yes, yes, I've told you over a dozen times. It's in great shape; don't worry. Besides, we've plenty of water jugs in case the radiator gets steamin' hot, and there are four spare tires in the back trailer. I'm sure we've prepared well." John grimaced and hoped he was right.

"But, John, the tires are bald. Are they gonna hold up?" Alice squirmed in her seat.

"Yes, they're in good shape. You and Marta should relax and try getting some sleep. Worryin' only adds to your stress. God knows where He's takin' us. Everything is in His care."

"John, we're short on cash, with barely enough for gas and a couple weeks' worth of groceries. There's no extra money for expensive car repairs."

"Alice, quit fussin'. Get some rest; you're tired. You spent a lot of time cleanin' the parsonage, and for what reason? No one's ever gonna live there. I believe no one wants to do God's work anymore. But that's over. Honey, please go to sleep."

Marta strained to hear her parents' conversation while pretending to sleep, and her doubt penetrated deeper. *Oh, God, please help us!* She glimpsed back at the eastern horizon they were leaving. A soft band of pale blue outlined the hills, indicating the sun would soon rise.

Meanwhile, darkness lurked outside her window. The road was empty except for a few rabbits running through the beam of the headlights. By the heat penetrating inside the vehicle, Marta felt as if it was already noon and not five in the morning.

She could faintly make out Joshua trees, their arms rising to meet the star-studded sky. They reminded her of an illustration she'd once heard in Bible school. It stated that Joshua trees seemed to raise their arms as if worshipping God. *Perhaps I should also praise Him in hopes of high and wondrous expectations in the new land?*

Before leaving their home, John had reminded them that the car, journey, and new home were all in God's hands. They must have faith in a faithful God. Marta tried to remember his words. As a preacher, he knew how to explain God's will for them. Still, Marta was fearful of the unknown. She couldn't imagine how God would provide for them, or whether his plans included reuniting the family again.

Linda woke up. After rubbing her tired eyes, she said, "I dreamed we had a Christmas tree in our new home. Marta, will the valley have pine trees?" Her childish voice was scarcely audible. Linda released a deep breath, exhaling the weariness out of her body. She was too young

19

to understand the difference in the many varieties of coniferous used during the holiday season, so she called them all Christmas trees.

Pink and orange sunlight spread across the desert as the sun rose above the eastern horizon. Marta made out the child's longing eyes, but she couldn't provide an answer. She didn't know. As she pulled the child closer to her window, she wanted her to see the beauty of the serene desert in dawn's morning light. Hundreds of creosote bushes swayed their oily branches as the wind drifted lazily over them. "Ah, smell that creosote, Linda. It smells like kerosene oil. It's heavy in the air!"

"Uh-huh," the child answered half asleep, not excited over the petroleum odor.

"And just look at those Joshua trees. They are bigger than life-size men, standing straight and still—like soldiers guarding us, or maybe escorting us out of Arizona. They're like brave Joshua in our Sunday school lessons."

Marta was melodramatic. She needed concrete evidence that they were in good hands and needed to remain confident. She didn't want to cave into fears or hopelessness, yet a part of her worried about Dad.

He wasn't a mechanic or handyman by trade, and if something broke, he'd be hard-pressed to fix it, especially their old rig. Trusting her dad's knowledge of fixing things wasn't easy. Remembering how he and Phil had overhauled the motor before Phil had left, made her relax. Thankfully, Phil had had an internship with the local mechanic back home and had learned the dynamics of car engines. *I'm so glad he helped Dad replace the motor.*

"Marta, will we find a pine tree for Christmas in

California?" Linda asked again. Still, Marta couldn't answer because she was in deep meditation.

Her concentration was now on the soft pink and orange sunshine creeping higher in the sky, casting a bright glow over the desert. Surely it had settled on their old home by now, publicizing its emptiness. The scene before her brought her thoughts back to their present state. The outside view was breathtaking. She never tired of seeing the desert country or any landscape nature had designed.

"I'm glad the sun is up," Linda declared.

"Yeah, now we can see how to fix this rig if it breaks down," Julian retorted glumly. He dropped his head against the glass window and stared at the back of the thick red seat in front of him. It kept him out of view from his dad's stare in the rearview mirror. His dad wouldn't see his obnoxious facial expressions he was making at Marta.

Marta kept quiet because she wasn't in the mood for talking. She tried reminding herself that God was moving them somewhere else because he had a mission for them, yet she wondered about this valley in California. *Why there, O' Lord?* She'd heard it had lush fields filled with crops of all sorts: fruits, vegetables, nuts, wheat, barley, and cotton. But they knew nothing about working with such vegetation.

"Just think, Alice," Dad said. "By late this afternoon, we'll be in Somerville. I can't wait to start lookin' for work. That community holds much promise for newcomers. Don't you agree, dear?"

Marta overheard the talk. To her, it sounded like he too needed assurance they were making the right decision. A deep pain hit the bottom of her stomach: it was fear making her gut coil and pull. While gripping her belly with the palms of her hands, she tried not to think of her dad's meeting with the family the week before they'd left, but the pain of that night still rang with fear for her.

"Alice, children," she remembered him saying, "I wanna let you know that we'll be leavin' for California next week. I know it's a sudden decision, but I received a letter from Sam Fowlerte." Dad had announced this as they'd sat at the table.

"I remember him," Julian had interrupted. "He's that man who stopped in for Sunday service last month while on vacation out here."

"Yes, he's the one. He wrote and told me there's plenty o' work in California. He has a rental we can rent for a small fee. The cottage will serve our purpose as we settle in the valley."

"John, it's a rash decision. Shouldn't we have time to think and pray first?" Mom had stated with fearful eyes.

"I have prayed 'bout it and believe it's God's will for us to leave. Listen, Alice, the congregation is trifling out. We've no other income 'cept tithes the people give. The copper mine has played out; everyone here is outta work. They'll be leavin' too."

"Yes, but John," Alice had started, looking like she wanted to cry. Marta remembered her teary eyes.

Dad had interrupted her. "No! There is no question about it. We'll be leavin' next week." His six-foot frame stood rigid. "Besides, it's summer vacation for the kids. There's no better time to make this transition. One more thing: work in the valley is goin' to slow down as fall approaches. We hafta hurry if we're gonna git work!"

He'd tried to calm the family's fears but also explain his urgency for leaving so soon.

Marta remembered her words to him, how she didn't want to go. But instead of convincing him to let her stay, she had only incited Linda with fear.

"Me too. I'm scared. I don't wanna go!" Linda had exclaimed, whale-size tears pouring down her chubby cheeks.

Dad knew how frightened they all were. They were making a monumental move that would change their lives either for the better or the worse. He also knew that his bewildered family trusted him, and he couldn't betray their trust.

Marta couldn't forget the ominous shadows in the kitchen that night. The light of the kerosene lamp elongated them against the wall and ceiling, teasing her thoughts with insecurities.

"Dad, if we stay here in Arizona, I could find work. Being seventeen has many advantages." Marta had tried sounding convincing.

"No, young lady. The answer is no!" He was adamant about his decision. Usually the family voted on circumstances, but not on the day he'd announced the dreadful news. He would not hear of it. He was in a rush to beat the valley's ending harvest and settle into the rental before dense fogs rolled in.

"Dad, what about Phil?" Marta had exclaimed.

He hadn't answered due to thinking of things that would only confuse them. He had kept his feelings to himself and had changed the subject quickly so as not to seem heartless.

Marta couldn't sleep that hot night as the summer

heat, and her thoughts, suffocated her. *I hate Dad's plans. No one can vote. It's unlike him to make such a rash decision without our support.* In her fear-ridden mind, a deep sadness had overcome her. How engrained would this grief become in her mind?

Chapter 5

Entering California

John and Alice were silent, and Marta didn't like it. Something had to be wrong. *Why aren't they talking? They can't understand my viewpoints on this situation. They're losing so much. It seems senseless to move to a place we don't even know exists. Trust them, trust them.* She talked herself into a whimper. After placing her face into a geometric Navajo blanket wrapped around her and Linda, she fell asleep.

Through the rearview mirror, her dad had noticed her sad demeanor but said nothing. He left Marta to her thoughts and wondered himself, *What unforeseen events lay ahead? Help us, O Lord. You know best.* Then he turned his full attention to the road ahead.

Marta awakened to the feeling of cramped toes. The small compartment was getting to her. She threw her pillow over her seat and felt a little more comfortable, though it was still difficult stretching out her legs and feet. She was glad to be sitting next to a window. There was no reason to whine about her dilemma. Daniel and Linda, sitting between her and Julian, had it the worst. She knew they too were feeling the same tightness of space. Marta consoled herself that the drive would soon end.

"We're enterin' California," Dad hollered over the radio's static. "Honey, wake up! Alice, look—we made it to California. Isn't it grand?"

Marta stared at the surrounding scenery. It appeared identical to the Arizona desert they had just left.

"Mom, when do you think it'll get cool?" Marta hoped to hear *soon* as the answer.

"Well, probably when we get into the Tehachapi Mountains. They lead into the valley. I hope so, anyway. It'll be a nice change for us this time of year." Alice looked into the distance ahead. It didn't provide much of an answer for Marta, but she knew that any cooling down would be better than the blistering heat.

Outside, the wind had picked up, with bursts of sand blowing around the vehicle. Marta stared at the sparse bushes lining the road ahead. Their waving branches created mystical images as if hurrying the family on their journey. The unknown country ahead was daunting to her imagination.

Then she looked behind and thought of home, sitting sorrowfully empty. "Mom, we'll miss our home, church, the barn, and animals. We were self-sustaining. And when Dad killed a deer during hunting season, it provided extra food, helping us financially. Now, our home and lifestyle are far behind. Have you considered the life we'll lead now?" Marta envisioned their home abandoned in the clay valley beneath the Organ Pipe Cactus hills, never to be occupied again.

"I know, dear. But your dad has made a good bargain

on a rental. It's in a town called Somerville. This town is big enough that we can make a decent living there."

"Mom, this place, Somerville—we know nothing about it or its people. What if they don't like our customs or attitudes, or we don't like theirs? How will we handle this problem? I don't know whether we'll be able to adjust to their traditions or culture. And what if they detest our family and run us out of town?" Marta's eyes filled with hot tears, and her body trembled with fear.

"We'll add this concern to our daily prayers, honey. Only God knows what's ahead for our family. He won't let us stray away from His blessings. You need to relax."

"But, Mom, we are leaving so much more than our home, not to mention our relatives." Marta sobbed.

"Yes, that's true. But look at it this way: there'll be wonderful possibilities too. We'll get our routines back, and we'll have a nice place. Later, God willing, we'll purchase a home. We will!" Alice tried sounding optimistic.

"How much farther till we get to Somerville?" Marta asked, rubbing the sleep out of her eyes.

Dad didn't have time to answer when they heard a popping sound. The vehicle began swerving on the road, and maneuvering was difficult. "Hang on, everyone. We have a flat!" He controlled the steering wheel as well as he could and applied the brakes gently, and the vehicle was soon safely off the pavement. The sandy-topped ground was packed hard enough to give the vehicle traction.

"Whoa, that was unexpected." Dad got out and began inspecting the damage. "Julian, get out and help me unload the trailer. There are spare tires in the bottom."

Julian did as he was told, moaning softly when his dad wasn't looking. After throwing his pillow at Marta, he stretched out his long legs and let them fall to the sandy ground with a thud. He ambled to the back of the trailer, wishing the flat hadn't occurred.

"Oh, man! Why did it have to happen here? I haven't seen but one gas station since we left home." Julian spoke with a tone of anger and glanced around, hoping to see a vehicle coming so he could flag it down for help. *They'd help Dad with the tire,* he whispered to himself. He was weary from the drive and didn't feel up to helping.

"I'm glad there's daylight to see by, but I can't say I appreciate this heat." Julian wiped moisture from his eyes so as to see what was in the trailer. "I can't imagine how much hotter the day will get. Hopefully this day will end soon, and we'll be in the rental before dark falls." He pulled out one of the tires, inspected it, and said, "Dad, this tire is nearly bald. You think it'll hold for a long while? And look—it's one of the better ones." Julian turned the tire over and around, checking for sturdiness. He picked it up waist high and dropped it as if it were a ball he could bounce.

"Well, at least it's aired up enough." He rolled the tire next to the flat and prepared to help without complaining— not too loudly, anyway.

"Julian don't you go sayin' anything about the tire to your ma. You mustn't worry her any more than she already is. You hear?"

"Yeah, yeah, I hear. Don't you worry none. I'm goin' to be thinkin' about getting to the new place and taking a long nap. I can't wait."

Dad was grumpy and tired and wondered whether Julian was going to keep quiet. This worried him some more. "All right, everyone, get out. I gotta fix this tire," he said wearily. He'd been up half the night loading the trailer while Alice and Marta fixed scrambled egg sandwiches, enough for three meals. They'd not be stopping to buy food, only gas, because money was tight.

The rising sun was relentless, and its hot rays shined upon the rig and its inhabitants. The stifling heat parched their lips and made their throats feel full of sand. Marta, Daniel, Linda, and their mother took refuge behind a Joshua tree, one of the few left on this side of the country. It was barely enough to shelter them from the penetrating morning sunlight.

After fixing the tire, John and Julian checked the radiator's water. Everything seemed all right, and soon they were off traveling again. The barren desert didn't hold a single building anywhere. There were scraggly sage brushes and creosote bushes as far as the eye could see. A few rolling hills lined the desert valley. The desert seemed to be an endless abyss for Marta. "How much longer do we have to travel? And will we ever make it?" she whispered into the window where no one could hear.

Chapter 6

Talents

Marta was leaving her comfort zone. It was coming time for her to grow into her new faith. Alice had been praying for wisdom on how to respond to her daughter's questions. After their family's meeting and hearing of Marta's fears, Alice had taken her aside. The conversation was fresh on Marta's mind.

"Honey, remember this: there are talents, values, boldness, and strength available to you. These gifts have been entrusted to you. They're just waiting for you to grow in your belief."

"Will these talents help me through my coming trials? I was acquainted with all the things that could go wrong living at the parsonage, and I knew how to battle those. But now I feel so unsure of everything ahead. If what you say is true, Mom—and I trust you are—I want to use my faith along with these talents. Do you know why? I wanna help you and Dad with our finances. And I know I gotta have faith to do this."

Marta thought of her mom's words but couldn't see how these gifts or talents might come to fruition in her. She didn't feel any special training existed in her except sewing, cooking, and singing church hymns. As far as she knew, she would end up marrying a minister and living as her mother had lived. She'd be at her husband's disposal. "Mom, I wished this small community offered more in training for young people. I want to help people, and I can do it through teaching or nursing, but we're stuck out here in the boondocks." Marta loved living in the sticks, as some referred to their area. To her, it was home.

"You just remember, the Lord has you in His care. He'll provide what your heart desires. If that is your dream, keep it in prayer. God will answer in His way and in His time." These were the last comforting words her mom had given her before they'd left. They lingered in her mind, along with everything else that had happened to them over the past year.

Lord, don't let me suffer too much as I come to receive and grow in these gifts. Bless our family in a way that suits You best. Amen.

She didn't know whether their journey's outcome would end with a blessing or a curse. It would all depend on her using her talents and faith to pitch in and help. Her fears expanded with every unanswered question. Traveling in the heat added to her anxiety. Desperately, she pulled her Bible from her bag resting next to her feet and began searching for scripture to comfort her. One powerful verse stood out: Isaiah 41:10.

"Fear not, for I am with you;
Be not dismayed, for I am your God.
I will strengthen you,
Yes, I will help you,
I will uphold you with My righteous right hand."
After reading it, she contemplated on God's goodness

and repeated one of her favorite prayers, Psalm 91. A calmness came over her. Talking to God always relaxed her. "Thank You, heavenly Father, for being here with us," she whispered into the sultry air inhabiting the cab.

"Marta, how are you doing back there?" Mom tried to sound as if everything was normal, yet Marta's fears of strangers bothered her. "Marta, remember how easygoing, kind, and friendly you are? These traits will help you adjust. Don't you agree?" Alice was indirectly reminding her daughter not to give in.

Marta couldn't agree; thoughts of the future seemed so muddled. "Mom, do you think we can have a normal life like back home?"

"I don't see why not. It'll be a matter of setting priorities once again and staying focused on them." Alice was glad her daughter's thoughts were on routines and schedules. This was a sign of hope that she'd not given up.

"We can start a priority list at the rental," Daniel interjected.

"That's true," Alice replied. "Just like we did at the parsonage. It'll be a running list of everything we need to do. We'll hang it in the new kitchen and get organized again." Alice felt hope for her children. At least she had one who still carried his wits.

"What will happen to us if we don't establish routines and get rooted again?" While waiting for an answer, Marta bit her fingernails. "You know, Mom, survival routines need to be the first focus. But by the time we get them situated, something evil could overtake us and destroy the people we've become." She looked down at Linda and Daniel. They were sound asleep and wouldn't hear her conversation. She waited for an answer. Alice was quiet.

"Mom, how am I going to use whatever other talents I have to help the family?"

"Marta, you're looking at your own strengths and neglecting to include God in your plans."

"I guess I am, but there are so many unanswered questions that I get distracted."

"Well, Marta, we must trust the Lord; He'll keep us in everything we do."

Marta couldn't let go of her many concerns. She was unaccustomed to outsiders and different lifestyles. Could she handle the upcoming incidents without falling apart? Meanwhile, the morning waned, and noon drew nigh. *I wonder how much longer we must travel? The little ones are tired.* Marta moaned with anticipation. She could hardly wait to see Somerville.

Chapter 7

Travel Fatigue

The heat grew intense as the family sat squeezed into the moving station wagon, their bodies stiff from lack of movement. Music on the radio went silent; later, it came back with a loud static, indicating radio stations were out of range as the car moved farther away from civilization. Marta picked up her Bible but felt it futile trying to read. Travel fatigue was taking its toll on her.

She could either concentrate on her physical pains or the problems facing them ahead. She tried to think of hopeful events that might occur in Somerville, though it was difficult due to not knowing how things worked there. Instead of happy thoughts, she thought of the worst. *What terrifying things will we come to? It's all so sudden, so cruel, like Daniel thrown into the lion's den.* Pain shot up her back. The pillow she'd placed there felt like a boulder.

Her nerves had made her skin crawl, and her back pain caused her hips and shoulders to throb with a sharp ache. Sitting in the same position wasn't easy on her legs either. She wanted to stretch them out, bend her knees, and wiggle her toes. With physical and mental anguish, her anxiety crept in, and her breathing became abrupt. She calmed herself by examining the changing scene, but it didn't stop her anxiety. *Placing my head on my lap might help.* After a while, she stopped thinking wearisome, doubtful thoughts and started breathing again.

She also thought to pray. *Lord, help me accept this new existence. None of us expected this strenuous journey, but it's not the end of our lives. Please continue to provide for us and give us hope. Let me not feel sorry for myself. Remind me to be an anchor for my family. Amen.*

"Well, Marta, will there be pine trees in the valley?" Linda asked again, sighing and not expecting an answer back.

Suddenly, Marta woke up out of her reflections and self-pity. "Why, sure, pumpkin. I'm sure we'll find us a lovely tree. Quit your fussin'. Put your head on my lap and go to sleep." With gentle strokes across Linda's straight dark hair, Marta soothed her to sleep.

Marta pondered the question with great seriousness. *One more thing, Lord: please provide a conifer for our Christmas so we may get rooted in our traditions again.* The word *rooted* gave her confidence. It meant stability, growth in many positive ways, and staunch tenacity not to stray.

Marta had heard her dad give many sermons on being grounded but understood it to be rooted in God's Word. This meant receiving God's protection, guidance, faith, and abundant blessings. She'd also come to understand that being rooted could also apply toward having established routines for performing daily chores, for scheduled meditation, and for finishing schoolwork. It meant having time to fellowship with the people involved with the family. *Ouch!* The pains in her body reminded her of their trip.

Travel fatigue was exhausting her. It seemed to be worse on her mind. Being cooped up with nothing to do allowed her too much unnecessary thinking.

Perplexed, Marta asked, "Mom, why is God allowing this to happen to us?"

"God is leading your dad in doing what is best for the family. He's in charge of our well-being. We have trust he's in God's leading." Her mom exhaled, pulling out a large paper sack filled with sandwiches and fruit from below her legs. She carefully reached over her seat and passed out the food. "Julian, there's a jug of tea behind you. Pull it out so everyone can have a drink, please."

"This isn't comfortable eating in here. Dad, can we pull over and have a break?" Daniel asked in his politest voice.

"Sorry, son. We've gotta make it to Somerville before dark; otherwise, we won't have daylight to see by and unload." John wished they could stop, but time was of the essence. The rental was on hold for one more day. After that, the owner, Mr. Fowlerte, would rent it to someone else. John had kept this secret so as not to worry his family. If they broke down on the road and had to travel the following day, they would be homeless. He prayed that it was God's will for them to make it there before morning. Plus, he wanted to be up early to hunt for a job.

His family's well-being mattered to him. He felt God had entrusted him with his family, and it was his duty to do the best for them. Besides, what little savings they had would soon run out. He didn't want to hear his wife say how they were out of groceries. Neither did he want to hear how they didn't have their laying hens and milk cow anymore because of his decisive decision to leave home.

"Marta, grab the tea jug from Julian and let me have it, will ya? Marta, are you listening?"

"Yes, Mom. I was trying to get back to sleep." Marta wasn't hungry; the sleep had come, but she was shaking it off to concentrate on her mother's instructions.

"Marta, it'll be all right. I'm sure we'll find wonderful people in the valley." Linda spoke in low tones to her.

Marta didn't want to discuss her the seriousness of her concerns. Linda wouldn't understand. The family would work through hard knocks or realistic and compelling actions that might arise against them. They would have to rely on the good Lord and accept challenges as they arose.

Linda said, "So you're right: things will be OK. God is with us." Marta hugged the child and then rubbed her palms together, trying to keep from scratching her nervous, itchy skin. The last thing she wanted to do was frighten her parents into thinking she was ill while they were so far from a doctor.

She hoped the traveling wasn't difficult for her younger siblings, Daniel and Linda. *Their little bodies are limber; they'll adapt. And Julian over there, I don't care what happens to his body. He deserves every bit this lengthy drive will inflict on him.*

"Quit being so nervous, scary cat!" Julian bellowed, not caring that his parents heard. "Dad is right. We'll be better off in California. There'll be all kinds of work for us."

Marta recognized that look on his face. It was his malicious features that came over him for no reason at all. Mom and Dad had never noticed these reactions, but she had—many times. When he looked that way, he often took to pulling her hair or throwing baseballs at her back with such fast speeds that they left round red marks stinging with burning, bruising pain.

She noticed the trip wasn't bothering him. He too was wrapped in his thoughts. *At least he isn't hurting any of us, not now anyway.* Marta worried about her brother's transformation since he'd entered his teens, but only because they were all suffering due to his changes. *I wish he was feeling fatigued as I am. He deserves more physical pain than any of us. If he had any, he might stop giving me his evil eye. I wonder if I'll end up hating him more or learn to forgive him? Only God knows.*

Chapter 8

Marta's Disdain for Julian

Marta tried to pray for Julian, but her disdain for his malicious behavior seemed to cut into her hope, causing further doubt to penetrate deeper into her mind. There was one consolation, and that was sitting with her parents. Julian couldn't hit or pull her braids around them.

She knew how callous, lazy, and dishonest he could be. He appalled her. She realized there was no limit to his meanness. It amazed her how their parents hadn't noticed. Perhaps it was because nobody ever tattled on him for fear of retaliation.

He was two years younger, stood five inches taller, and weighed twenty pounds more than Marta. She found him threatening with his petulant demeanor. By now, she'd learned how to defend herself and her siblings from his bullying tactics and quick temper.

His tyranny, unbeknownst to their mother, was overwhelming. It didn't matter to him that their mother expected respect and kindness toward each other. How much he'd taken her lessons to heart was obvious when their parents had business in town or went ministering. Then his dreadful traits stood out against his siblings.

Marta tried not to judge him and sought to tolerate him in hopes he'd outgrow his cruel ways.

She thought of his abusive manners. There was the time she needed to pick up a few groceries for her mom. How well she remembered that event. "Julian, you want to come and help me carry groceries?" Marta knew better than to invite him but had to show kindness to him, and she needed the help.

"Yeah, sure. Can I buy a Popsicle?" Julian laughed as they walked the dusty road to the store. He'd picked up a long stick and began whipping the air. It was an intimidating gesture meant to alarm Marta, who'd been quiet because she didn't want to instigate trouble. She tightly gripped the grocery list.

He'd whirled the pretend whip high, snapping at flying insects. His cruel laughter had broken the silence as he' stomped past her. He gazed at her large, brown eyes filled with fear of him.

Being determined not to let him sense her fear, Marta responded casually. "Julian, you know there's no money for that! I have to follow Mom's grocery list. There's only enough money for these groceries, and I can't charge it."

She'd hurried to the store, trying to get there without harm from his snapping whip. The menacing gestures were his way of telling her he was in charge. "Ouch!" Marta screamed. Julian had laid the stick with substantial force on the back of her bare legs. Her dress was too short to protect them from his cruel act.

"Yeah! Take that, you dumb girl," he replied, snapping the stick to the back of her bare legs again.

Marta had not run after him because he controlled the situation. He would only bruise her harder. "If you can't behave yourself, go home. I can carry the groceries by myself. Ouch!" she hollered above the sound of the whipping switch.

Julian snickered and kicked the back of her right sandal, glad no one could stop him from inflicting her with pain. He hated how she was in charge of him since Phil had left. He didn't enjoy being ruled by a girl. It hurt his pride and manhood.

"Ouch! You brat, stop that!" Marta finally decided to run, hoping to get to the store before he could inflict further pain on her legs.

"I won't go home—you can't make me!" His uproar had carried into the small market, and shoppers stopped to stare. When they saw it was Julian yelling, they returned to their shopping. They were used to his antics.

Julian ran to the cold box and picked out a vanilla Popsicle. Before Marta could stop him, he tore off the wrapper and chewed on the frozen treat.

"Ha ha, you must pay for it now!" Julian bellowed. Marta tried reaching for the Popsicle but received a shoulder block from him.

"Hey, stop that!" Mr. Jenkins, the grocer, came over to help Marta. "You're a preacher's kid—you ain't supposed to do that!" He stood over Julian, his hands resting on his hips. His deeply set black eyes bored into Julian's dark, malicious spheres with great anger.

Julian laughed a hideous roar filled with scorn and cruelty. He hopped around Mr. Jenkins and then ran to hide behind Marta, the Popsicle now gone. "Ha ha, you can't catch me! What's the matter, old man? Am I too fast for you?" With the ice cream devoured, Julian gave

Marta's raven-black braids a hard tug and then ran out, leaving her to pay for the treat.

Marta continued in her thoughts of that incident. Yet her life with Julian, filled with such horrid events, had eventually caused her severe anguish. Marta's memories continued.

"Marta, you forgot the salt," Mom said as she searched through the bags.

"No, I didn't. I had to pay for Julian's ice cream." Marta announced her brother's crime and didn't feel this was tattling.

"Oh, that's all right. He's earned it. He's done his share of taking over Phil's chores. We can do without salt." Their mother continued putting away groceries while Marta went to the icehouse to grab ice for the raised whelps behind her legs.

She skipped snitching this part of the whipping for fear her dad might lose his temper and take a switch to Julian. This action would cause Julian to regret his deed but possibly hurt him to an extreme. Marta knew how hard her dad could strike at the fifteen-year-old, to the point Julian would lie unconscious after one strike. But then, she remembered that was before he had come to the Lord.

Even though he was becoming a changed man, Marta couldn't chance him losing his temper and doing something he would regret—possibly while in jail for his cruel act. She remembered his bad temper, but since becoming a Christian, he had tempered it down.

As a minister, he'd have self-control, but disciplining Julian this old way would have caused him to backslide.

Marta didn't understand her dad's faith and how strong it was; otherwise, she would have tattled.

Marta wondered if pitying Julian was perhaps a terrible thing. He needed the discipline, but not Dad's method. Therefore, she kept many of his obnoxious and contentious acts to herself, even at the expense of the pain he caused her.

After his threshing, she'd gone to her bedroom with a bag of ice in her pocket. Rubbing the ice pack on the back of her legs soothed the heat out of the red wounds. She decided that for his sake, she'd not hold back on his misbehavior anymore. Her pity for him was understandable, knowing her dad's treatment of him after Phil had left. But now he was becoming far worse than overbearing.

Marta remembered how Dad had at first whipped Julian into submission when Julian rebelled against doing Phil's chores. He'd become defiant and didn't understand why he had to take over those duties. As for his discipline, he took it the wrong way and blamed his punishment on his siblings.

On top of his bullying tactics, he became spiteful toward Marta, Daniel, and Linda. Marta knew he'd always had meanness in him, but it was getting worse. His harassment never ended and only increased. He became deceptive with his actions of cruelty. Marta, however, loved him beyond his cruelty. She trusted he'd change for the better, and soon.

Julian could be obstinate and unlovable, and he could demand his way around them when their mom wasn't looking. He demanded things from her when Dad left the house. He exemplified evil for the younger children, yet they knew better than to mimic his behavior.

"We need to forgive Julian," Linda once announced when Julian had sold one of their mom's frying pans for a few pennies. Like Daniel and Marta, she had a kind heart.

Alice had taught her children to love and forgive each other, as well as many moral rules. But Julian was a unique breed of person who'd become disrespectful, rude, annoying, loud, boisterous, a bully, and narcissistic. He'd become worse since Phil had joined the service.

Phil had been in charge of Julian as Mom and Dad traveled ministering during the midweek. He reminded Julian to help Daniel with his math. Since Phil's departure, Julian had helped him only because he knew their dad was listening to Daniel's plea for help. Julian didn't do it out of the kindness of his heart or because he cared for his younger brother.

Marta recollected the many times he hid her house slippers. "Has anyone seen my slippers?" She woke up one chilly winter morning to find them gone.

"Not me," everyone answered at once. Marta noticed Julian had a smirk on his face, and she knew better. He was up to his dirty tricks on her again.

"Julian, where are my slippers? Give them back." Marta crossed her arms and tapped her right foot, showing impatience with him. Though she wore cotton socks, she felt the chill of the tiled floor.

The next day, she found them where they belonged, under her bed. She was furious but tried to control her temper and not hold a grudge against him.

Julian's conduct wasn't funny to anyone, only to himself. He enjoyed being cruel. He'd roll with laughter at his selfish, mean pranks. There were the times he had hid Howie's bones in the trash can. Howie was the family's dog and had passed away of old age months before Phil had left home.

The children, including Phil, carried the pain of losing their beloved dog. However, Julian never mourned the loss of the old mongrel or shown remorse for fooling him. He didn't even show up when they buried the dog on the hill behind the church.

Marta tried not to hold that against him either, but in her heart she yearned to have Howie back. She never let on to Julian that she missed the dog. She realized his cruelty knew no bounds. He'd only taunt her about the dog, rubbing in the pain of his death and rejoicing in her agony. He could be deceptive and cunning, always looking for means to have fun at the expanse of hurting someone.

But around their parents, he acted as if he was kind and a team player. Marta, Phil, and Daniel knew him better but never tattled on him. Dad didn't approve of such behavior. This was why Marta wished Mom had never left them alone with him. He'd pull their hair if he wasn't happy with their answers or when he demanded something out of them. If one of them responded with, "I don't want to," he'd run after them until he caught them, pulling their hair and ripping bunches by the roots. Dad was oblivious to this cruel behavior. They weren't supposed to tattle on each other; it was their parent's number one rule.

Marta and her young siblings never told their mom about Julian's mean tricks; he'd deny them, anyway. Later, he'd play meaner pranks on them as payback. Their mom would not even admonish him when seeing him causing trouble.

He took advantage of the fact that their mother needed him to run family errands, so she tried to stay on his good side. Some of these errands included having him take funds to pay the grocery bill, or the cleaners when picking up their dad's Sunday suit.

Since Julian had taken over Phil's duties, he felt equal to him. Their mom was so dependent on him that she'd overlook his misbehavior.

"Mom, it's not fair how you take up for Julian!" Marta had complained many times before. Yet their mother thought it was sibling jealousy and dismissed the misbehavior.

Marta had developed a hate for his misbehavior. She knew she had no love for his poor traits and began to resent his existence. According to her dad's sermons, she was to forgive and love him, but it was getting difficult to do either. His obnoxiousness grew with great fury.

Why did God tell us to love one another? she thought. *Julian is as cruel as cruel can get!* Hot, painful teardrops had rolled down her cheeks many times. She didn't know whether they were tears of pain, regret, or hate. *God, heal my heart of hate.* She hoped He would; it was an awful, sickening feeling that kept her awake most nights. She was tired of resenting his conduct.

Eventually, Marta tried changing on her own will, showing Julian kindness and hoping he'd get the message and change for the better. In her heart, Marta hoped he might do so, but his constant cruel behavior made it difficult for her to show him any further kindness. Her feelings of him became enraged with anger against his rebellion. She thought perhaps praying more often for him might help her change her viewpoints of him.

Her disdain for his attitude caused her to shun him, making him feel rejected. He thought the entire family felt the same way, increasing his inferiority complex. His insecurities caused him to act up further, but Marta was not aware of this. He continued feeling inferior to his siblings, though he thought his meanness showed him superior over them.

Marta made it a habit to pray for both of them to change. She didn't want to go on hating him. She wanted the best for him. A prayer of forgiveness was always in her heart.

However, this battle of hate ignited daily in Julian because of his whimsical and selfish actions. *Lord, give us a life without hatred and bitterness;* Marta prayed silently.

Marta's thoughts returned to their journey. They were a spiritual family, and she felt he should behave kinder and more responsible. *God, deal with him.* Then she thought about herself. *Help us all, O' Lord.* She stopped her thoughts to stare at Julian. Whimpering softly, she turned her eyes away from him, not wanting to see any more of the glares he was giving her. She wondered what was on his mind. There was something there; she knew it.

Julian spoke. "I'll work like everyone in this family. You'll see. I'll make you and Phil proud of me!" He'd been looking over at his mother to see if he was getting her approval.

Marta stared at him with rejection. *Sure*, she thought. *Will he scathe with unreasonable excuses?* His shifty eyes made her cringe. *Meanwhile, how long must I bear his detestable behavior?*

Chapter 9

California Country

While she held her long braids, Marta heard Dad speak. "We'll be enterin' the San Joaquin Valley in a few hours. Then we'll locate Somerville. I have a mental map of where we're goin'." He spoke with excitement.

"Don't any of you worry! God will meet our needs," their mother added confidently.

Marta relaxed and looked into the distance ahead. There, she saw steamy waves rising from the sizzling road. The unending shrubbery and pale sand reflecting sunlight were intolerable. *If only there were trees of any kind. Our eyes would get a break from all this brightness.*

"Wake up, sleepyheads," Dad announced. "We're comin' up to a range of mountains called the Mojave. Then we'll be in Tehachapi."

"I don't see conifer trees, Dad! When will we see 'em?" Marta asked uneasily.

"I'm not sure?" He seemed to be wondering himself.

As they drove down Tehachapi Pass, they came to a city. "Is this Somerville?" Daniel asked in astonishment.

"No, it's called Bakersfield. Somerville is a few miles north," Dad announced. "It's not this large, but it'll be of fair size. Look—there's the Sierra Nevada Range." He pointed to the east, where tall mountain peaks stood behind the yellowing hills.

Marta saw the possibility of locating a conifer tree in the nearby mountains. Their outline appeared as a violet ribbon in the east. *Surely Somerville must be near them too?* Her heart danced with joy and hope. They continued their journey and they passed almond, orange, and olive orchards. The rumble of the vehicle's engine put her into a peaceful, deep sleep for the next few miles.

She awoke to the sound of something hissing. After sitting up, she saw a white mist rising from the front of the vehicle. "Oh, no!" Marta groaned.

"Julian, let's get out," John bellowed. Then he raised the hood. "Alice, you and Julian fetch the water jugs! The rest of you get out and stretch your legs while I add water to the radiator."

Great clouds of scorching spray spewed into the air when he unlocked the radiator cap. He jumped far from it and said, "Stand back! The steam is hot. Stand back, all of you." John hollered again and moved his family farther away.

Marta hoped the sizzling vapors didn't burn him but felt better after seeing he waited a few minutes before approaching again.

While John worked on the rig, Marta took Linda for a brief walk. Alice joined them, hoping to stretch the soreness out of her joints. They saw plants neatly planted in rows, but they weren't familiar with them. Marta picked up a handful of dirt and noticed it wasn't sandy anymore. It was a sure sign they were out of the desert country. "My, but this soil is rich. It's like the kind we bought in bags from the hay store to fill our garden pots." She got excited at seeing it, giving her hope things might be this splendid in Somerville.

"Oh, can you smell wet dirt? It smells earthy!" Alice looked for the water source.

Marta walked to the side of the vehicle and viewed the scene. A musty odor filled the air, and the sight of wet furrows was an overwhelming experience. The sky didn't appear as blue as she remembered, and the sloping hills beyond appeared as stepping stones for the peaked mountains above them.

Marta marveled at the steamy heat and blazing sun, which had dried tall grasses on the sloping hills, painting them straw yellow. The dry hills rose above the bright green fields below them with a sharp contrast. "Marta, what's growing there?" Linda pointed to some foliage behind a water ditch. Large, white fluffy balls covered it.

"I don't know. I've seen nothing like that!" she wondered herself.

"It's called cotton, and it's ready for pickin'." Dad overheard them as he finished pouring water from two jugs into the radiator.

"You mean cotton as in our cotton clothes," Daniel announced. He knew that because his mom soaked the white cotton clothes in a tub of bleach on wash days.

"That's exactly the same!" Dad smiled at his son's innocence.

"Who would've thought our clothes were made from plants?" Daniel replied excitedly.

After leaving Bakersfield behind, they entered deeper into the valley. They traveled past migrant camps and hamburger stands along Highway 65 with giant billboards standing next to them, announcing the best burgers and shakes. One stand looked like a huge, round orange. *Oh, what wondrous sites!* Marta could hardly wait to eat at one of those stands, but then she thought, *Oh, my, but we're out of money. Maybe after we've settled and found jobs, we'll get to do that someday.*

Chapter 10

Pine Trees Can Wait

"I don't want to hear any more talk 'bout pine trees," Dad commanded. "We've other things to figure out, like findin' our way to town. When the time comes, I'll find a nice tree." He'd heard Linda and Marta discussing trees for the umpteen time.

Marta thought when it was time, she'd help her dad with this tree mission. He would have enough to worry about in California. She'd use her faith to find a decent conifer. Then after recalling her geography lessons, she remembered something of the valley. It was flat land surrounded by the high Sierras.

How far away are those Sierras? Do they hold my miracle? Are they close to town? Then Marta had a strange thought. *I've never seen Somerville on the map. Have we headed the wrong way?* She hoped not and reminded herself to trust Dad and the Lord.

Upon noticing navel orange orchards, her attention returned to the rental waiting for them. She was glad for it and the hope it held.

"I don't want us to break down anymore. It'll be dark soon. If we do, we must wait till morning to get help!"

Julian said with particular concern. He looked at Marta but pretended to look out her window.

"Daddy, do you think we'll be able to have a tree for Christmas?" Linda asked sweetly. There was no reply. Dad was concentrating on every sound the vehicle made. It worried him because they were low on water. His silence overwhelmed them. When he acted this way, it meant something troubled him. No one spoke, afraid they'd aggravate his temper.

"Alice, I mean to make our lives as normal as possible here in California. I'll get around to Christmas planning, but do you understand it's too early to think of that right now? I have major planning to do before that, and I need you and the good Lord on my side."

"I understand, John. But the children mean no harm by asking for a tree for Christmas."

"Listen, my dear," John lowered his voice. "Let's both make plans to have a merry Christmas for the family, even through all these new changes. It'll all work out if we wait upon the Lord. It always does. So let's not encourage the children to wish this early for something we don't know whether we'll get it for them. We'll pray about it and let God move on our plans."

Marta could hear some words they spoke. She heard the part about waiting upon the Lord. *How right they are!* she thought. *We must have faith and wait. Except I feel I'm running out of patience. Help me, O Lord.*

Marta leaned against her seat, wondering how much farther they had to go before arriving at Somerville. She was so tired. *I'll never travel like this again unless God calls me to do so; otherwise, I'm staying put.*

"Marta, do you know if we'll get us a tree for

Christmas?" Linda whispered, hoping her upset parents didn't hear her.

"Linda, I'm sure we'll have a tree, but let's concentrate on getting to Somerville. Can you imagine what the town will look like—I mean how big it might be? Maybe it'll be full of canneries. My teacher said they have many packing houses there."

"What do they pack?"

"Oh, there're oranges, lemons, other fruit, and vegetables."

"Why do they do that?" Linda couldn't imagine why they'd want to pack food away.

"Well, they ship it through trains and trucks to other towns and cities who need the food."

"Do you think there might be a train station in Somerville? I've never seen a train except in picture books. Hey, maybe they haul in Christmas trees!"

"There might be a train station; we'll see. Let's get some rest. We're almost there." Marta hoped her answer satisfied the child. Her dad was right: conifer trees could wait. There were many other important things to worry about besides conifers. Still, Marta worried their Christmas wouldn't be Christmas without them. Linda was right: they had to have a tree. It was the symbol of their unity as a family, which included traditions of celebrations filled with good food, friends, peace, joy, and hope for their future.

Chapter 11

Nearing Somerville

The road sign read, "Somerville, five miles." It was a welcoming sight for them. John felt assured they could travel this distance with no more problems. The sun looming near the western horizon gave its somber light to the weary travelers. It perched upon them and bathed the countryside in a thin blanket of golds and reds. Overhead, rays of orange hues streaked into dark purple clouds hanging over the Sierras. They blasted the snowless mountain tips with rusty tones as they waited for darkness. It was a reminder to the family that their journey had finished.

Upon nearing town, they saw towers of dust taking shape high ahead. The sight was daunting. Marta and Daniel noticed a red and gray tractor on the roadside.

"Dad, why is that machine raising so much dirt?" Daniel asked, bewildered at the scene.

"Son, it's late summer season—time for weeds to die. They become fire nuisances, so farmers keep 'em at bay by ploughing 'em with tractors. Makes agriculture easy to contend with."

Marta had kept her window open, not expecting the dust to infiltrate the cab. It made her uncomfortable as the swirling dirt irritated her eyes and throat. She wanted the blowing wind to blow through the cab and cool them off, but instead the dust circulating along with the air made it impossible to breathe. Then the wind was stifling hot, making them more miserable. *We can't tolerate any more, Lord. Please give us Your strength. Amen.* She was thankful their trip was over.

They saw cotton and alfalfa fields surrounding the town and a dust cloud hovering over the redbrick buildings.

"We're almost there!" Dad hollered above the noisy rattle of the loaded station wagon. He smiled at Alice, who sat motionless and looked frightened.

Marta's stomach growled with hunger. *Thank God we have supper ready; egg sandwiches are better than nothing.* She helped Linda sit on her lap so she could also take in the view.

A huge cotton gin on their right awed them, and across it stood a large schoolhouse. "Dad, will we live near a railroad? Maybe they'll haul in Christmas trees on it. Do you think?" Marta asked eagerly.

"I don't know if there are trains, stations, or tracks around here. I'm sure we'll find out soon enough. We have to trust God for our provisions," he said pensively.

"I hope he'll supply a coffee kettle and a frying pan," Mom half whimpered.

"What happened to yours?" Marta asked with puzzled look.

"I forgot the box containing them on the kitchen floor after I fixed our traveling meals." It perturbed her, but it was too late to correct the problem.

We can't go back and risk burning the engine. Lord, there's no money to make these purchases. Please provide Mom with these provisions. Such thoughts stole Marta's thrill in the new town.

Chapter 12

John

While swabbing his forehead with his forearm, John looked in the rearview mirror to see his sleepy children slumped in the back seat, weary from the long drive. They had just left Bakersfield after the radiator incident. He kept from complaining out loud. *Lord, I'm exhausted. Soon we'll be living in our new home.*

Droplets of sweat caused by the muggy air beaded down his brown eyes, heavy nose, and thick black mustache. He pulled out his white handkerchief, wiped his face, and then removed his suede hat, revealing wet black hair mussed around his crown and ears. After wiping grime and moisture from his neck, he hoped his family couldn't see his haggard face. With the faint light, they'd recognize he appeared to be on his last leg, even at his age of forty-eight.

"I'm gonna get up early in the mornin'. I wonder where I should first look for work?" he said in low tones to Alice. "There's a variety of fieldwork available for a man. There's more than enough for both of us." His faint smile betrayed the weariness in his body.

"I've never done fieldwork. How hard can it be?" Alice

moaned softly, fanning her face with a church flyer she'd been reading along the trip.

John knew he'd handle it but wondered whether his family could. His plans included having the children work when school was out. He hoped it wasn't difficult and tried not to worry himself or them about it.

Worrying for Phil and Grandmother had put a strain on John. He didn't want these worries on his mind, not until they had settled in well. His priority was in his immediate family and the jobs that waited in the valley. He wondered how much work they'd get in before winter, when the crops froze. He hadn't mentioned this to Alice or the children so as not to take away their hope.

John thought of the many days and months they had to work before freezing weather arrived. *After September, cool winds from the north will hail in fall, and then the freezin' winter will arrive. There'll be no more jobs until spring, when cotton choppin' begins. We've got to secure work while it's available.* He prayed. As a man of God, he felt it was his duty to model faith. He'd remain resilient and faithful.

John, like the family, didn't understand the ways of the icy valley in the winter. The damp fogs rolling in at evenings and lasting until late morning hours were to be a surprise for them. They would soon learn that fog occurred because of the rising sun, which warmed the damp earth.

John worried they might not get situated enough before the bitter cold arrived. Besides needing funds to get established in the rental, he also considered saving money to carry them into springtime. If it was possible, he'd even set aside extra income for a home mortgage.

We'll be without work for a few months in winter, but having a nest egg will be helpful.

John worried he'd not get his family situated before Christmas. They'd have to make do without essentials so he could save for gifts. Also, he planned on making the purchases without spending his secret stash he'd stored for emergencies.

Meanwhile, sizzling heat affected him the most. He'd stopped the station wagon for three gas fill-ups, to repair a flat tire, for the family to use the restrooms, and for a radiator water fill-up. Strained muscles caused him to hurt bitterly, including his lower back. Yet he didn't let out loud moans, even when his sore shoulders ached from maneuvering the stiff steering wheel.

In May, Alice had noticed him give out soft moans when bending to pick up things, and she wondered how he'd injured his back. She suspected he was moonlighting but dared not mention it to him. Hoping to get a confession of his pocket money, she'd volunteer to rub his sore back.

Alice knew only what the children had told her. They'd gone up to the mountains a time or two with him, looking for cypress trees. Then they'd watched him cutting firewood, but obviously it wasn't theirs, because he took it straight to town. Alice could speculate what he was doing with the wood but kept quiet.

With winter not far off, summer was the best time to cut and gather firewood. John got paid well for his work, allowing him to give Alice grocery money and still have enough for savings. This was for their journey to California. It had to last until they made it to Somerville.

John prayed for wisdom and discernment regarding the care of his family. He knew God would provide everything required for their new life in the new town. The strain of maintaining his family's well-being overwhelmed him, but he never let it show. His mind had become busy with their affairs and with Julian's growing careless attitude. He hoped this was a childhood phase.

John concentrated on his driving and wondered of the rental's condition. "Alice, I pray the rental is in suitable shape. I'd hate to see it dilapidated and useless. Hopefully it'll be in useable condition, and I won't spend our savings on fixtures."

"I hope so too! There's no telling how soon you'll be able to get a job."

"Honey, I've gotta tell you something. Mr. Fowlerte is saving if for us through tonight. If we're not there by mornin', he'll rent it to the next person on his list. He said he couldn't hold it any longer for us. Migrant workers are also looking for rentals."

"Oh, John. You didn't tell me this."

"I didn't want you to worry. Besides, worryin' won't accomplish anything for any of us. We made it before nightfall, thank God. We can relax for now."

John couldn't say any more that might discourage his wife. They'd made it through the worst of the journey. *We can almost call it a day,* he thought.

Chapter 13

An Omen?

At the edge of Somerville, before nearing a large cotton gin, they heard a loud popping sound, and the vehicle began swerving. Marta's heart dropped. *What's wrong now?* she wondered, sitting up to look outside. *Whatever it is, I hope isn't serious.*

"I've got a tire going flat! Hold on, everyone. Thank God I was going slow enough to keep the trailer from turning over." Her dad tried to sound hopeful.

The orange glow of the late afternoon sun provided them with enough light to fix the tire. Marta looked out the window and examined the area. The worn-out road made her wonder about Somerville's prosperity. The lush green fields around the vehicle appeared well cared for. The buildings ahead appeared well kept.

Marta saw her dad's face pale when the noise sounded. *Did he suspect something worse? Are we off to an inauspicious beginning in the new town?* Marta worried, forgetting her faith. The family was tense and dared not move for fear of something worse was happening to the old rig.

"Are you OK, Alice?" John asked.

"I'm fine. Are you children all right back there?" Alice turned apprehensively to check on them.

"Mom, what happened?" Linda asked, her face showing fear of the unknown.

"It's OK. Sit back until Dad tells us what to do," Marta said, and she hugged the child to assure her there was nothing to dread.

"Everyone, get out," Dad ordered. "Julian, help me change it, would ya?" John walked to the trailer, removed the top furniture, and pulled out a worn spare tire, waited for him. He inspected the tire and was thankful he had it. It was the best he could do under their financial strain.

Marta stood alongside her mother, holding Linda's hand. Even this late in the day, heat from the hot pavement rose around their legs. The steamy air smelled foul, and it was difficult to breathe. While looking for the source of the stench, she saw a large metal building on the right side of town ahead. A sound of grinding gears resonated from it, prompting Marta's curiosity.

She observed sights and smelled valley odors. It was all so different and exciting. After taking in a deep breath, she realized there was a faint scent of roses, honeysuckle, and cucumbers—scents familiar to her.

The roadside, plowed under, was now covered with upturned dirt and dried grasses. There were crops planted on the right and left of the road, all the way up to the town. Excavated narrow ditches lined the fields, parallel to the road. There were furrows of cucumbers on one side of the road and sweet alfalfa on the other side. "If we have to, we can walk that distance to the rental," Marta said to her mother.

"We could," Alice replied, but she sounded uncertain

of something. "But we need to wait for Daddy to fix the flat. If he can't, then we'll haul our pots and bed clothing there."

"It's a minor miracle we didn't have a flat way back yonder." Marta spoke lowly so as not to worry the two younger children. She didn't state out loud what she most feared. It was the idea that the flat occurring as they entered town might be a sign of doom, an omen warning them to stay away. Her fears of the future shot up in her mind again, though she was not superstitious. Her dad wouldn't allow this, but having the flat occur near the town seemed an omen to her.

A vehicle pulled up next to them. "Hey, there! Do you need any help?" a young man behind the steering wheel of an older model truck asked.

"Hello! No, thanks. I think we've got it. Don't we, Julian?" John looked at Julian and winced, seeing him struggle with the lug wrench.

"I can't get these bolts to give!" Julian heaved. "They're overtorqued."

"I have a hammer in my truck. Let me pull over, and I'll get it," the young man replied. He pulled off the road in front of the station wagon, got out of his truck with a hammer in his hand, and approached the rig. "Here, let me try her." The tall, young man wore a large-brimmed beige hat, and he held a ball-peen hammer in his hand. He fell to his knees next to the flat and began banging on the lug wrench. "There you go. They're loose. Let me help you with that tire." He wasted no time in helping John change the flat. He noticed the baldness of the tire but said nothing and kept his thoughts to himself. *God, help these poor people. It's a miracle they made it on these old, bald tires. You were watching over them. Bless them to get out of this poverty. I know You love them. Amen.*

"Let me introduce myself," the young man said, dusting himself as he stood up. "My name is Henry Barnes." He smiled, placed the wooden handle of the hammer in his back pocket, pulled out a handkerchief, and wiped his hands.

"Pleased to meet you," John replied, reaching to shake his hand. "This is my family: my wife, Alice; my oldest daughter, Marta; my sons, Julian and Daniel; and the young'un is Linda. My oldest son, Phil, is in the army, stationed in Korea."

"Pleased to meet y'all. What brings you folks out here, if you don't mind my asking?"

"We hope to find work after we settle into a place a friend of ours owns. He's holding it for us." John said no more about the rental arrangements.

"That's mighty kind of him. Well, don't let me keep you any longer. It'll be dark soon, and I'm sure y'all would like to get settled in for the night." With one hand, he pulled off his wide brim hat, and with the other he ran his fingers through blond hair. Then after plopping his hat back on, he appeared to open his mouth as if to say something, but John interrupted him.

"Excuse me, do you know where this address is?" John handed him a paper.

"Sure, I do. Just drive down this road, turn left on the second street you come to, and then go to the third street and make another left."

"That's easy enough. I should find it. Thank you. Nice meetin' you. Good evenin'." John shook hands with Henry, thanking him for his help. "OK, everyone, let's get goin'."

"If you folks need anything', just call me. I work next to the post office, over at the hay store, at the end of this street. Good night, everyone. Hope you enjoy livin' in Somerville." He got in his truck and drove away.

Marta stared at its red taillights heading down the main street until they were small, beady red eyes. She wondered if they'd ever run across him again. *Was he to be the warrior fighting for them against the omen meeting them at their new community? It wasn't a coincidence that he came along.* She wondered who he was.

Chapter 14

Henry Makes an Impression

Marta couldn't stop thinking about Henry. She noticed his healthy appearance by his dark tan, which stood out under his blond hair. His blue eyes and ready smile displayed his pleasant nature. His noble mannerisms made him stand out. *He's like Phil,* she thought. *He's also helpful to strangers. It complements his handsome appearance.*

Henry's chance appearance reminded Marta to reconsider their future in Somerville. *It'd be grand if my siblings grew up to be like him. He appears to be twenty-five years of age, yet his maturity is that of an accomplished individual. Have the town residents encouraged his polite behavior? Maybe he has a religion that inspired his attitude?* Marta saw their hope and future in Henry. Upon realizing she had a new viewpoint to consider, she beamed with gratitude.

Her prayers now included backsliding. *We've got to keep this evil out of our lives and find a church to attend. Meantime, Mom and Dad will continue having prayer and Bible studies at home. That'll help. Please, dear God, provide us with a church, and soon!*

While reflecting on Henry's demeanor, Marta's inexperience with strangers caused her to doubt his goodness. Though young, he had a decent job, showed kindness and respectability, and appeared responsible. If the residents were accountable for shaping him, they might have the same influence on her and her siblings. Marta's curiosity prompted her to desire to know more about him.

Chapter 15

The New Home

The vehicle rolled into town, and the silence of the settlement making the rattling of the engine sound louder. Marta paid no attention to the clamor because her concentration was on the size of the place. It had tall, redbrick buildings on both sides of the street. When they got off Main Street, they saw wooden houses standing in neat, long rows. *What a curious place. They're not staggered and built of adobe.* She stared bewildered and amazed.

In the light of twilight, she saw beige dust covering everything in sight, including the empty streets. It made the town look abandoned.

"Why is it empty?" Marta asked her parents. Neither parent spoke up.

"I hope they weren't deceived, and this is a ghost town," Daniel murmured to Marta.

"No, it can't be. We met Henry. He was for real, all right." Marta hoped for the best. *God wouldn't allow us to make a mistake this huge.*

"It's not. It just looks that way. The residents are probably working, or maybe they're in a town meeting," John said, looking for the next street according to his directions.

"It seems late to be working, don't you think?" Alice spoke softly, keeping the alarm out of her voice. "See those lovely yards? They have grass lawns. How do they trim the grass? And such tall shade trees, taller than any that grew in our town." Alice was beside herself at seeing such wonders.

"Mom, did you see those rosebushes in those yards? And look at those white picket fences. I wonder what kind of vines those are running on top?" The neighborhood thrilled Marta.

"I bet it's their orange, trumpet-shaped flowers producing that perfume scent," Daniel commented.

"It smells familiar, like Grandmother's bedroom." Marta spoke in a low voice, as if speaking any louder would disturb the stillness of the town. Grandmother's perfume always reminded her of love and harmony. The aroma depicted security for her, and she associated it with Grandmother's strength, courage, and faith in God. The family elder knew how to take care of anything that became threatening to the children. Marta inhaled another whiff of the pleasing aroma, hoping to keep it in her nostrils for a while.

John drove along the quiet streets. They passed dusty fences and electric streetlights that cast a luminous glow on the empty streets. An occasional dog barked at the family's arrival.

John missed his turn, so he drove into the next road on his left, hoping they hadn't lost their way. The homes on that street were not as neat as those they'd seen earlier. Unlike the paved roads between the lovely houses, this was a dirt road. It released dust clouds under the tires. He drove slowly so as not to hit the many potholes, and then he turned onto the street he'd skipped. On the right, they saw an uncultivated field filled with wild weeds.

A small tumbleweed patch.

"Here's our street. OK, everybody, look for this house number." John called out the number as he drove slower.

"There it is," Dad noted with relief. "Looks like a good rental. We'll make a real home out of it in no time!" He pulled up to a small house with fading white paint, most of it already chipping.

A dingy front porch stood out, surrounded by tumbleweeds that had blown in by the brisk summer winds. There was a broken picket fence around it with a fallen mailbox by the front gate. In a corner of the front yard grew a peach tree topped with small peaches.

Alice opened the vehicle's door and got out hesitantly, a tote bag hanging on her right wrist. "Come, children. Let's have a look at the place before we unload." She ambled along the cracked sidewalk and stretched the stiffness out of her arms, keeping a scant distance behind John. He held the lit kerosene lamp high so as to see the inside of the dark house.

Marta's sore body sluggishly moved out of the car. She was aware that they needed to unload but thought of the weary children. "Mom, we're so tired. Can we have a rest and a snack before unloading?" Mom reached over to hug her. Marta wasn't thinking of herself but of Daniel and Linda, who were exhausted and hungry. They were her responsibility because she was the eldest daughter. No one had to remind her; it was part of her culture.

"Sure, we can." Alice turned around and hollered, "Daniel, bring in the lunch bag, will you? And Julian, get the tea container. It's half full, so be careful."

The boys hurried to the wagon. Meanwhile, the rest of the family walked slowly into the shabby house. It was as if they expected some weird thing to pop out and grab them.

Marta noticed the beige linoleum floors were level, unlike the loose tile in their old place. A ripped piece of linoleum by the entrance to the kitchen door was an eyesore. It appeared as if someone had taken the corner and pulled it up, ripping it as they pulled. The walls and doors, swabbed with years of grime, had peeling paint. The shavings curled into small rolls that hung loosely on the wood. They needed scraping and painting.

A small wood stove sat on one side of the compact living room, its rock slab appearing broken in half. Its pipe lay on the floor. A large, dirty picture window overlooked the street. After walking into the kitchen, they saw a wooden table with words carved on its top and surrounded by eight battered wooden chairs. Behind it stood a counter with a deep sink. A large window stood above the dirty sink. It's two grimy panes appearing as two hoot owl eyes peering down at their entrance. Two old appliances, a tiny gas stove and a refrigerator, stood side by side next to the counter.

"Mom, look at that thing. It looks like our icebox back home, but bigger," Linda exclaimed, amazed at the size of the white appliance.

"I think it's electric, Mom," Julian quipped.

Perched on one side of the kitchen was a small porch. The bottom half was closed in, and the top half, made of steel screen, was now rusted red and brown. Leaning against one dirty wall stood an old box-spring mattress. A tallboy with missing nobs stood beside it. A box stacked with crumpled newspapers sat next to a broken washing machine.

"Mom, God answered your prayer." Marta held the oven door open for her to see inside. "Someone left an iron skillet and a coffee kettle in here!"

The discovery elated her mother. She rushed to pick up the skillet and held it to her chest. "Oh, my. God is good." She placed it and the kettle on the stove's top and continued examining the home.

After closing the oven door, Marta moved to the kitchen window. She looked out and she saw an enormous dark pile sitting in the backyard. "What's that enormous thing out there, Dad?" she asked with a startled look.

After looking out the greasy glass, he studied it carefully. "It looks like a junk pile. Maybe the former tenants left their stuff out there instead of hauling it away. Oh, look behind the pile. I can see what appears to be fruit trees. Praise the Lord! We'll get a better look in the morning."

Alice pushed in between them for a peak. "Trees? Fruit trees? Thank God for such a miracle. But come on, let's have a seat and eat." Her drained voice suddenly held a burst of joy. She found the house to be satisfactory for their needs.

"We'll decide who's having the bedrooms; there are two. We can use the large back porch for another bedroom. There's one bathroom, so I'll make a schedule for bathing times." Their mom reached for the kitchen faucet. "Oh, look, we have running water." Alice stood aside so everyone could see the wonder.

Julian flicked a light switch next to the refrigerator, "See? The electricity works. We have instant lights!" he shouted with glee. "Let me try those in the other rooms." Soon he came back scowling. "The living room doesn't have electricity, but the other rooms do." He sat down and waited for his mom or dad to give them further instructions.

"Yep, it does!" Linda exclaimed with a giggle, flicking off and on the kitchen light switch. This was a miracle to the child, who was accustomed to the amber lights of oil lamps. The sudden burst of light above them was an enormous delight to all of them.

Alice clutched her hands and rested them on her chest. The thrill of having a place to call home overwhelmed her with hopeful assurance. She could raise her family with many conveniences, making life easy and comfortable.

Alice pulled her Bible out of her tote bag and held it to her heart. Her family's spiritual concerns pierced her mind. There was so much hope around them, more than she'd imagined. She'd been praising the Lord silently since they'd arrived. N*ow the family could hear her praises. She sang a favorite hymn,* "Amazing Grace," while they unloaded, and later that night, she sung her children to sleep.

The next morning, Marta walked out back to check the enormous yard. The early sun washed it in soft, pale light, revealing the immense pile of trash. Fruit trees, loaded with fruit, circled the picket fence. The large apples, oranges, and lemons gave her an immense surprise she didn't expect. A cherry tree beside the side gate had dry cherries lying underneath, its fruit-producing season now ended. There was also a tree her dad called a persimmon, bursting with large orange fruit. What she hoped to find, a conifer, wasn't there.

Marta walked back into the house and found her mom fixing breakfast. "Mom, can I help with something?" she asked, looking at the breakfast schedule her mother had posted on the inside of one of the cupboard's doors. Marta began pulling out ingredients to make pancakes.

She took her time preparing the batter. There was a question she wanted to ask, but she didn't want to seem hasty. "Mom, do you have ideas where we might locate an evergreen tree for Christmas? It's just a few months away," she said while mixing ingredients, appearing to hold an everyday conversation.

"We'll put that on our prayer list because I don't know the answer. Don't you all agree?" Mom spoke joyfully as the children waited at the set table.

Marta heard, "Yes, Mom," from the others, which comforted her and confirmed the faith in her siblings' hearts. But how long could she hold on to her faith? *Father, praying for a conifer tree for Christmas seems a big request. But I need to trust You for Your blessings. As for now, I'm grateful for the safe trip and the rental waiting for us. Help us establish roots again.* Her spirit cheered up for a while. But how long would she last in this euphoria with the many trials lying ahead of her?

Chapter 16

Settling Down

The dilapidated house gave Marta an eerie sense of doom. Then she wondered, *Is it giving me that impression, or is it me with my misgivings?* The doom sensation tried to overcome her gratitude. Thinking of their situation caused her to further doubt their future in Somerville. *Why did Mom and Dad leave our beautiful home? For what reason—to come to this unforeseen world? It's filled with dust and such heavy humidity. Agriculture surrounding town is a barrier fencing us in, prisoners to a way of life. It leads nowhere. And what of our finances? We're low on funds. Will there be jobs for them?* With these thoughts constantly haunting her and robbing her of hope, she often cried in her room.

She tried not to think of their financial condition and put on a jovial face for her siblings' sake. Though acting and speaking in positive tones, she still sank deeper into despair. It was difficult for her to find hope when all she saw was her parents searching for jobs and stretching out their last dollars. She too did her share of helping with the finances by helping create cheap casseroles on the gas stove.

Her heart ached to be back at the parsonage where life was simple and familiar, and where she felt safe. Plus, Phil would return there after the war. The parsonage was also their grandmother's home, where she'd lived out her life with her son, John, and his family until her stroke.

Alice had noticed how negligent Marta had become with prayer and Bible study time. *She puts no effort into any of it,* she noted to herself one afternoon. "Marta, why the long frown?" Alice asked while setting the table.

Marta didn't answer.

"Honey, listen to me. I understand what you're going through." She spoke softly. "Come outside with me. I wanna talk with you."

Alice pulled the iron skillet out of the oven and left the muffins to finish baking. After pulling back loose brown hair strands, she then took Marta by the arm. "Let's go, while the kids are getting ready for supper." They walked down to the front gate, where they were far away from prying ears.

The smell of freshly cut alfalfa mingled with drying plums was heavy in the summer air. They saw a devil duster spinning around the field at the end of their street. Alice looked up the road and hoped to see the station wagon coming. The setting sun glinting off the trailer parked by the house told her John was having a long workday.

"Marta, I know you're concerned with our life here in the valley, but we must work together as a family and trust the Lord. Quit your fretting, honey. You must curb your thoughts of hopelessness. It'll take time to adjust, but we'll manage, and you'll survive your doubts and fears. You can't lose your faith!" Alice spoke agreeably, keeping any alarm or reprimanding tones out of her voice.

Marta turned to the east and looked off to the distant mountains, her eyes damp with tears. "I have faith, but sometimes it's not enough. Whenever something awful happens to me, I get scared, and my faith weakens. Then when I try to work with the family, I come up short and consider myself a failure. I always expect terrible things to happen to us. So I can't do my share of helping, and it agonizes me. And then there are our finances. I'm failing you and Dad. I should be out there working, but I fear meeting unfamiliar people. And you know Dad gets upset if we talk to strangers. Am I wrong?"

"No, dear, but worrying over things won't make you get things done faster or better than what God will provide. You can't let your guard down either. You need to trust Him for His timing in our lives. Also, change your viewpoint of this town and its residents. You're being too harsh on them. They're as normal as people back home. Before you know it, not one of them will be a stranger."

"Yeah, but Mom, it's not just that. I have a sense of being lost. We might not learn to adjust or gain new friendships. And celebrating holidays as we're accustomed will disappear, forgotten forever, not to mention our culture. Losing them makes me uncomfortable. There's so much pressure inside of me, as if I'll burst and disappear." Frustrated, Marta tapped the toe of her sandal onto the packed dirt, tears rolling down her pink cheeks. She clasped her hands to her face and sobbed sorrowfully.

Alice wondered if hormone changes were adding to her despair. She pulled her daughter into her arms, and both cried. She carried fears herself, but in her case, she didn't have to contend with dizzy hormones. "I'm a little fearful myself, but I gotta keep activating my faith. I trust your dad's plans 'cause I have faith God is leading him." Alice stopped her sobbing and smiled at her daughter. She continued portraying strength mentally and physically, though there were days she felt she couldn't manage.

"I'm sorry, Mom. Maybe I'm missing Phil and Grandmother too much, or perhaps I'm feeling sorry for myself. We've never been in this kind of predicament. I'll work on my patience and trust you and Dad more, 'cause I know you're both working hard for us. I'll try doing my share. Mom, I don't want to be one of your problems."

"It won't be difficult starting our old traditions, making friends, and getting rooted in our familiar ways again. As for Phil and Grandmother, they'll be back with us. And as for culture, our culture is that of Christians. Wherever we go, the Lord goes before us. It's His culture we seek and follow. It'll take time settling down, but we'll make it," Alice said gently.

"That's true, but this is different. I fret we won't fit in this community and that our outlook of this place will be stifled by whoever hates newcomers. I'll try to meet decent people to encourage me, but what if I don't find any, or Dad gets on me for tryin'?"

"Where do you get this idea of townspeople hatin' strangers, Marta? And as for your dad, I'll talk to him to be more lenient with you. Come, let's pray." Alice held her hands and prayed over their state of affairs. "Please help us be a blessing to each other and to our new friends. Bring kind people into our lives and show us how to be kind to those You send. Guide us to settle in Your peace and holy will. Provide faith when our measure is low. In

Jesus's name, we pray. Amen. Now, let's go eat, honey." Alice placed her arms around her daughter's shoulders and walked her up the porch steps.

Marta stopped before entering and said, "P.S., dear Lord, provide us with a tree for Christmas. Show us where we can find one if it's your will. Amen." She couldn't forget Linda's Christmas tree and a reminder of her hope.

"Don't concern yourself with that now. We'll get a tree when the time comes. We've never made do without one." Before stepping inside, Alice and Marta wiped off any residue from crying. Alice stopped upon hearing the station wagon pulling in; John was home.

That evening, they had a hot meal with iced tea, which was a bit of a pleasure they enjoyed together. "John, is there any news today?" Alice asked this question every evening at suppertime.

"Not much, except the neighbors are friendly. They wave when they see me. I hear they and everyone in town are value centered and dependent on each other."

"That'd be difficult for us to do, not knowing anybody," Julian said with a mouthful of food.

"I can say one thing for 'em: they're a tight-knit community. I heard that's how the town's founding fathers decreed it to be when they first settled. Even today, they carry their tradition of meetings and discussing Somerville's future. They're supposed to have a town hall meeting once a month." John looked off into space, wondering how those gatherings worked. What he also didn't know was they'd planned to expand the town boundaries, with the funds for the city projects coming from a founding family named Somerset.

John wanted to understand the residents' mindset. He'd

heard that at these meetings, the townsfolk announced their needs, objections, and visions for the town's growth and survival. Socializing such as this appealed to him because it would develop trust among the citizens. It was a trust that accepted everyone's spiritual beliefs and judged no one as better or worse than others. The other way to learn to trust them, John gathered, was by attending one of their churches or a town hall meeting. He thought of all the churches he had seen around town.

Somerville contained seven churches, each with a different belief. Upon hearing from Alice at a town hall meeting that John was a minister, some of the townsfolk decided they would like to give him a try at ministering. They had already accepted his family into their fold. However, John and his family were unaware of this information, so they continued their cautious conduct toward the local folks.

That evening, before their Bible reading and prayers, John wanted to assure them they'd made a worthy move. "I spoke to some men gathered at the post office this afternoon. They informed me the people here are polite, kind, and easygoing. I figured they're similar to our people back home. I mention this 'cause I too fretted about the locals. I can tell you there's no need to fret, so let's relax about them. OK? Now, where did we leave off in our reading?"

"John," Alice interrupted. "What else did they say?" She sensed he wasn't telling them everything. "If there's something else we need to know, then do tell us. The kids need to know what's going on in town so they can be extra cautious not to step on any toes." Alice's facial expression showed her impatience, but her voice remained calm.

John noticed but stayed calm himself. "They mentioned that the town leaders expect newcomers to adjust to the rules and their traditions. Otherwise, they'll have to leave the same way they came: forlorn and broke."

"That's tough to swallow," Alice replied.

"I didn't want to mention this, but it's just as well y'all know how they feel. I figured we'll adjust and join in the teamwork. I don't want us to be ostracized. And by the way, they welcome the hardworking migrant."

John agreed with the townsfolk's belief toward negative attitudes that might jeopardize their bylaws. They couldn't have rebellious people taking part in their town meetings. Such people could hinder teamwork and social events meant to raise money for the town's growth. The patriarchs understood this and worked hard to keep the town running peacefully and orderly. They even posted their doctrines outside, under a glass case, on the city hall walls so every person passing by on the sidewalk would have an opportunity for reading them.

John considered these rules and principles and wanted his family to abide by them. He hoped they might fare better. He wanted them to become town builders as the early patriarchs intended for newcomers. John finished the Bible reading, and later that evening, he explained more to Alice on what he'd heard.

"We must encourage the kids to be amicable to the locals and not judge them so harshly. They're normal people trying to make a livin', as is everybody else. We need to work together with them. So come next week, you and me are goin' to a town hall meeting to introduce ourselves."

"If that's what you think is best, then we'll do it." Alice

wasn't sure this move would work, but she trusted her husband. *It'll help us adjust sooner than later,* she thought.

After attending a meeting, the townspeople accepted John and Alice as members. They found them to be hardworking, honest, and sociable people. Thereafter, John always had steady work and made enough wages to keep them afloat. There would even be extra money for fixing the rental.

"This home meets our needs. Except look at those brown rings on the ceiling—this place leaks. I'll patch the leaky roof before the next rainfall. Alice, have you been saving tin lids from the canned goods? Remember me asking? I'll be needing them for patching holes." John said while looking out the kitchen window. The clouds forming in the east warned of approaching storms.

The next day, he took inventory of his equipment before fixing the roof. He needed to build a ladder out of store-bought lumber. This project would take money from his savings, and he didn't know anybody well enough to borrow things. Even if he did, he was too proud to ask. He could borrow a ladder from somebody in the town hall committee but didn't want to appear a beggar. That, and he was not a user of people. He gave in and purchased ladder-making supplies.

"All right, Alice. I've got the roof patched. It'll stay thataway till we can afford store-bought roofing materials. The same goes for those pipes under the bathroom and kitchen sinks. If you notice any leaks, let me know right away." John was serious. He meant to fix things as breakages occurred so the home would be cozy and functional for them.

"Thanks for fixing things, John. You know, it'd be nice to have electric light in the living room like the kitchen has." Alice was fishing to hear, "I'll fix that light next."

Instead, John answered, "That's not a priority, Alice, but I'll get around to it. I gotta go see 'bout a job at the melon shack." John pulled his suede hat off the hat rack and placed it on his head. After tipping the brim on his forehead so as not to look sloppy, he stepped out into the sizzling heat.

"Mom," Daniel said, noticing his mother's frown because she wasn't getting electric lights—not that day, anyway. "Didn't Dad do a wonderful job in our room? It's not a screened-in porch anymore. And I'm proud to say I helped him nail boards on the top half," he declared with pride. "You know where that rusty screen was? And you've been using the washing machine, right? I helped with that too. It makes clothes washing much easier. Huh, Mom?" He was fishing for praise.

"It sure does, and it saves my fingers from wearing out on the scrub board." After preparing biscuit dough and letting it sit under a kitchen towel, Alice went outside to bring in the wash.

John arrived, bringing home exciting news. While washing his hands, he noticed Alice outside taking down the dry laundry. "Guess what, honey?" he hollered out the kitchen window. "I got both of us a job: cleaning the melon shed!" He grabbed a green tumbler, pulled the tea pitcher out of the refrigerator and filled it with tea, and met Alice at the back door. After taking a giant gulp, he leaned back on the open screen door, letting her in.

Alice had an armload of clean clothes. "That's wonderful news. Tell me what happened while I fold these clothes." She threw them on the table and began folding them.

John placed his empty tumbler in the sink and gave an enormous possum smile. He turned toward Alice, grabbed her, and kissed her.

"When do we start?" Alice asked, placing folded towels in a pile.

"On Monday. It's part-time work, and they pay good wages." John picked up his clean coveralls, folded them, and then folded his shirts.

After finishing their work on the front gate, Marta and Linda turned to go inside. They'd missed most of their parents' conversation and heard only the last sentences as they started up the porch steps.

"We'll talk 'bout this later; I gotta get to the toolshed and find our cleaning tools. That's one reason I got the job: I told the supervisor I had my tools. Plus, someone gave me a great recommendation. I'll tell you more tonight after we put the children to bed." John skipped down the porch steps. "Hello, my lovelies!" He patted the girls on the head as he passed.

"Dad got a job?" Linda asked, jumping with joy. "Yippee!" She waved her arms and ran to hug her mom.

"Yes, he did. He'll give us more details later. Here, put these clothes away, girls." Alice handed Marta and Linda bed linen and towels. Then she pulled out vegetables to prepare for dinner.

Meanwhile, Julian wandered from wall to wall in the living room, checking out the wall sockets. Though he could hear his parents' conversation, he couldn't care less. Julian asked, "Are we ever gonna get the electricity fixed in here, Mom? This is the only room without it. I think it's that broken ceiling fixture causing the problem." Julian wished they had electricity in there so he could see television shows, but Alice wouldn't have the TV set placed in any other part of the house containing power. This was her plan to save money on the electric bill.

"Why? Because you wanna turn on Grandma's television and see if it works?" Daniel winced, taking his clean clothes to his room.

"Sure, I do. There's nothing else to do. I'm bored, and that set ain't meant for a decoration," Julian snapped.

"All right, stop this!" Alice admonished, putting a casserole into the oven.

"What's wrong with the living room lightbulb, Marta?" Linda said, looking around to make sure Julian wasn't listening.

"Well, pumpkin, see those wires sticking out near the light fixture up there? They need attaching to something. But don't you fret. Daddy will fix them soon," Alice replied, hoping the answer satisfied Linda because she didn't know the answer either.

Julian, who was inspecting a wall socket behind the sofa, heard the girls' conversation. "Yeah, except Dad is fixing the priorities first. That fixture isn't one of them, and that's why we have to use the oil lamp in here. If he fixed it, I bet the electric wall sockets might work too. I can't wait to turn on the TV and see those neat westerns." Julian spoke blissfully while pushing the sofa back against the wall. Then he walked into the kitchen and opened a cupboard door. "Here, Daniel, make yourself useful. Help me set the table." He grumbled as he handed Daniel the plates.

"Why do I have to help you? That's your job," Daniel complained at having to help Julian with his chore.

"Yeah, well, I was busy checking the wall sockets in the living room!" Julian retorted. "I'm behind my chores. Now, hurry it up and help me!"

Marta was tired of this talk of the light fixture, so she took the broom and went outside to sweep the front porch. Gray clouds forming in the east warned of an incoming storm. She wondered whether heavy fogs would roll in after the rain. She didn't understand how it might affect them, not having experienced this weather condition. *Dear Lord, don't let them hinder our survival. Please help us know how to survive when it gets here. Otherwise, it'll be doom in the gloom for my family. Amen.*

Chapter 17

Alice

"Work in a packing house?" Marta exclaimed. "Doing what?" She stopped cracking store-bought eggs into a bowl. A stream of morning sunlight lit the kitchen as the sun reached the top of several fruit trees, casting its orange light on their tops. The summer heat penetrated the glass windows and smothered the home.

Alice spoke excitedly over their new friend. "Well, do you remember that nice young man, Henry, who helped us with the flat tire? Dad ran into him at the Waters' store. He recognized your dad and inquired how we were getting along." She pulled out the milk and she poured it into the aluminum tumblers. After emptying the glass bottle, she set it outside on the porch for the milkman to take on his next round.

The children, who were taking their seats at the table, heard the conversation. "Mom, you didn't tell us Dad had talked with him!" Marta cracked the last of the eggs and scrambled them.

"Yes, he did, and guess what? He directed Dad to go to the packing house and look up the manager. Henry told 'em to mention his name, and we'd have jobs there.

He gave us good recommendations too. Praise the Lord!" Alice couldn't contain her joy as she set the plates and then moved on to the oven to remove hot biscuits.

"What will you do there?" Daniel asked while picking up his burgundy aluminum tumbler and taking a sip.

"Dad and I will clean the melon shed. It's part-time work, but between the both of us, we'll have nice paychecks next week. They pay weekly. That'll help us with finances, plus they're located nearby."

"Can we have eggs now, Marta?" Linda begged, not caring about her mother's conversation.

"Wait a minute! Mom's gonna make gravy," Julian snapped, his fingers wrapped around an aquamarine tumbler.

"So when will you start work?" Marta inquired, taking out the flour from a cupboard and the milk from her green tumbler to use for the gravy.

"We'll begin in the morning and be back by noon. Kids, you must clean the house and do your reading afterward. Your dad and I don't want you wandering the streets when we're not home. Is that understood?" Alice declared authoritatively, hoping they took her seriously.

"But, Mom, we've read those same books so many times, and there's no library that I've noticed so we can check out some books. Can we walk over to the pavilion and sit and wait for you and Dad instead?" Daniel put on his sweet face, hoping to convince his mom to say yes.

"No. Do as you're told and behave yourselves/ That goes for every one of you—especially you, Julian. Did you hear me?"

When their mother's face was turned away, Julian smirked at her as if she was his enemy. His disrespect was obvious to everyone except to her. "Sure, I will, Mother." Julian smiled when she looked over at him.

"You'll give us a terrible reputation, and nobody's gonna want us here if you don't behave. You must obey me!" Alice didn't enjoy raising her voice, but without doing so, Julian would do as he pleased. She understood him better than anyone else because he had seen Phil in the same phase when he was Julian's age. Still, she acted as if she didn't understand Julian but was only bothered by his obnoxious ways. "One more thing: you're not damaging our good name in this town. You ruined it in Arizona, but I'm keeping my eye on you, Julian. And you will not throw spiteful fits here either—not in front of the townspeople. You understand?" Alice kept from clenching her teeth. She'd never been this upset with him.

I oughta tell John about Julian, but he'll take the razor strap to him. I can't bear seeing such cruel discipline. Lord, how do I tell him of Julian's mean streak and cruel antics against his siblings without John losing his temper? Though the law allowed spanking, she'd rather not use such measures. She was lax with discipline, and she prayed God's conviction upon them that they might learn proper behavior. She hoped they'd obey Him.

While serving breakfast, Marta noticed Julian's glare. She wondered why he was doing this. It could be anything since he'd become sensitive three years back. Marta turned her eyes away from him, hoping she was wrong.

While making fists under the table, Julian aimed them at Marta. He wished his mother wasn't there so he could punch Marta because he couldn't stand admonishment in front of girls. His manly attitude, exhibiting itself with pride, caused him to readily lose his temper. Yet he restrained himself with all his inner force, instead dog-staring at her. It shamed him having women picking on him. He blamed Marta for it, though he knew she hadn't tattled.

Alice hoped he'd outgrow his meanness soon. Meanwhile, she and her husband worked in the packing house for the rest of August.

On weekends when she was off work, she'd have the children clean the backyard. "OK, kids, let's fill these gunny sacks with junk. We're gonna remove this burned pile and grow us a sizeable garden in its place." The blackened pile stood high to her waist. Though she couldn't see it being cleared in one day, they'd work steadily and make dents in the giant mass until it was gone.

They filled the sacks with rusted cans and pieces of dented pipes, broken dishes, charred chair rungs, and other strange and gnarled rubbish. Alice gave her children continual praise for their labor. By the middle of August, they'd cleared the space of the waste. Alice finished raking the charred ground and visualized where she'd make furrows for fall vegetables.

"Children, place the sacks by the front gate, would ya? Dad will haul them to the dump next Saturday." Alice leaned on the rake and looked up to heaven. *Thank You, Lord, for every wonderful thing happening to us. Especially for my children, who are doing their work without too much complaining.* "We'll sow vegetable seeds in this spot. I'll be able to grow enough vegetables to can for winter."

The children, grateful because now they'd have space for playing games, stood in awe at the wide space. "I'll have Dad build a fence around the garden patch so y'all can play around it."

"I don't think I want to play out here—not with Julian!" Daniel retorted with an unsavory smirk. He'd had enough of Julian's meanness back home and would not allow that routine to start over. He stood firm with his arms crossed. A look on his face spoke defiance as he faced Julian and stated, "I'll stand against you now, brother. You ain't getting away with it here. I'm bigger and smarter than I used to be, so stand back!"

Noticing Daniel's firm stance and angry words, Alice spoke up. "Now, wait a minute, Daniel. Julian ain't gonna act thataway anymore. He's not gonna fight or pick on you kids anymore. If I hear he's acting up, I'll tell your dad." Alice acted tough, though this wasn't in her character— and Julian knew this.

Alice saw that Julian's misbehavior had become a nuisance and pure trouble. *I have to retrain his attitude, and fast. And how will I encourage Marta's viewpoints against him to change? Help me to help them change before it's too late, Lord, and they become intolerable and useless to society. O Lord, don't let Julian ruin our dignified name here.*

She told them, "Listen here. God has given us a fresh start in a new town, where the residents don't know of your misbehavior and my inadequacies as a mother. You'll work on your attitudes, and I'll work on my motherly skills. I asked God to forgive my incompetence, and I take responsibility for your failures and problems. You'll change your behavior starting today. We're all making amends. That includes disciplining you. I'll be consistent and won't lapse on it anymore." Alice was adamant about ensuring her children grow up as respectable and responsible people.

Julian stood back, wondering what he'd done wrong. *I've been behaving and haven't hit them since we arrived in Somerville. Why am I getting lectured now?* He picked up his shovel and walked to the shed. Before the others came to put away their tools, he stood there and cried. There was something annoying him; it condemned his callous behavior. He recalled the horrid ways he'd acted back home and hated himself for being so cruel and ruining their image. He didn't understand why he played awful tricks on his siblings. After wiping the tears back with his grimy hands, he turned to go in the house and wash up before they saw him in that condition.

Lord, let it be he's regretting his mean behavior, Alice thought as she noticed Julian's sorrowful demeanor. She said nothing because she didn't want to bring attention to his composure. The children would question why he was acting this way. She couldn't explain it herself.

Though she wanted the best for them, teaching certain behaviors such as kindness, goodness, patience, and faith was challenging. She'd worked on her discipline measures but had yet to find a balance. *Perhaps it's been the way I discipline,* she thought. *I give them warnings but never follow through with punishment.*

"Mom, we're tired. Can we take a break?" Daniel tried speaking without moaning.

"Sure, let's go in." Alice had a pitcher of ice tea ready. After sitting at the table, they relaxed and talked amicably.

"Mom, what's it like in the melon shack?" Daniel asked, gulping his tea from a golden tumbler.

"Well, the stench is overbearing. Your dad and I have to throw out a lot of rotten melons that've fallen off the steel conveyor belt. They roll and hide in conspicuous places and rot there. So we have to find them wherever they've rolled. Then we throw them in steel trash cans and sweep the place. At the end of our shift, we dump the cans into trash bins located alongside the road."

"That sounds awful. I never want to do that job." Linda grimaced, keeping her lips together and hiding her two missing front teeth.

"And you won't have to. That's why when school starts, I'm gonna enroll you kids in school. I want you to get an education, unlike your daddy and me. I want every one of you to speak proper grammar so you can have better jobs, not dirty work as we're doing. You must work using your brain, not your backs. At least, that's what my mama always said." Alice smoothed Linda's loose hair strands and stroked her ebony braids. Linda smiled, exposing her front gums.

On the first day of September, Alice put on her newest-looking navy blue dress and her straw hat with matching flowers, and she walked her children to school. Her fair skin stood out against the dark blues. Thereafter, every morning she'd walk them there while the packing house was closed for the season. After dropping them off, she'd go shopping or search for other work.

As a Christian mother, Alice taught them the meaning behind cleanliness. On weekends, she'd have the kids scrub the house. Though the children complained, she didn't admonish them and simply reminded them it was their Godly duty.

During the weekends, they peacefully performed their assigned chores. "Marta, your job is to scour the doors and walls. Linda will polish the furniture, Julian will sweep, and Daniel will scrub the bathroom. I'll clean the windows inside and out."

"Mom, don't forget the picture window in the living room," Linda reminded her.

"I won't. I'll clean out the woodstove too. There's no telling how long it's been since its belly was cleaned out, and good. From the looks of this house, the previous occupants probably left it piled high with ashes." Alice wondered how dirty its inside was and how much time she'd have to spend doing the job. Her schedule for the day was full, but cleaning everything thoroughly in the house was a priority.

"Mom, you want me to clean the wood box? I don't mind doing it," Julian volunteered. "I can clean out the creosote from the stove pipe too."

"No, don't bother. Your dad cleaned that when he reattached it to the stove."

"Do we have to clean every Saturday, Mother?" Linda asked with a scowl.

"Not this much, but yes, we do. We've gotta keep things clean and tidy. Your dad doesn't care for half-baked work—you know that!" Alice smiled at her youngest child, appreciating her concern.

After scrubbing the walls, Marta needed to empty the small aluminum tub of dirty water into the sink. She filled it with clean water and then walked back to the wall to finish the scrubbing. Julian stood with his arms stretch out in front of it, purposely blocking her way. Marta said, "Julian, move. I need to finish scrubbing the wall. This tub is heavy. Now move!"

Alice overheard the commotion. "Move, Julian! What has Marta done for you to act this way against her?"

She was upset with her son's abusive behavior, and she wondered why he did it without provocation. Alice knew he'd had remorse for his old ways, but why did he continue misbehaving cruelly? His mischief and moodiness increased daily, but she didn't mention Julian's behavior to John.

In the evenings, she made sure they said their prayers. This included praying for their neighbors, teachers, and the people they met in their lives. She hoped to encourage them to think optimistically of their new society. *They might come to accept this town as friendly, and feel secure,* she figured.

While she waited for other work to come along, Alice would cook supper every afternoon and have it ready for John and the kids, whom she loved dearly. When John came home from work grimy and sweaty, she said nothing mean to agitate him. "Oh, you're tired. Let me help you with your stuff," was all she'd say. She'd take his black lunchbox to the kitchen and empty its contents.

"Yeah, I'm dirty and soaked in sweat too." After placing his hat on the wall rack, he'd reach for his iced tea waiting on the counter. Alice was always glad to have him home. She saw past his outer appearance and noticed the wonderful man that he was. She'd have his tea cold and supper ready for serving, and on cool days, she'd have his coffee piping hot.

"What did you do today, Alice? It's gotta be lonely without the kids around the house," John said after his bath one day.

"I did the usual: cleaned house, prepared supper, and then walked to the school to pick 'em up and walk 'em home. Oh, and I got to socialize with other parents as usual." Alice sounded content. Her children were on track to setting healthy routines.

She thought of back home and the differences between the two places. The needs to run the homes were opposite each other. One place was self-contained, and the other needed money to keep it running. The adjustments they'd have to make for the rental were extreme.

Their needs for winter, spring, and the following summer needed careful planning. There were many goals they needed to complete before June. This included having enough funds every month to pay for the water, electricity, gas, trash, milk, eggs, and other food items. Back home, it was cheaper to survive.

When in Arizona, they didn't pay for gas, electricity, or water, which came from a well. The kerosene oil lamps provided inexpensive light, and a wood stove was used for cooking, with wood gathered from the nearby mountains. They had farm animals providing fresh milk and eggs. Alice made cheese and sold it along with freshly baked bread to the store. Their potted garden grew vegetables year-round. Bartering these products for supplies they needed helped them monetarily.

On her treks around town, she'd look for a church building up for sale, rent, or abandoned. Her dedication to God, returning her family to church routines, and her husband's mission as a minister caused her to plan to have a church of their own once again, resettling their roots in a lifestyle familiar to them. She wanted this foundation of faith that they might always stand strong, even throughout the most tumultuous times.

On her many trips around town, her focus was on

locating such a building. Then one day, she found a one-hundred-year-old small church. Its plaster had chipped, exposing red bricks. The white paint that remained had aged over the years and discolored. The parking lot resembled a war-torn airfield, and the withered bushes and trees around it stood in dry, cracking wood stocks.

Alice wasted no time searching for the owners and found it abandoned. She was eager to tell John of her discovery.

"Guess what?" Alice began her conversation at supper one evening. "I found an empty church building. After inquiring at city hall, they gave it to us in one condition: that we keep the doors open every Sunday for three years. John, are you listening? Do you agree, or should I cancel it?"

After biting on a biscuit, John asked, "You found what?" He couldn't believe what he was hearing.

"What do you think?" Alice said again. "I have the contract I picked up at the office. I know we can handle it for that period. Can we claim the building, John?" She took a spoonful of her chicken soup and waited for a reply.

"It sounds too good of a deal. I'll go with you tomorrow. I'm getting off early; Tom said it's been slow hauling gravel. I drove the truck only twice today, and then we cleaned the shop until we closed early."

"John, I pray our children's conduct will change once they attend church and hear your sermons. You'll inspire them for better behavior and make it easier for them to set roots in this town." Yet she wondered, *Have we made a mistake moving them away from their secure environment at their delicate age? I hope it isn't too late!*

Chapter 18

View of the Valley

Do farmers consider their workers to bless them, money wise? Where do farmers send the produce after harvesting? Marta thought. *Do farmers grow them because of an innate desire to farm, or to become rich? Is it satisfying work for them?*

It was an unfamiliar world to Marta and her family. Even in her outlandish thoughts, she never figured that such a world existed before they'd arrived in the valley. It was breathtaking and refreshing to the eye, and her backyard was as a small valley filled with fruit-bearing trees. She hoped before the cold weather set in, they'd produce enough fruit for her mother to can several jars.

The first thing Marta came to love about the flat country was the smell of wet dirt and clay. The intense earthy scent tempted Marta to think of digging in the soft soil. It reminded her of the damp earth back home after a summer rain, where afterward she and her siblings ran barefooted through the wet clay.

"Finish changing out of your Sunday clothes so we can go for a drive," Dad announced one Sunday after church services. He sounded happy and proud of his children.

He'd reward them with a countryside drive after church service every once in a while, if he had extra gas money.

"Oh, boy! Are we gonna have a picnic, Mom?" Daniel asked, smacking his lips.

"Sure, and we'll sit under that large oak growing by the river outside of town."

"I love those drives," Marta stated. "We'll get to see other crops too. There are so many varieties that I can't remember them all." Marta and her family would see fields and orchards with verdant furrows of fruit trees. There were also lush fields filled with patches of corn, chilies, cucumbers, tomatoes, artichokes, potatoes, and cotton.

"Dad, how many types of fruit trees do they grow out here?" Julian asked politely.

"I don't rightly know. But some orchards contain apricots, peaches, plums, oranges, lemons, grapefruits, almonds, pecans, walnuts, and olives, both the black and green kind. They grow wine, table, and raisin grapes too."

"The valley is a sight to behold for a person not accustomed to seeing so much green growth." Marta beamed with delight at the surrounding beauty. "I enjoy the green grass growing in yards. It lifts my spirits to see their lush growth. Can we grow our lawn like them, Mom?"

"I know what you mean, Marta. Maybe one day," Mom said longingly.

"Dad, what do you know of this agriculture?" Marta probed.

"I can tell you it's amazing how the farmers can dig such wide and straight furrows. The machinery they use is innovative." Dad was as surprised by the agricultural wonders as were the children. They had no idea such technology existed.

On their drives through the country, Marta saw the method used to irrigate the fields. "Dad, do they dig wells? There's so much water rushing up from the ground, filling those ditches. And how do they have it run from them into the furrows?" The gusts of water spewing from below the ground like cosmic activity awed her.

"Yes, they do, and they reuse them over again. The workers fill the ditches with this water. A long mound of dirt separates them from the furrows. Then irrigators dip one end of a short, plastic, half-circle pipe, called a siphon pipe, into these ditches. They hold slight amounts of water in them, and after quick swinging actions, they flip it over into a furrow. It lays over the dirt embankment. Water then flows automatically into the long furrow. They continue this process for each one."

"How did the farmers learn to irrigate, Dad?" Julian asked.

"I don't know, son, but I agree with you kids: I like how the gushin' water flows automatically from ditch to furrow. It's an ingenious procedure. Look over there." John pointed to the furrows they were driving past. "Look how the sunlight beams gleam off the water? They appear as streaks of flashing light in them furrows."

"My teacher said the valley is a cornucopia of fresh food. She said that once, the land was dry and growing weeds, including the tumbleweeds. Today, it's considered an irrigated desert," Marta explained proudly. "You can see how it looked when you see the weed field at the end of our street. It grows the same weeds that grew everywhere before they transformed it."

Daniel spoke up with pride. "I know that field. It's filled with wild sunflowers, goat's head, nightshade, wild tufts of grass, and tumbleweeds. That's what my teacher told us."

"The tumbleweeds are my favorite," Marta replied. "They have a lovely blue tint and grow in round shapes. They remind me of the Arizona cypress that grew in the mountains back home. Maybe they're not as tall and don't contain the aromatic pine scent, but I enjoy seeing them."

The family didn't know that after a long, dry season, these tumbleweeds, once broken at the root stem, eventually dried up. The crispy looking, round beige mass of needles become lightweight, allowing the blistering winds to blow them around, rolling them from field to field or across the roads. At times, devil dusters picked them up and twirled them in the air, settling them far from their growing spot. A few remained intact to the ground, their roots hugging dry ground and surviving on what moisture remained in the atmosphere. Otherwise, these tumbleweeds with fresh blue-green needles remained planted until the early winter, if frost didn't kill them off.

As far as Marta could see across the countryside, she saw flat, cultivated farmland. The Sierra Nevada Mountains stood far to the east. The valley was generous with its bounty. *I wish Phil were here to see this blessed country,* Marta thought. *I hope he's still alive.*

Chapter 19

Phil, Lost in North Korea

Phil's unit moved farther into North Korea, where they hoped to stop the aggression of communism. It was monsoon season; this wet season lasted from July to the end of September. The heavy rains poured nonstop, causing the rivers to swell. Their overflowing banks becoming dangerous.

As they moved to higher ground, the army unit also lost contact with their mail carrier. They'd been aware of the possibilities of flash floods occurring, something familiar to Phil. He'd seen their destructive power in his home country during their rainy season in August, though they were of a shorter cycle. He appreciated the knowledge he'd gained on their dangerous assaults, as when they caused flooding in town.

Phil had arrived in Korea the summer of 1951, after a brief training period. Now, he was tired and homesick. The excitement of visiting foreign shores had faded. There was no word from his commanding general when his unit would return to America. Because of severe scrimmages with North Korean, America had lost hundreds of army and marine personnel.

Many artillery duels, scrimmages, standoffs, ambushes, and ridge battles had exhausted the military personnel. They were pushing back the North Koreans but at a horrendous price. America was paying, with the bulk of casualties occurring during Phil's first year. He prayed they'd return home soon, with the war ending in the next few months.

The storm of bombings and shootings had stopped for a while. Phil rejoiced in the brief break. But overhead, another kind of storm crawled. It blackened the late summer sky, warning of tumultuous clouds ready to burst over his unit. Constant, torrential rains, which would batter the soldiers for a solid three months, were about to begin. Though Phil had survived last year's typhoon season, he hadn't adapted to its severe activity. It poured every day without warning and threatened anyone in its path with heavy floods.

In his two men tent, Phil sat on a tin pail writing a letter home while outside, the wind blew violently. Lightning struck, and rain pelted the land. While wrapped in a green wool blanket and stabilizing his notebook on his knees, Phil wrote a few words.

Hello, everyone,

I hope this letter finds everyone well. I am doing OK. I'm stuck in North Korea for now. They say we'll be moving farther north when the storms cease. I'm not sure what it's like up there, but I've heard stories. It shouldn't be so bad. We're pushing the enemy back. I'll mail this letter as soon as the mail run opens again. I miss hearing from everyone. Please forgive me for not writing any sooner. But it's been busy here. I gotta go. I love you all.

Phil.

The letter was brief, and Phil didn't want to say any more that might worry his loved ones. *They have enough problems of their own,* he thought. *If time permits, I'll write more later.*

"Do you think they'll get our letters out?" a young soldier sitting on a cot next to him asked.

"I don't know, Arnie. I hope so, and soon! I haven't received a reply from the last letter I sent them. What if they've moved? Dad wrote in his last letter that the local mine was shutting down and everyone was moving out. I sure hope they didn't move and forgot to tell me about it." Phil looked forlorn but knew he served a mighty God who was caring for them. He'd pray they were well. His daily morning conversations with God reassured his faith.

"You mean they moved and forgot to tell you?" The bewildered young soldier couldn't understand why any parent would do that to their children.

"That's not what I mean. Their letter is probably stuck somewhere between here and America. I don't think my parents would abandon me. I might be twenty-two, but I still need them, which includes Dad's sermons. Besides, I have the Lord watching over me. I'm not worried. I'll hear from them soon."

"So your old man is a preacher?"

"Yeah, he is! He's a real good one too!" Phil rubbed his eyes as if tired. He didn't want to believe they'd moved, and because he did not know where they'd gone, he worried he might end up losing them. Worst yet, he didn't know if he'd make it back home.

The war was getting fierce, and his unit was walking into its heart. He sat motionless and stared through a crack on the tent door, its flaps flapping in the fierce wind.

They shifted back and forth as the wind maliciously kicked them. The only light he could see outside the flapping flaps was an occasional flash of lightning.

The pouring rain fell heavily upon them. "This is what the locals call a monsoon?" Phil hollered his remark over the noise of the storm. "I heard it's worse in the south. The captain said earlier we've entered a protected valley amid the mountains, so we're getting it lighter here. What do you think, Arnie?" Phil was making small talk. With winter coming in, he knew they'd get the worst of the snowstorms farther north. The astronomical blizzards would surge without warning.

The land produced slight amounts of plant life, making locating wood for campfires a major task. And there was no guarantee they'd receive allowances for the petrol or gas needed to run their equipment.

Arnie didn't answer because he was reading a Western. Off in the distance, lightning cracked, and seconds later a peal of thunder rolled in the heavens. Phil prayed. Being the assistant pastor for his dad had prepared him with faith for the poorest of circumstances. Knowing that God was in control of every aspect of his life gave him hope. He put away his letter in his Bible, until he could write more, and he lay on his freezing cot.

Phil fell into a restless sleep as the violent rain poured. He dreamed of his family, including his grandmother, gathering for Christmas. They decorated the parsonage with green, red, and silver garlands. His dad had chopped an ice-blue Arizona cypress from the high country. His mother had baked sugar cookies, and a pot of pork hominy stew was boiling. Marta chopped lettuce, onion, and parsley for garnishes. Hot chocolate simmered on the stove as Grandmother finished knitting mittens for him. He sniffed the spicy scents of the hominy and the heavy aroma of chocolate. Strung popcorn hung around the tree. He awoke to a quiet morning with the storm blowing over for a while. The dream was fresh on his mind, and he wished it might come true.

Through the split of the canvas flaps, a beam of sunshine streaked across the tent's dirt floor, their flapping movements ending with the stillness of the storm. Phil jumped out of the cot and headed outdoors; the smell of wet dirt was pungent. The bitter cold striking his face brought instant numbness. It wasn't difficult for him to grasp the gravity of the cold.

He looked beyond their camp and saw bare, rolling hills that reminded him of those behind the parsonage. But the hills back home were covered with pinion pines, scrub brush, cacti, and tall grasses, which were a sight to behold. He consoled himself by getting his letter out.

There was no information notifying his unit of their next move, so he'd write more later. He'd wait for orders to move on, or reports notifying his platoon the enemy was a ridge or two away. He prayed they'd not engage in battle but that his unit's presence was enough to frighten the enemy to move farther north. But the next scrimmage was never too far away. *Lord, help me and our unit survive the next battle. I wanna make it home one day. I don't want my body left out in this forsaken land. Amen.*

Chapter 20

Marta Falls into Depression

With the terrifying dream, Marta experienced a long, weary night. She began mumbling and tossing with great turmoil after that. "No, I tell you, no!" she said in her sleep.

The dream went on. A wiry man, garbed in beige, waved his arms in the air. "There's no more copper. We gotta close the mine for good," the foreman announced.

"No, no, stop, stop, there's copper in the mine. You gotta dig a little deeper. Don't stop now." Marta stood outside the mine yelling at the man, trying to convince him of the abundance of copper. *If they'd only dig deeper.*

The man hollered his instructions again until they abandoned the place as trucks filled with men rolled away from the hill. The last copper ore load, less than half a truck, also left the region. Posted signs outside metal gates proclaimed, "No trespassing!"

Marta struggled to breathe as if she'd been running all night, and she vividly remembered the man's words in her dream. After sitting up in bed, she recalled the images of copper, rocks, shovels, men walking away, and trucks driving out from the mining district for the last time. It frightened her. The mine had closed forever. The event had caused her anxiety, and that, coupled with Julian's rebellious conduct against her, deepened her stress. Marta noted Linda slept quietly. Marta was glad the child hadn't heard her frightful words.

"What's wrong, Marta? Are you OK?" Alice walked into the dark bedroom, trying not to fall. After sitting on the bedside, she hugged her daughter. "Shh, hush, my girl. Mama is here." Alice worried. She could see that the heavy stress of moving and settling into the rental had become too big a burden for Marta. It had disturbed her deeply. *Was she replaying old problems in her mind, causing her unnecessary stress?* Alice speculated. She didn't understand why Marta was suffering mentally.

Alice appreciated John's powerful, faith-based sermons, and she hoped they were enough to lift Marta's spirits. Besides, they had a deeply rooted prayer life, and Alice made sure they established routines keeping confusion to a minimum. Still, they had failed to notice Marta's gradual decline in her well-being. Neither she nor John had noticed it until it was too late.

Thinking back to Marta's mood swings, Alice remembered her concerns when the announcement of the mine's closing occurred. She was still unaware of its consequence on Marta's outlook of life. She recalled a few choice words Marta had used to characterize the foreman and the mine supervisor. Alice didn't take this well but had faith and patience Marta would outgrow this bitterness.

Alice tried not to pay attention to her mean comments as she took their ruthlessness to be common among teenagers. *Hopefully she'll outgrow it. Having teenagers is difficult.* She thought of Julian, who was also experiencing hormonal spikes.

What if they aren't hormonal spikes? What if they're simply not adjusting in some way? Alice didn't know what to think. *When will they go back to normalcy? And how well will they fare when it's over?*

"Oh, Mom," Marta sobbed into her mother's shoulder. "What's happening to me? I thought I'd passed away. I couldn't breathe." Marta held on to her mother as if that night was to be her last.

"Honey, what's going on?" Her dad walked in holding an oil lamp. He didn't want to turn on the light switch and risk waking everybody with the bright lights. He placed his arm around his wife's shoulder. Upon seeing Marta's heavy breathing from the panic attack she had suffered, he knelt by the bed and held his daughter.

"Dad, it was awful," Marta sniveled.

"Don't talk now, Marta. Let's get you up and have a cup of warm milk. Would you like that?" John helped her out of bed while her mom pulled her robe around her.

While feeling around the floor for her slippers with her bare feet, she stopped and muttered, "Mom, I can't find my slippers. Julian hid them again." Marta began bawling again as if her missing slippers were a tremendous loss.

"Marta, calm yourself. Here they are." Her mom helped her put them on.

"What's this? Why is Julian taking her slippers?" John sounded infuriated at what he'd heard.

"Oh, it's nothing. She's having a nightmare," Alice answered, hoping this was the truth.

"What do you mean, it's nothing? It sounds to me Julian has been a problem to her. I can see it in this anxiety attack," John said angrily.

Alice didn't answer as she walked into the kitchen,

opened the refrigerator, and pulled out the milk bottle. She changed the subject. "Let's have a glass of milk and cookies. It's midnight. We can sleep in—tomorrow is Saturday. We don't have to start work till ten in the morning." She kept her eyes from meeting John's annoyed look. She realized she should have mentioned Julian's misbehavior sooner. Instead, she'd been putting it off, hoping he'd improve on his own.

"I'm going to bed. We'll finish this talk tomorrow, Alice." John turned to go into their dark bedroom, leaving the kerosene lamp on the kitchen counter.

After drinking her warm milk, Marta could speak again. "It's those miners, Mom. They shut down the copper ore mine. Why did they have to close it?" After talking it over with her mom, she felt sleepy again and returned to bed without her mother's help. Everything was normal again once she remembered they were living in Somerville. They were far away from the mines and the desert. It gave her a sensation of relief things might turn out well. They were in a new town filled with fresh hope.

The morning found John chopping wood while Alice hurried to get ready for work after preparing breakfast. "Marta, wake the kids and come eat breakfast. I've got it ready. You'll hafta serve them. Will you do that for me?" Alice removed her apron, revealing her work clothes.

John heard Alice and decided it was time to stop his morning chores. He'd finish praying for Marta's situation on the way to work. He'd have Julian finish piling the chopped wood in the toolshed after breakfast. Then he made a plan to speak to Julian, but he thought, *how might Jesus handle this crisis? Certainly not with angry words*

or a proud spirit. Show me, Lord, how I'm to do this.
Marta's anxiety attack bothered him. They'd not come
this far in their existence to be destroyed by their health.

As he thought of her attack, he recognized this was the
reason for her slacking up on her chores and appearance.
John understood she was suffering, and as a minister, he'd
take this problem to the Lord every day. He'd remind Him
of the seriousness of this problem and of His pr*omises.*
*After all, God said to remind Him in Isaiah 43:26, "Put
me in remembrance."*

Marta's condition infuriated John. It should never have
gotten this severe. He remembered her characteristics,
signs that something was wrong with her health. On the
journey, he saw her crying in the rearview mirror. Her
countenance should've been a sign for him to assess her
troubles. He'd never given a second thought that she was
suffering mentally. He always thought of his children
as resilient. *God has a plan for her. He won't let her
emotional state decline.*

John recognized she wasn't a child anymore but a
female teenager, coming of age into adulthood, and he felt
guilty for not being aware of her sensitivity. *How could I
have overlooked this need?* He didn't understand women.
As he continued to think of her illness, he remembered
markings on the back of her legs. Then there were the
bunches of hair lying on the bathroom floor, thick with
roots. *Could her mental anguish have anything to do with
these signs of cruelty? Did Julian cause them?* He'd ask
Marta when the proper time presented itself, or ask Alice.
It bothered him to see his daughter neglect herself.

Since he had become saved many years ago, he
had trained himself to keep his anger from exploding.

Therefore with Marta's problem, he aimed to be gentle and patient. It couldn't have been anything she'd caused. This case required facts, wisdom, and self-control. In the meantime, he'd relax and listen for any confrontations among the children. And when he'd gathered evidence, he would plan on meeting with them as soon as possible. Whatever ailed Marta needed to stop, and soon.

Upon finishing breakfast, John gave a strict order to them with as much gentleness in his voice as he could muster. "Kids, your mom and I hafta go to work today till this afternoon. I don't wanna hear of any fighting between you. You're goin' to get busy cleaning the backyard. Girls, you're to stay away from the boys till I can talk to y'all; maybe it'll be tonight. So after you do your chores, git to your bedrooms and read till we get home. Issues are going on in this family, and I wanna get them cleared up before they escalate to bigger problems. Is that understood?"

They agreed they'd do as he asked. None of them could absorb the complications created by Julian, and they'd never seen their dad working so hard to stay calm when his red face said otherwise. He hugged each child before leaving for work and assured Marta of positive changes that'd take place.

"I'll take care of things, Marta. If anyone doesn't obey me, I want you to tell me when I get back from work. Is that clear to everyone? Marta will keep track of your behavior for me." John looked at his children with a stern look that seemed to state, *Don't defy me.* "Be ready tonight for a discussion. Alice, I'll help you clean the kitchen after supper so Marta can take a break."

Julian scooted back when his dad approached him for

a hug. "Julian, you're the man of the house. When I am gone, I expect you to treat your brother and sisters with respect. If you can't do this, Marta has my permission to give me reports on your behavior, and you'll not get even with her for doing that! Do you understand?"

"Yes, sir!" Julian looked fearful. His dad had given him the right act.

Marta looked at him and felt anger for him. It was an emotion she didn't want and wished she'd change her viewpoints of him. There was something wrong between them, and she couldn't figure what it was. *Hopefully whatever it is will get cleared up at the meeting tonight.* Praying didn't occur to her.

"Alice, as of now, our responsibilities as parents have escaped us." John spoke over the loud engine's roar. "The confusion and calamity existing in our home are both our faults. Do you know when Marta's depression and fears began?" John was sure she'd know because she spent more time with her. He waited for a reply, but it was slow in coming. *What's wrong? She has to have an answer for me. Indeed, she wouldn't lie to protect Julian, would she?*

"Alice, what do you suppose came over Marta? This fear of miners and such. I mean, there's gotta be more than that to her phobias. Do you know anything about it?" John looked at Alice with questioning eyes. He drove slowly that he might have time to talk to her. Besides, they were early as usual.

"John, I meant to talk to you about this, but we've been so busy with our lives that I forgot to mention it."

"Well, we have time before we have to be at work."

"I realize now that we've got to get to the bottom of the source of this anxiety. It has to stop. I remember she mentioned a phobia she had of the town's residents. She feels uneasy with them. Maybe if she was to explore the town and its residents, she might learn to trust them. That would eliminate part of her problem with fear."

"John, you do what you think is best for her, but don't forget she's emotional over everything. I don't understand her sensitivity; she's so delicate." Alice was beyond herself as to how best help Marta.

"I think we oughta let her have free rein in this town. Marta would be free to delve into the shops and experience associating with the people running 'em. She'd find they're as normal as folks back home in traditions and social habits. This might help her relax and gain confidence."

"I agree, John. You're the decision maker. I only ask you not to be too harsh and strict on her. Go lightly with your discipline toward her. She's so frail and impressionable."

"Look, I'll make any amends so Marta may sense her security and well-being. I realize it's partly my fault. I've worked long hours and haven't devoted enough time to her or the other children. Having church services on Sunday might not have been enough time for relaxing. I vow I'll make plans to take them for country drives and picnics more often. I'll spend evenings chatting with them instead of being immersed in my Bible."

"I like your idea of giving her more free time in town. Allowing her to socialize with the townsfolk will help familiarize herself with this community." Alice was grateful her husband was coming around to seeing his children as people in need of his guidance.

"I can tell you one thing, Alice: I don't care for her disheveled appearance. Also, her chores are left incomplete. I pray to the good Lord it is not too late to ease her pains. We need to help her grow healthy during her teenage years."

"I understand, John. I'll do what I need to do as a mother and help her."

"What kind of dad or minister am I, if I fail my family?" John placed one hand on his mouth and nose as if sobbing. "From now on," he said, taking his hand down, "I'll be the disciplinarian with all the children, not just the boys. Alice, I mean to promise God that I'll take the reins and manage the kids before they land in juvenile hall." He pulled into the melon shack parking lot.

Alice was relieved at hearing her husband's plans. She felt the pressure of being the disciplinarian removed from her.

That evening, John held a family meeting in the clean kitchen. Marta noticed the swept floor, a chore she'd often forgotten to complete. After seeing the seriousness on their dad's face, everyone took their seats quietly.

He stood at the head of the table and waited for them to get quiet. "Before we start the meeting, I want the girls to go brush their hair. Boys, let me see your hands." Squeamishly, the boys sprawled their dirty hands before him. John scrutinized them. "Go wash them. They're filthy!" he demanded, checking everybody equally so as not to bring attention to Marta's unkemptness.

"All right, now that everyone's back, we'll begin." John sat pensively, looking at their appearance again. He'd been praying on how to conduct this meeting with sensitivity yet using a firm and gentle tone. "Let's pray before we begin."

They held hands and bowed their heads. "Heavenly Father, guide us in what we are to say. Let us speak truthfully with an open heart. Let nothing be kept back that can destroy, deceive, or tear us further apart. In Jesus's name, we pray. Amen."

Everyone waited respectfully. "What are we meeting for, Dad?" Daniel looked at his siblings, noticing the seriousness on their faces.

John replied, "First, I want to thank every one of you for carryin' on with your chores. We've made progress in the past few weeks. It's not been easy, but we're gettin' situated comfortably. You must continue doing your best in keepin' the family afloat. Whatever your job may be, do your finest. I don't want you leavin' anythin' half-baked. When we do a chore for anyone, God expects us to do it to the utmost of our ability. We do everythin' for His glory and accordin' to His holy will for us. Let us close with prayer." They bowed their heads and waited for their dad to lead.

After prayer, Marta wondered why he brought up topics they already understood. *Or do we?*

Also, don't let me hear that you kids are hurtin' each other, playin' mean tricks, or lyin' and screamin' to each other or your mother. And you won't be negligent in completin' your chores. God loves each one of you very much. He's keepin' an eye on you to make sure you are growin' properly, healthy, and safely. It's not His will for you to fret; leave that to us. If you have a concern, please bring it to my attention. I'll meet with Mother to discuss the problem or problems happenin' here. We'll get back to you individually. Are there questions?"

"I have one. What if one of us is misbehaving? Can we snitch on him, Dad?" Daniel tapped his feet on the chair's rung and wiggled in his chair, fearing retaliation from Julian after the meeting.

John noticed his disposition and gathered something was wrong. *I'll ask Alice later how far back this feud has been going on.* In a soft yet firm voice, he stated, "Yes, Daniel. Y'all can tattle, but only for the next two weeks. We'll meet again then and see how things are goin' among you. There is one request I ask when you tattle: it's that you do it in private with me, that you tell me the truth, and that it be serious. With that information, I'll figure out what's going on here. Then the culprit and I are gonna have a talk. Trouble between you kids is gonna stop. If you feel neglected, unloved, insecure, hopeless, afraid, or doubtful, please speak up." John waited a few minutes, looking to see if anyone raised his or her hand. He knew where the trouble stood but dared not insinuate or cause further division.

"Are you going to spank us, Dad?" Julian looked calm while asking the question.

"No, son, I'm not. I can tell you I'll find a punishment fit for the culprit. If the punishment is not severe enough, I'll talk to Sheriff Rodgers over in Tuleville and plan to have that culprit clean jail cells. I've had to meet with him to minister to prisoners there, so I know him well. Don't think you're above this punishment. I'll not hesitate to take you up there and leave you there for a week. Do you understand?"

"Will the girls get that punishment too?" Alice considered the wisdom of her husband's discipline strategies.

His wife's naïve attitude annoyed John, but that was one reason why he loved her.

"They're innocent. They've done nothing except try easing the household burdens. I am proud Marta and

Linda are continuing to do their best in completing their chores. As of now, I am giving Marta permission to walk to the post office after school and check for mail. Any letters coming from Phil should come to our new mailbox. Also, Marta, you can stop at the store any day of the week and buy a Coke. Don't bring it home to entice your siblings, though; charge it to my account. You deserve it for the work you've done to help keep the house and children in order while your mother works. I know she appreciates it too."

"What about me? I'm also innocent!" Daniel exclaimed.

"I'm sorry, Daniel. You are that. I'll reward every one of you with a treat at the end of each week."

Daniel smiled with anticipation and looked up to see Julian frowning. Daniel was glad Dad had called this meeting because now they would know Julian was the culprit. Daniel had kept from tattling but was bent on doing so next time Julian misbehaved toward them.

Marta was also beside herself at hearing such wonderful news. She'd be able to visit Henry at the hay shop and Mrs. Waters at the small store—two local people she'd met and liked. They never treated her as an outsider or as a country bumpkin but showed respect for her. Suddenly, it was as if a breath of fresh air entered her soul, giving her renewed life. *I'm to have liberty to meet people and have friends, and I don't have to fear Dad's wrath for being sociable and getting home late? Perhaps he'll let me skip my senior year so I can pitch in and help more often with family matters.*

"I'll get home as soon as I'm through with errands. I'll have time to fix dinner if Mom is working." Marta couldn't believe what she'd just said. Her heart pounded with excitement. She was being allowed to take her time in town and not worry about rushing home. This was a rule that'd always created anxiety for her in the old place.

She recalled those times. If late, she was punished for stalling. She wondered why her dad had changed his opinion. "Dad, who'll care for Daniel and Linda?" she asked, not showing her delight.

"It's OK, Marta. Julian is old enough to watch them for a few minutes till you get home. Isn't that right, Julian? And if you've hurt them, you're gonna answer to me. Do you understand that?" Dad looked sternly at Julian as if to say, *You're not getting another warning.*

"Yes, sir. I understand. I can help them with their homework until Marta gets home. Then we'll help her get dinner ready. That's if you and Mom are working late sir." Julian fidgeted in his chair, knowing he had to straighten up or else meet Dad's strict discipline.

"One more thing, Alice," John said without hesitating. "I want you to take Marta to the hair salon and have her choose a style she'd care to wear. And do something with her jacket—perk it up if you can. She'll wear it till we earn enough income to buy coats for everyone. I think we oughta treat Marta as a seventeen-year-old girl oughta be treated, and that's with respect and patience. Do any of you have questions?" It got quiet after he voiced his orders. No one dared speak back or come against his wishes.

Julian was shaking with fear that his siblings might tattle on him. His guilt concerned his well-being, but otherwise he cared nothing of the horrific schemes he'd plotted against his siblings. Now, he understood punishment was on its way. After the meeting, he'd changed his ways toward them because he didn't want to clean jail cells. Gulping hard, he feared a big quest ahead and decided it was time for him to start praying again. He needed supernatural help.

"One last thing," John's voice rang out. "Does anybody here wish to make any apologies?" He stared at Julian and kept his gaze upon him. It was his way of telling him, *You need to consider repenting.*

Julian understood the message and spoke up, if only to please his dad. "Dad, I wanna say I'm sorry for my behavior with everyone here tonight. I didn't mean to be cruel to anyone. I wanted to have fun. I am sorry if I've hurt anyone, especially you, Marta. Will you forgive me? I won't hurt you ever again or tease you."

"Is that a promise, Julian?" John looked at him sternly.

"Y-yes, sir. It is." Julian appeared to be sorry for his actions, so much that he shed tears. That startled his siblings.

His answer satisfied John. They were on their way to a fresh beginning with improved attitudes. John hoped this would also improve their relationships with each other. "Very well. This meeting is over," John said in a softer voice. "Let's hold hands and say our bedtime prayers."

After the kids went to bed, John and Alice spoke softly at the table. "We hafta keep a better eye on 'em, Alice. Between both of us, we must make sure they get along. These lousy attitudes our teenagers have developed must stop. We hafta help 'em unite in friendship, respect, and love for each other. I'm sorry I wasn't aware of what was happening between 'em. From now on, I want you to let me know if this happens again."

"I understand. I didn't know it was this severe between them either." Alice sniffled and reached for John's hand.

He covered her hand with his and said, "You and I are both ministers for the Lord. We cannot have our family destroyed by the enemy and before our eyes. We'll not slack up on discipline. I believe we've been leaning upon God too much to raise our kids. We have to do our share of that job. Don't you agree, dear?" John gently spoke his remedy and waited for an answer from her.

"I know, honey. I'm so sorry I've let us down too. May God forgive me for my irresponsible motherly conduct. I closed my eyes when seeing trouble between them. May Marta forgive me too."

John cradled her hand. "Alice, talk to her in the morning, before the others wake up, and repeat those words to her. It'll do her good to hear she has your support." John got up from his chair, kissed his wife on the forehead, and muttered, "Let's go to bed. It's been a trying day for us. I'm sure we made issues clear for Marta and took a heavy weight off her shoulders. It'll help decrease her sadness, God willing. We'll keep it in prayer between the two of us. Is that agreed?" John wiped his face with his hands. His children were in real trouble. He'd caught it before escalating to tremendous problems for them all.

After walking into the bathroom, John clasped palms and thanked the Lord. Blessings were on the way; he had no doubt. He couldn't wait to see Marta's attitude and appearance improve. They'd all settle comfortably and peacefully in their new town. *Surely we will. Faith, don't fail me now.*

Chapter 21

Setting Goals

Why did they have to make the move to the valley during my senior year? It all seems unfair. It'd be wonderful to graduate! It'd be one more hurdle jumped and closer to being on my own helping people. But there's so much activity in this house! How can I handle school work? I might have no choice but to drop out of school. Will I have to? Marta asked herself.

"Mom, this family drama is too much to handle. I'll help you and Dad with finances like you ask, but don't ask me to give up my schooling," Marta stated one morning before the others were up.

Alice had no idea where this sudden comment came from. "All right, dear, if that's what you want to do. It sounds fine to me." Alice went along with the conversation, hoping she'd said the right words. She dared not ask again for Marta to hold down a job for fear of stressing her.

"The way I see it, this town will help me fulfill my vision for my future." She wanted to apply herself to her schoolwork. She'd have one chance to get it done, even if it was to be at Somerville High School.

"We're not asking you to quit altogether, but to hold up

on your schooling for a few months until we get situated better." Alice was beside herself, trying to convince Marta to help with their finances. *When did she suddenly become interested in finishing her senior year?*

Marta didn't know how she might carry out her personal goals if she had to place them on hold to assist the family. She slept uneasily that Friday night after talking to her mom in private.

Saturday morning, Alice and the children were in the garden weeding. After finishing, they took a break and sipped a glass of iced tea. Alice was proud of her children, who'd completed the first week of school with no problems. There was excitement in the household as they discussed their teachers and school-year goals.

"How was your school week, kids?" Alice asked, excited for them. The children all talked at one time, unable to contain their excitement. "Wait, one at a time. I can't hear what you're saying. Linda, you go first, then Marta, then the boys." Alice laughed to see their eagerness.

Linda began telling of her exciting week and the many students she had befriended. "Mom, I've made lots of new friends, and I love my teacher. She's so kind."

"That's wonderful, dear." Alice turned to Marta and noticed her faraway stare. "Honey, it's your turn."

Marta, in her dismal thoughts, didn't hear her mother speak.

"Marta, did you hear me? It's your turn," Alice said.

"I'm sorry, Mom." Marta tried to conceal the thoughts flooding her mind. *No one understands my concerns for my future. Will I graduate in June as planned, or will family matters choke my aspirations? What will become of me after graduation? What skills do I need that'll help sustain us? I wish I could go into teaching, but it's such a huge dream for me.*

"How was your first school week?" Alice sipped her tea nonchalantly, hoping she'd get Marta to talk. Something had been bothering her. Alice understood that listening to her daughter and accepting her recent interest in graduating were important.

Noticing Marta was quiet, Daniel spoke up. "Mom, it was worth cleaning that trash pile outback. Our garden is sprouting cabbage, kale, lettuce, and onions." Daniel, in his wisdom, knew he had to change the subject.

"Yes, Daniel. I'm glad you're happy. Now, hush up and let Marta speak." Alice was getting impatient waiting for Marta to voice her concerns.

"I like my school and my teacher, Miss Jones. She gave us an assignment that made me think of my education. The students discussed their plans of attending college after high school. I had to lie about my plans," Marta replied soberly.

"What did you write?" Alice asked, feeling sorrow for her daughter.

"I made up a story I'd be going to college and studying to be a teacher or a nurse. I wrote it to finish my essay, but not because I meant those plans. There's no money for me to pay for college. I've no idea what I'll be doing then. Though I bet I'll get a good grade on that essay. The other best thing is, it got me thinking about my schooling. If it's possible, I wanna study for one of those two professions."

Alice appreciated her daughter opening up and talking, especially regarding her future. She needed to encourage Marta while reminding her there was time to do proper planning. "Graduation is so many months away.

If you wanna attend college after that, then we'll make a plan for you to attend. So it won't be lying. Don't worry so much, Marta." Alice tried soothing her daughter's guilt.

"I wonder what that college near Main Street offers?" Marta dreamily said.

"You're still in high school, and you're thinking about college!" Julian barked.

"Julian, be quiet. It doesn't hurt to talk and plan. Marta, I know you'll do your best with your plans. Don't fret over your chores. I'll finish whatever needs doing when I get home from work." Alice determined that day to have her daughter educated, even if it meant Alice had to work full time to help her financially.

As the days wore on, Marta daydreamed of college. No one had ever mentioned this topic to her. "Mom, how come we never discuss college?"

"Well, I suppose it's because our people have attended nothing higher than the fifth grade. It's splendid that Somerville offers students twelve years of free schooling. And for them to provide college for small fees is encouraging!"

"I wanna graduate high school and maybe later attend college. It'll train for a skill I might enjoy, a career where I won't get paid minimal wages. Mom, before the essay assignment, I had no plans after graduation except to work in the fields alongside you and Dad. I didn't see any hope in Somerville for any of us, and I saw it as a dead-end town. But that assignment, and hearing the students talk of their plans, got me thinking. I want to go further with my schooling." Marta spoke single-heartedly, but her thoughts were otherwise.

I'll end up working my hands raw, picking fruit or vegetables in the mud, come sizzling heat or heavy fog. It's miserable being poor. I don't care for it; it makes me feel as if I'm in a gutter, and I can't get out.

"Marta, your plans are outstanding, so I'll talk to your dad. I'm sure he'd like that for you too."

"I'll accept whatever God wills for me, Mom." Marta kept from frowning and ran her fingers nervously through her hair.

Julian snickered and then pretended to choke on tea, but secretly he wanted to kick Marta's ankle underneath the table. He then remembered his promise to his dad. The thought of cleaning jails filled with convicts frightened him. He'd hold his anger back until he could hurt her in private. He hated how his parents favored her.

"We'll add 'attend college' to our goal list, OK, Marta?" Alice pointed to the cupboard next to the stove. "I'll tape it there on the inside of the door." She got up to write Marta's goal on the list.

"What will we do after we do that, Mom?" Linda asked suspiciously.

"It'll help us get organized. As each one thinks of a goal, chore, or errand, I want you to write it there. Get your worries off your mind. Don't let them become head-draining problems 'cause from now on, they'll be waiting on that list until you cross them off as completed."

While sipping from her green tumbler, Alice went back to contemplating whatever fascinations might run in Marta's mind, other than college.

"Linda's Christmas tree will be first on it." Marta patted Linda on the shoulder, forgetting her ideas of education.

"Why don't you give that a rest? That's all we've heard out of you since we came out here," Julian stated peevishly.

"Stop that tone of voice," Alice demanded sternly.

Marta looked at Julian, wondering what bothered him. He seemed anxious, kicking his feet on the chair rungs and running his fingers back and forth across the tabletop. It was his behavior for showing aggression. But then again, she was used to his restlessness, which didn't surprise her. She turned her gaze to her aqua blue tumbler before he'd take it the wrong way and act insolently. He didn't care about being stared down and went into spiteful rages. When away from their mom's range, he'd pull her hair or kick her shin. Then she remembered his promise to their dad. It echoed in her thoughts and brought relief from her fears of him.

"Kids, I need to talk something with you," Alice began slowly. "Your dad and me will be working in the grape fields harvesting grapes. It'll start next week and run through fall." She examined their facial responses and noticed their jaws dropping.

Gripping their tumblers as if they'd keep them from falling off their chairs, they exclaimed in chorus, "Work in the grape fields? What about school?" The bleakness in their eyes showed they were beyond understanding this new outcome in their lives.

Alice began picking up the empty tumblers. "Don't get upset. You'll work after school. Dad and I will figure a way to get you to the grape field."

"Mom, can Linda and I stay and fix supper?" Marta looked up at her mother, pride beaming in her eyes.

This was an opportunity to show her growth in family responsibilities.

"We'll see, Marta. But if you help alongside us, it'll aid our finances. We'll plan it so you can have days off to run errands." Alice didn't want to see her children's faces filled with discontentment, but she appreciated their willingness to help.

By giving Marta freedom, John hoped to give her relief from Julian. She needed time away from him. It'd also increase tranquility in their home. Plus, she'd get acquainted with the townspeople and maybe lose her anxiety about them. Her mental health meant more to him and Alice than any earnings she'd make.

"I hope it's simple work, 'cause it'll be difficult going to school the next day. We'll be too tired." Marta was keeping pessimistic words from her conversation, yet she felt she needed to voice this concern. The younger children couldn't survive this schedule. She worried they were too young to recover from the hard work.

"Remember, negative thoughts aren't helpful, Marta. They'll staunch our faith and hope."

"Those aren't negative words!" Marta snapped at her mother. "I'm sorry, Mom. I don't mean to be disrespectful, but I need to speak up for them." Marta didn't care if this was disrespectful to her elders; she needed to voice her opinions for the little one's sake.

Alice changed the topic. "Which reminds me, do you kids remember Isaiah 40:30–31?" She spoke cheerfully, avoiding Marta's irritated glare.

"I do," Daniel said as he lifted his right arm to get his mom's attention.

"Recite the verses, please, Daniel."

Even the youths shall faint and be weary,
And the young men shall utterly fall,
But those who wait on the LORD
Shall renew their strength;
They shall mount up with wings like eagles,
They shall run and not be weary,
They shall walk and not faint.

When he was through with his recital, Alice patted his brown hair. Her smile reassured him of her confidence in him.

"Those are excellent reminders of promises I keep forgetting to claim," Marta started getting up to help wash dishes. "Kids, go take a nap. I'll fix supper later. Go on now." Alice waited for her children to go to bed before going outside with Marta.

"Honey, sometimes we must reach deep inside of us and find the motivation to carry us through each day. But you have to depend on your reservoir of faith. Allow it to grow by leaning on the Lord. Remember, everything is already in His care; you must trust Him completely."

"Mom, thank you for your encouragement and support. I'll try to get motivated. Oh, I need to add something on the priority list: it's trusting more in God. Mom, I'd like to attend college."

"I happy to hear you say that, Marta."

"Can you and Dad see a way to help me attend? I figured I could work in one of the local shops and save money for that. Without this hope, the future's so despairing. And this college plan is exciting. It'll keep my mind occupied with encouraging ideas."

Alice patted Marta's hand. It was a start in the faith

direction. She was proud of her daughter for attempting to better herself with this ambition. *Can we help her make it to college until she completes a degree in teaching or nursing?* she thought. *Thank you, Miss Jones, for bringing this idea to Marta. And thank You, Lord.*

Chapter 22

Godsends

The rental, with its yellowed white paint, stood out like a decaying lemon. The disgusting site shamed John and Alice. Now, thanks to Mr. Fowlerte, they had supplies to fix and update its appeal. God was blessing them and meeting their needs. Painting the eyesore before starting a new job was John's goal. They couldn't wait to have a charming home. They wanted to contribute to Somerville's beauty and laid-back charisma. Mr. Fowlerte, a godsend, had made it possible for them.

While stirring a can of white paint, Marta overheard her parents talking. "God is sending kind people our way," Alice said, taping window frames.

"Yes, He is," John agreed, moving painting equipment closer to the house.

"Dad, the paint is ready. I'll start at the other end." Marta pointed to the front porch. Plodding along with paint tray in her hands, she thought of their conversation. *It seemed easy for them to see blessings.* Marta perceived only difficulties and uncertainties, even though their new community had many conveniences, making it a comfortable place to live. However, her faith kept trying to take a plunge, especially as she considered the upcoming Christmas season. *How prepared will it find us?*

One day at Mrs. Waters's store, Marta asked her concerning conifers. "Mrs. Waters, I have a deep concern that never seems to lift from my mind. I need to know if anybody in town sells Christmas conifers." She took a sip of Coke and waited patiently for an answer.

"There are two shops that sell 'em. Jake's General Store, down on Main Street, and over at Henry's hay shop," The woman said while filling candy containers.

Her shop, like Jake's and Henry's, was considered a mom-and-pop shop. Only two long streets contained such businesses. They intersected in the middle of town, and there at one of the corners, stood a small park and gazebo. The quaint town had many friendly people who always had a smile for Marta.

Every day after school, she strolled to the post office. Afterward, she visited Henry if he wasn't too busy, or she bought a Coke at Mrs. Waters's. This free time from her siblings gave her time to relax and think of her future.

While relaxing at the small store, she watched customers as they interacted with Mrs. Waters. She enjoyed observing them, listening to their various accents, and learning their mannerisms, habits, and lifestyles. They made her feel comfortable with their easygoing manners, as if they'd known her all her life. She appreciated their traditional way of life. She had come to realize they were like folks back home.

"Marta, I'm glad you have time to spend with me. My head can get overwhelmed with work. It's nice to have you to talk to during the slow periods, even if it's for a few minutes. Customers come in as bunches of grapes. Then it's quiet." Mrs. Waters smiled while putting away huge, empty pickle jars. "Tell me, Marta, do your siblings like their teachers?" Unbeknownst to Marta, she was pursuing gossip.

"Yes, they do. And I'm fond of my teacher, Miss Jones."

"And Mr. Fowlerte likes your folks, doesn't he?" She prodded for more information.

"Yes, he does. Do you know what he did one day when he came by for the rent money?" Marta didn't hear a reply from her, so she continued. "Well, he took a peek into the backyard, noticed the fall garden filled with vegetables we had planted, and asked where the rubbish pile had gone. My dad told him we had hauled it away to the dump. He was so thankful that he offered Dad lumber, nails, and cans of paint. He told him he could pick them up anytime and use them to fix the porch or anything he wanted to around the house."

"My, but it's generous of him. It sounds like he's taken a real liking to your family," Mrs. Waters said before returning to work. She turned around to climb the short ladder, where she reached a top shelf and dusted the cans sitting in neat rows.

"Well, he told my dad the neighbors didn't care for the stench reeking out of the backyard. They'd been after him to clean it up for two years. I guess my family saved him a lot of headaches by removing it."

"I can also imagine. I have heard people in town say it even saved a lawsuit." Mrs. Waters continued with her dusting, glad to hear the new family in town were hardworking individuals who appreciated a lovely yard.

"You know, important things as hauling away that trash will bring up our town's value. It's something we take pride in, our lovely yards." She couldn't wait to tell her customers of this hardworking family.

Henry came in late that afternoon to purchase something for dinner. He hadn't been there but a few seconds before Mrs. Waters began her conversation about Mr. Fowlerte's new tenants, the Rodrigos.

"Henry, have you met the Rodrigos? You know, that nice family."

"Oh, yeah!" Henry cut her sentence short because he didn't want to hear or say too much about them. If he gave Mrs. Waters information, she would pass it to someone else as she searched for tidbits of gossip.

Mrs. Waters waited for him to say more, but then she spoke up when he kept quiet. "This class of newcomers is what city hall wants: caring, responsible, diligent, and hardworking residents. They are a godsend. Do you know anything about them?"

"No, I can't say that I do." Henry paid for his groceries and was ready to leave, he heard her ask one more question.

"Do you know anything about their boy they call Julian? He seems to be a handful, always acting up when he's in here with his older sister—the one called Marta."

"Nope. Don't know anything about him either. Have a good night." Henry walked out of the small store when he heard Mrs. Waters's last words. He thought, *I'll keep my eyes and ears open for him. He's gotta be an interesting character.*

After stepping out into the hot evening, Henry wondered, *Is Mrs. Waters a godsend or foe to this family? I'm gonna add her to my prayer list that she doesn't start trouble for them.*

Chapter 23

Phil's Letters Arrive

John felt they should have heard from Phil again because Phil was writing and sending letters as often as he could. It was a warm afternoon when John checked the post office and found mail from Phil. Hearing from his eldest son excited John.

After taking his hat off, he sat at the table and called the family to a meeting. A ring of bliss etched his words. The children stopped their reading, rushed into the kitchen to hear what Dad had to say and took their seats. They could only speculate what the gathering was about. Meanwhile, Alice and Marta took out fixings for dinner.

"Ladies, please sit down too. I've got a wonderful surprise for you," he said, pulling out the letters from the inside of his denim jacket.

"Oh, you have mail! Are they from Phil?" Linda asked, squirming in her seat.

"They certainly are, little miss!"

The children were beyond joy. Marta placed the bread on the counter and took a chair next to her mother. "Read it, Dad," she cheered.

John tore open the earliest postmarked letter and read.

Tears welled in Alice's and Marta's eyes. After reading both letters, they sat still. It was more than they had expected. Two letters in one day! It was a momentous day for them.

"We need to give God praise for this blessing," John said gravely. They were thankful Phil was not dead.

"When is he coming home?" Linda practically hollered.

"He didn't say when, but we'll write him a letter," Dad said, picking up the letters. "Later tonight, I want everyone to do that. Make sure you write something cheerful. Marta, will you take them to the post office tomorrow?"

"I will. I'm telling him we're living in California and about our new home, its location, and the school." She didn't mention that she'd also include the school's address in case he needed more information as to their location.

Phil received the heavy package filled with the family's letters in late fall. It was a surprise difficult to believe. *The planes must have flown only for mail deliveries*, he joked to himself. But in reality, he was thankful for the people behind the mail deliveries.

The bulky package contained one letter from each member of his family. They had stated how much they missed him and couldn't wait to see him again. He wondered why they'd moved to California. He sensed from reading their letters that they yearned to be in Arizona with Grandmother. After praying for their situation, he included a prayer for all military personal and the War Department to allow the soldiers Christmas furlough as they saw fit.

Chapter 24

Searching for an Evergreen Tree

On their many drives through the valley, Marta had never seen conifer plantations or groves. *So how do these people get trees for Christmas? Oh, my, do they even celebrate it? Are their traditions that much more different?* In stealth reconnaissance, Marta intended to begin her conifer tree search. The townspeople wouldn't understand her reasons for searching, especially so early in the year. *Where is the best place to look during this September heat wave?*

One Saturday after breakfast, Marta announced, "Mom, Dad, do you mind if Linda and I go for a walk?" After putting dry dishes in the cupboard, she waited for a reply.

"Marta, where are you going so early this morning?" Mom asked while putting breakfast leftovers in the refrigerator.

Marta fidgeted with the dishes and then answered, "I want to check out the town. May I?"

"Please hold on to Linda's hand. We don't need trouble in this town," Dad commanded, coming in the back door with an arm full of tools that needed oiling. He'd heard her request.

"I will. I'll get us back home safely."

Marta began her trek near Main Street, passed the small park and college, and then walked to the west edge of town, where houses stopped and fields of alfalfa began. She dared not go any farther with a young child in tow.

"Linda, do you suppose there are farmers somewhere near here who grow pine trees in this rich soil?"

"Maybe, but we haven't gone far enough to explore."

"You're right! That's what I was thinking. Dad mentioned there are dairies that way. Before we go, let me lift you up. Check if you can see anything that resembles pine tree tops, would you?" Marta was determined not to let this opportunity go without checking thoroughly.

Linda wistfully peered up the country road as they headed west. "No, I only see fruit trees and alfalfa fields. Marta, I'm tired. Can we go home?"

"Yeah, let's go home," Marta replied, holding Linda's hand tightly.

The girls made it home safely. Satisfied she had begun her search, Marta got ready to help with dinner. She had enjoyed her brief tour of the town and had learned more about its dimensions and of the many businesses available to the residents.

Conifer trees were always on Marta's mind. *Perhaps they're brought in through trains. I gotta find out if this is possible!* After passing by the gravel pit on the way home from school one day, she spotted a man standing by a truck. After the truck left, she stopped to talk to the man as he began walking toward the office. *He would know about trains—probably does business with them. But come to think of it, I haven't seen tracks or heard train whistles.*

"Excuse me, mister. My name is Marta Rodrigo, and I want to know if there are trains that come through here. You see, my family just moved in, and I'd like to know."

"Miss, we don't have any coming through Somerville. The nearest town they come through is Tuleville. That's about twenty-five miles west of here. You'd have to check there for those questions," Tom, the supervisor, informed her.

"I'm curious about something. How do local businesses bring in merchandise and equipment?" Marta didn't want to show her conifer concerns, at least not yet.

"We gotta drive up there in trucks and pick 'em up."

"Well, is there a business here in charge of evergreen sales, or, ah, conifer shipments?"

"Yes, Henry at the hay store orders them in November or early December. Sometimes the general store, owned by Jake, will order a few too. Do you know where his store is located?"

"I do. Thank you for your help. Have a nice day." Marta blushed, feeling ignorant for asking such a dumb question.

Somerville was a medium-size town. It contained various businesses that provided the family with many comforts and hope. It had a gravel pit with a dozen bulldozers, a post office, a school that had heaters under the floors, and a hay store that carried nursery plants, alfalfa, grain, and farm equipment. Other buildings included a large cotton gin, a plum-drying gin, two stores, seven churches, a water district office, a small bank, a small college, a hair salon housed in a private home, and a long building that housed a drug store with fountain drink conveniences. These redbrick buildings stood tall and appeared strongly built. A few paved roads lined with sidewalks allowed the stranger thoughts of civilization, whereas those off of the main cross roads were still hard packed dirt.

Every now and then, Marta would stop at the hay store and chat with Henry. As she searched for him through all the equipment and hay stacks, she simply had to look for the blond hair. That and his tall height divulged his location.

"Marta, I ain't gonna get noisy with you, but where have you been the last few days? I thought you'd quit coming here," he said as he handed her some gum.

She liked him as a reliable friend whom she could trust for advice, and his knowledge of the town and its inhabitants was comprehensive. Yet he never gossiped about them. "Oh, I've been around. Can I help you water the potted plants?" Marta asked.

"Don't you have to stop at the post office and check for letters from Phil first?"

"I did that. There weren't any. Have you put in your order for conifer trees yet?"

"No, I haven't. I think I'll let Jake order them. Most years I do place an order, but it gets expensive unless I sell 'em. I'm changing my mind and might not order them at all. So, you wanna help? Grab that hose over there." Henry pointed to a green hose rolled up against the office wall.

Before picking up the hose, Marta stopped to peek in the office. "Henry, I gotta say your large, black Bible is identical to Dad's and Phil's. They both have that large print version." Marta pointed to the desk in the office where the Bible sat.

"You have a sharp eye on you." Henry marked off

something on a chart and placed it back on a hook near the office wall.

"There's something else why I think you're like my brother Phil."

"Yeah, in what other ways?"

"Both of you are hardworking. You're as old as he is, almost. You enjoy reading your Bible and are polite. Do you have time to read during work hours?"

"Sometimes I do during lunch." Henry wondered what she was getting at, or whether she was making small talk. Then she asked another question regarding conifer trees. In the few weeks he had come to know her, he could see through her. He saw her innocence and appreciated that in her; there was nothing brutal, conniving, or selfish about her.

Marta found Henry to be a gentleman and felt safe around him. He produced fruit of the Holy Spirit—a lesson taught by her dad's sermons. He always admonished his children to desire these fruits: love, peace, joy, forbearance, kindness, goodness, self-control, and faithfulness. She'd discovered this one Saturday, stopping by the shop after picking up the mail. She noticed him relaxing on a bale of hay.

Henry was having a late afternoon snack, and upon seeing her enter, he placed his Bible next to him. After greeting her, he offered her a part of his sandwich and coffee. He'd displayed kindness, one of the fruits. *He's bound to have others,* she thought.

Henry enjoyed her company even though he knew she visited because of her conifer problems, in hopes he'd solve them. *Only time will tell how her Christmas is to display itself for her and her family.* Henry hoped for the best for her.

One day, Marta came to the shop again, asking for evergreen trees. Henry gave her the same answer. "Marta, I told you, I won't get any shipments until December, and that's if I order them. But it's too early for that decision. I've given it some consideration; I might order those in five-gallon cans with sprawling roots bursting at the can's bottoms." He smiled at her, and pity for her filled his heart. She was decent and didn't deserve disappointment come Christmas.

"Marta, why don't you check Jake's store and see if he might have some trees that arrived early? Usually he orders perennials at this time of year. Ask for Jake. You can't miss him—he's a giant of a man with a crew cut." It was late in the day, and Henry had been putting away tools. After wiping his brows with a checkered blue handkerchief, he walked her to the door.

"Thank you, Henry. I'll go right now. Goodbye!" she hollered, picking up her steps.

Henry's heart was heavy for her. He wondered what would become of such an innocent, caring girl. He noticed she had upright morals, which included being dependable, hardworking, and honest. His sister, Erin Jones, Marta's schoolteacher, had described her to him when he'd asked about her. He'd learned she was a believer too. He made up his mind to add her name to his daily prayers. These prayers would include that she graduate next summer.

As of now, he saw a young, immature girl who didn't seem to understand the importance of an education, as she'd mentioned once she'd rather work. He understood the importance of her desire to help her family with their finances, but he prayed she would see that an education would one day land her a good job. He hoped she'd been kidding, but he noted that having a Christmas tree was of prime importance to her. He wondered why.

Upon entering Jake's store, Marta began looking for the man. A tall fellow came out of the back office. Recognizing Jake by the description Henry had given her wasn't difficult. He was rather tall with short, white fuss standing on top of his head.

"Hello, can I help you, little lady? Wanna buy somethin'?" he asked in a low, Southern drawl familiar to her.

"Well, well ..." Marta's words caught inside her throat. "My family and I are looking for a small pine or fir tree we can use for Christmas." Marta swallowed and tried to put on an air of maturity. Knowing not to speak up for her parents, she felt guilty but couldn't stop herself.

"Young lady, I have leftovers from last year. They have roots so as people can plant 'em' outside after the holiday. They're beautiful and smell good too! Do you wanna see those?" Jake sounded eager to sell his trees, and he pointed out the side window. A yard filled with containers holding small and tall plants was visible.

"Yes, please." Marta followed him. She saw a wide variety of conifers ranging in height from short to tall. The excitement of seeing them overwhelmed her. "How much are they?" The question popped out of her mouth before she could finger the pine needles and whiff their resin scent.

"The small ones are five dollars. Come Christmas, their price will go up to ten, and twenty for the taller conifers. They're shipped in from up north on the Tuleville trains. That's expensive. I've another order ready to send out, but those won't come in till early December. I just hope I don't forget to send it out." He laughed jokingly and then placed one hand on each hip, making him look rigid and authoritarian—intimidating traits to Marta's confidence.

"Very well," she spoke timidly. "I'll let my parents know." After shifting the concern to them, she turned to leave. *There's no way I'll be able to save that much money.* "I gotta get home and tell my parents, but thank you for helping me."

"Mom, Mom!" Marta was out of breath when she entered the kitchen where her siblings were having a snack. "Mom, guess what? There are conifers trees for sale at Jake's store. They are only five dollars each. They're growing in cans. Do you think we can buy one and save it for Christmas?" She spoke fast before her mother interrupted.

Alice pulled her daughter into her arms and hugged her. "You are impetuous. Christmas is still a long time away. Quit your fussing; God will bless us with a perfect tree when the time comes. Besides, money is tight. Those five dollars will buy us enough food for three days." Alice wasn't trying to put Marta on a guilt trip, but they needed every dollar for their survival.

Marta noticed the children had stopped eating. Had they heard their conversation? The ghastly look upon their faces told her they had. After taking her seat, she ate her snack quietly, reprimanding herself for discouraging the children. She resigned herself not to mention conifer trees again around them. *If God wants us to buy one of them, He'll give us the funds and the tree,* she reminded herself. However, she intended to continue her secret search.

Chapter 25

Marta Desires Stability

Marta ran into the bathroom crying for no reason except that she didn't want to be around Julian when babysitting her siblings. Never knowing when his meanness would come out stressed her. Circumstances never changed. Negative disruptions continually interrupted her stability and stole her hope. There was no consistency in her life, nothing she could classify as dependable and empowering her with security.

"Mom, Julian ruins all our days. Why can't he be nice like the rest of us?" Marta asked her mother one day after they had returned from ministering to a neighbor.

"Marta, you need patience with him. He's going through growing pains, and that's hard on a boy." Alice felt for her son, recognizing the change in his behavior only because she experienced it with Phil during his phase of growth. After this experience with Phil, she wanted Julian to have an easier time of overcoming his adolescent changes. She first noticed the unique developmental shifts when she'd heard Julian's voice crack. It'd changed into a deeper tone, giving her fair warning. Alice hadn't realized that Marta, as a female, was also going through bodily and character changes and also needed her understanding.

Marta tried to hold back mean language with her mom, knowing not to disrespect her but to honor her as the Bible taught; she kept from screaming at her. "Mom, there's been a change in me as well. I don't know who I'm becoming. I'm going through bodily changes. That's what my teacher told me when I broke down crying over some ants that got into my purse! She took me outside and spoke to me about it." Marta was disappointed her mom took up for her brother. "Phil never acted as awful as Julian, and you keep protecting him. He's a natural brat."

Marta didn't receive an answer. Left hanging to consider Julian's behavioral changes, she wished Phil was back to take over his disciplinary role. He would understand the reason for this changing attitude and help Julian if there was a need.

Marta felt she couldn't survive her bouts of depression. *Phil, come home soon, please.* Marta continued weeping. Feeling the weight of their problems on her shoulders caused her breathing difficulties. Crying in privacy for a while quieted her nerves.

What's happening to me? My faith in my family's well-being is slowly fading. My hate for Julian overwhelms me to the point of constant anger. Being around him weakens my legs. After several sleepless nights, she performed her housework with minimal effort, overlooking several steps to complete her chores. Now, after losing a few pounds, Marta felt skinny and unattractive. *What will become of me? I hope this will end soon. I can't handle this emotional state anymore!*

One warm afternoon, Marta got in a hurry to visit Henry before she forgot some questions she had for him. *Perhaps he has the answers.*

"Hey, Marta, what brings you out today?" Henry asked upon noticing her sad disposition as she entered the shop.

"Hi, Henry. Do you have a minute you can spare?"

"Yeah, let me put this money away—just had a customer."

Marta took a seat on a stack of hay and waited for him to finish. She practiced phrasing her questions in her mind first. There was so much she wanted to know and understand about Julian's behavior. *Perhaps another male may have an answer for his misbehavior. Knowing what's going on with him might stop my fears of him.*

"What's on your mind?" Henry took a seat next to her, extending his long legs onto the graveled ground.

"Might you answer a question or two for me? It's about my brother Julian."

"Sure, I'm listening. Ask me."

Feeling tense, she tried to begin. After gaining courage, she asked, "Do you know why a nice boy like Julian turns mean and almost evil once he grows older?"

Henry thought about her question then asked, "How old was he when you noticed the change?"

Marta thought back. "I think thirteen."

"How old is he now?"

"Fifteen."

"Julian is passing through puberty. His body is changing from boyhood to manhood, if that makes sense."

"Does that mean he'll end up a mean, cruel man one day?"

Henry laughed softly at her innocence. "He'll certainly transform. The way your family has you all in church learning verses, I believe he'll switch for the better. But when will this happen? Boys, like girls, will make physical adjustments. It's called puberty and takes a few years for teenagers to come out into their own character. If I were you, I wouldn't worry too much about him, but keep him in prayer. I'll do the same."

Henry then got up to go back to work. "Are there any other concerns?"

"No, but please keep me in prayer too. Otherwise, I won't last around him."

Noticing her anguish, he said, "Come on. Let's pray and ask for forgiveness, strength, patience, and discernment for the plan God has for you and your family. That's why he brought y'all here to Somerville. There's something here He wants you and your family to do. I don't know what that plan is, but He does."

Marta felt better after talking to Henry, but much of what he said was beyond her comprehension. She smiled to herself as she gingerly walked home, mulling over Henry's words. Thereafter, her days seemed filled with joy as she kept forgiving Julian's mean acts. She quit taking anything he did to her personally, and she no longer feared his malicious antics. *Henry said God will help him change. I need to believe that.*

In time, Marta came to heal of her depression before it became deeply embedded. She began praying for

Julian more often. Hating him was not a choice for her; it left her bitter and angry. She didn't want these foreign characteristics as part of who she was becoming. She was thankful Henry had answered her questions, giving her renewed hope in Julian.

"Marta, you've improved on your work," her mother said one day as she and Marta were cleaning the kitchen. "You're now focused on your chores, and your prayer life has increased. I'm glad for you, daughter."

"Mom, I want to change to do my best. I'd hate to grow into a bitter, hateful woman. I'm also working on my grades; I hope to raise them. It bothered me that Phil was gone, but I've faith he'll come back to us alive."

"Thank you for making a wonderful impression in town. I've heard people tell me what a polite daughter I have. You make me proud, you know. Anyone would enjoy being around you. You're kinder and more polite than you used to be, even as of a few weeks ago."

"Mom, I want stability in our lives. I don't want us to move again. I've got to trust that the Lord brought us here. At least, that's what Henry at the hay shop thinks."

"He's a blessing for you to have around, isn't he?" Alice comforted her daughter.

"Yes, he is. He's as good as having Phil around for advice. He's so kind to me too."

In the middle of their conversation, Julian burst into the kitchen, bumping into Marta and making her fall. "Oops," he laughed, acting as if he'd done it by accident. Then he ran into the living room and out the front door.

"Mom, what will you do about Julian?" Marta asked upon seeing her mom turn to face the window without one scolding at him. Marta entered her bedroom, where she began praying silently. Her scope of drama with Julian never seemed to stop. *Why didn't Mom raise her voice against that obnoxious brother of mine? Help me understand, please, dear God, and change him. Amen.*

Chapter 26

Marta Is a Blessing

Cold, foggy days were ahead in the valley, but Marta and her family were unaware of the coming severe weather. The children would need winter clothing to meet its challenges. None of them had a clue of how damp and ice-cold the air could get. It filled with dense water vapor, creating blankets of fog that flowed near the ground. They moved in to envelop everything in their path with utter, freezing cover. Its bitter wetness penetrated deeply into everybody's bones. It was a silent foe. This formidable force began its trek in November. For now, the family would have plenty of time to prepare for the foggy winter ahead.

Marta's family didn't know this formidable opponent rose in the low valley, which was below sea level, making it a perfect place for its presence to rise. The young family had yet to learn how it formed at night or near the dawn of morning, when temperatures were at their lowest. Then the rising sun lent its warmth to the chilled earth, causing steam to form and rise. The two elements were the perfect ingredients for this phenomenon to occur.

As for now, Marta appreciated the warmth of

September, except for the high humidity. It was the monsoon season on the other side of the Sierra Nevada, where an occasional rain spilled into the valley. These storms were a creation of tropical warm weather sweeping over Baja California and into the Sierras, causing a precipitation phenomenon. This weather wouldn't have bothered Marta if it had reached them. These storms were familiar in Arizona.

Occasionally, they'd bring small torrents of rain to the valley, spoiling crops such as grapes. Raining on them in September was their demise the farmers feared. The grapes would then be ruined, with every harvest wasted. But the foggy weather, which would soon arrive, would be a different matter for her.

"Mom, I've heard of the fogs coming in around fall. I'm worried we won't be ready. The kids need winter coats. It's gonna be miserably cold. We need to save what we can to buy thick coats." Marta stopped and stared out the kitchen window pensively, a potato and peeler in her hands. Alice stirred some greens in a skillet, and biscuits for dinner were ready to bake in the oven. The children had finished their afternoon snack except for Daniel, who sat quietly, enjoying every bite of a stale biscuit while listening to Marta.

"Marta, you're not telling me something I don't already know. That's why I'm helping Dad in the grape harvest. I'll need help here at home while I do that." Alice winced at her daughter's remark. She didn't need to remind her daughter of the family's needs, but she appreciated her caring love.

Money for the family was still scarce. Marta had wanted to help her parents with this problem. Since her dad had realized Julian's meanness and she was receiving prayers from Henry, she felt less stressed and capable of working.

"Mom, I can help with getting Linda ready for school while you and Dad work. I'll be sure to help with as many chores as I can." Marta felt weak in spirit, but if her parents needed her, she would gather her strength and step in and do the job. This was no time to complain or whimper. She was willing to help, no matter the cost to her health.

"Marta, there'll be so much for you to do. I'll make a list of chores that need doing daily and split them up between y'all."

"I already do most of them. Mom, I won't forget to wash clothes, make bread, clean the kitchen, fill the oil lamp, and polish its globe."

"You're such a blessing," her mom commented with pride.

"Don't worry, Mom. I'm happy contributing to our survival. I carry my weight, don't I?"

"Marta, you do more than carry your weight. Dad and I appreciate you so much." Alice couldn't say anymore without crying for the blessings her daughter provided to the family. Then she thought of Marta's depression. *Dear Lord, don't let it return to that ever again. Find something to ignite her hope in Your plans for her. Please, Lord. Help me trust You'll do this. Amen.* Alice bit her lower lip. She had to trust God for His provisions; otherwise, she'd have a nervous breakdown.

Chapter 27

September Grapes

September began with a heat wave, muggy and sizzling. Marta wondered if they'd be attending school all year, part time, or not at all. Her parents' talk of taking the children to work in the fields whenever possible bothered her. She couldn't imagine performing field labor. This conversation had placed doubt in her mind that they would finish their education.

"Mom, what's all this talk about us kids working in the fields and harvesting grapes? Will we have to drop out of school? You once said you'd like for all of us to get educated, including yourself." Marta had nagging thoughts of dropping out when they'd only just begun. She tried concentrating on her work. Peeling potatoes wasn't one of her favorite chores, but preparing supper was a priority.

"No, no! You won't have to. Your dad will think of something so as you all can help but also keep up with your school attendance."

Marta was relieved at hearing the news, and she trusted her mother's words. "I hope we can help you and

Dad. I just don't see how it's possible to be at two places simultaneously."

"We'll figure it out. I'm so excited about all this fall harvest work available to us. I can't believe our fortune. Ain't God good?"

"Mom, you mean 'blessings' and 'isn't God good?'" Marta didn't want to correct her mother, but if she were to change for the better, it would have to begin with proper speech. Marta meant to improve herself, and speaking incorrect grammar didn't appeal to her sense of self-improvement. She felt the need to talk Californian even if the residents themselves used a few incorrect words.

"Yes, that's what I mean. I'm sorry, dear."

"And yes, God has been good to us, Mom." Marta was glad her mom took her recommendation cheerfully.

Alice took a deep breath, relieved her daughter wasn't ashamed of her God. Her thoughts were on the Lord once again.

"Are these grapes the kind we used to buy at the general store back home? Those sweet, juicy ones?" Marta remembered the purple grapes the grocer stocked during some years when he could get them.

"What your dad tells me is there are grapes of all varieties and colors here. They are green, red, and purples that vary from light to dark shades. I can hardly wait to get started. This work will last at least two months, through the end of October, anyway."

"Maybe we can help you pick 'em after school," Daniel stated, drinking the last drops of his milk.

"Mom, so what you're saying is we might go pick grapes after school with you and Dad?" Marta finished peeling the potatoes and waited quietly for a reply.

"Mom, couldn't we afford eggs for supper? They'll taste good with these biscuits. Otherwise, it's gonna be a meager meal," Julian said nicely.

"That reminds me, Mom. I need to let you know the flour barrel is running low, and so is the salt and baking powder. There's enough to make two more batches of biscuits."

"Payday is two days away; we'll make it. Quit fretting. And yes, we'll fry some eggs to go with the biscuits, Julian." Alice stirred the dark green lamb's quarters the children had picked from the weed field.

"Mom, I'd like to help you and Dad with grape harvest. I'm old enough to work. I could skip school once or twice a week. Do you think Dad will allow me so the children can stay in school?" Marta hoped to hear a yes. She could always catch up, unlike the younger ones.

"We'll see, dear. It would benefit the family if you helped us, but you also need to stay in school and graduate. Your dad will have an answer for us on how this is going to work out."

"Mom, you and Dad aren't making enough wages. We need winter clothes and extra groceries to stock the cupboards. With my working full time, we could afford some of those things." Marta didn't want to give up her education, but she saw no way around how her family could catch up on family needs.

That evening, Marta went to bed worried about the coming winter and the thick coats and stockings they would need for the winter, which lasted until April. *Dear Lord, please let my parents allow me to work with them, even if it must be during school hours.* After a while, she relaxed enough that she fell asleep.

Every morning as dawn approached, John and Alice left for work. Marta took care of her siblings and the house chores that needed doing after school. One day after supper, their dad announced, "Children, we're gonna have y'all help us with fieldwork. The boss said it's all right to bring you along to help. After school, Mom will pick you up at home and bring you to our workplace. I'll stay out in the field and continue working till you get there; then we'll all work together."

"That's right," Alice answered. "You'll start on Monday after school." She sounded fatigued and looked worn out since she'd been working with John picking grapes from sunrise until near sunset every day for the past week.

Marta's sensitivity to her mother's health was admirable. Knowing the hardships they were facing was difficult for her mom, and Marta understood. Yet her mom appeared to tolerate every pain, never showing signs of body oppression. Still, Marta kept watching over her delicate health and pitching in whenever possible.

Seeing her mother dragging made Marta feel hopeless once again. Her life had become so busy that she'd stopped reading her Bible. Also, the hardships of daily life took their toll upon her and her family. Her prayer life had ended. She couldn't even thank God for her meals. Her mind was always heavy with worry for Phil, Grandmother, their finances, and the Christmas season. Trying to remain resilient on her schedule took her strength and dwindled her faith.

"What does a grape field look like, Dad?" Julian asked civilly.

"Well, I can describe it this way. The furrows, like the ones we see on our Sunday drives, are ruts created by tractors. Well, these furrows have high walls on both sides. On top of these trenches, grape bushes are planted so many feet apart. They are watered by ditch water that runs in 'em so they can reach the roots with ease. Wooden poles are buried between the vines to help stabilize the bushes. These poles hold up wire that runs from pole to pole. The bushes grow tendrils on their vines that will eventually grab the wire and help hold the bushes upright, so it doesn't fall into the trench. Then these vines crawl along these wires, growing to reach the vines of the next bush. This allows large clumps of grape clusters to hang underneath the leafy vines.

"Now, between this row of bushes and the ones across lies nothing but flat, soft dirt. That's the middle of the furrow where farmers have field hands lay empty boxes. These need fillin' with bunches of grapes. They won't irrigate during this time of pickin' so the dirt under the boxes don't get soaked. Does that make sense?"

Daniel spoke up. "I can't see how the rows are set up."

"It'll be easier when you see them," Dad said.

"Are you going to show us how to pack grapes?" Julian asked on Monday afternoon when they got to the field. He noticed how neatly grape clusters lay in someone's boxes.

Marta and her siblings, though tired of a long day at school, didn't complain. Continuing work in the fiery heat seemed brutal to her, but she understood their importance of helping. They would continue work from late afternoon until almost sunset.

"Yes, I am. Now pay attention, I'll be showing y'all how to cut clusters and how to pack them. Once you've got them cut at the stem, you'll place them gently into your five-gallon buckets. From there, Julian will help me pick up the filled cans and empty them into those boxes sitting in the middle. Is that clear?"

"John, show the children how to handle the knives." Alice wanted to make sure the children didn't hurt themselves.

The knives were short and curved. The children had never seen such a tool. John took a knife out of a leather bag slung around his shoulders. "Children, notice how you are to keep the bunches together without breaking 'em apart." Carefully, he showed them how to hold the grape clusters with one hand while the other cut the stem above it.

He handled it gently and placed the large, purple mass in a five-gallon pail sitting on the ground.

Marta tried to mimic her dad's movements with her knife but felt unsure of the procedure. Still, she gave it a go, not wanting to disappoint her dad.

John looked around at his other wide-eyed children, who seemed perplexed at the work details. Upon noticing their confusion, he exclaimed, "You'll do fine. Watch me again!" He performed the cutting procedure again. "See how easy that is? Any questions? Now, y'all get started. Holler if you need help." John didn't wait for a reply and turned around to walk to his workplace. He fell to his knees under the vines and began cutting grape bunches.

Marta worked without fear of stabbing her hands or destroying any bunches. She found it easy work once she got the hang of it. Once buckets were filled or half filled, her dad or Julian emptied them into wooden boxes that held twelve bunches of grapes. "Linda, stay near Mom," Marta admonished her little sister. "Don't wander away from her." Though there was no one else working this late in the day, Marta wanted to make sure her little sister didn't get lost in the hundreds of grape furrows. She felt proud to be helping in all ways possible.

Under the vines, Marta scooted on her knees and moved her pail farther alongside her, using her knees; she found it to be too heavy to move, otherwise. Moving it against the sandy soil would cause a pileup of dirt on its other side, acting as a wall, forbidding the can's movement. At that point, she had to use her arms to lift it over and move it. Then she'd continue scooting herself on her knees.

"Dad, this can is full. Will you please empty it for me?" Marta would rather her dad emptied her pail; she avoided Julian as much as possible. She hated how he always fussed about something she'd done wrong, even if it wasn't serious. Keeping a distance from him minimized her stress so she could concentrate better on her job.

The grape-picking process wasn't difficult to comprehend, but it was monotonous and labor intensive. Even so, Marta was glad they weren't chopping cotton. It was late in the season for that, anyway. Still, she'd heard how farmworkers had to be in the cotton fields as early as six in the morning. The dew was the heaviest on plants then. The dew would wet workers' shoes, ankles, and pant legs. With every step they took, they kicked dust around their legs, causing it to land on their wet legs and feet. This created mud, which grew thicker as their movements continued. As the mud dried with the rising sun, it became weighty and cumbersome to haul.

But unbeknownst to her, dew was everywhere early in the early spring and fall. This phenomenon didn't occur in Arizona because the air there was always dry.

Come Saturday, the family would begin work at six in the morning, and Marta would experience this phenomenon for herself. As for now, they worked afternoons after school hours. By then, the late sun had dried the dew. The next worst problem, the blowing dust created by their movements and gentle breezes, was an enemy to be reconciled. It landed in their hair, nostrils, and mouth, and through any openings in their clothing or shoes. Obviously, it was due to the dry ground.

"Dad, will we be here every afternoon?" Marta asked while carefully placing a cluster of grapes into her bucket.

"Yes, and if we're very blessed, we'll probably work grape harvest another three or four weeks, maybe through the end of October. Children, remember you have to finish your schoolwork at school. There won't be time at home in the evenin' for you to finish." Dad spoke fast, as if speaking would take extra time from their work. With quick arm movements, he emptied a pail of grape clusters into a box.

"I am glad we're coming after school. It's cooled down by then. I don't think I would enjoy scorching heat in the middle of the day, or cold fog in the fall," Daniel said with an air of maturity. He placed a bunch of grapes in his pail. "Can I eat a grape, Dad?" he asked longingly. "They're tempting me right now. I am so hungry!"

"Son, we ain't supposed to eat them. They might have chemicals on them. They need washin' first," Dad admonished.

"Why is Julian eating them?" he groaned, placing a bunch into his pail.

"Julian, quit eating grapes! We'll be taking a break soon. Now, hurry! We need to fill our quota of grapes for the day!" Mom didn't sound happy. Her hands and arms were tired from the fast-moving action of cutting bunches, yet she showed no appearance of slowing down.

"But Mom, I'm hungry. Can't we stop and take a break now?" Julian's complaint was reasonable. The children had left home without an after-school snack. Alice came home from cutting grapes early in the afternoons, leaving John in the field by himself. She'd prepared and pack a quick supper and then hauled the children to work.

Marta heard her mom's complaints and agreed. Their priority was to finish packing as many boxes as possible. Payday would come soon enough. Their parents needed a large paycheck to meet their family's needs.

"Mom is right. Maybe we'll get paid an enormous sum, so we can purchase new shoes and clothes for school, maybe even some coats. None of us got anything new this year, remember?" Marta reminded the children. She didn't want to mention that her shoes were so tight that sometimes she'd go without socks, making extra space for comfort.

With careful movements, Marta moved from vine to vine, carefully cutting grape clusters. "Linda, move away from Mom. You're too close to her knife." Marta noticed her mom's cutting movements were faster than was safe. "I'm sorry, Mom. I just don't want you or Linda to get hurt." Marta never gave up worrying for Linda.

"Thank you, Marta. I'm proud to have you help me care for her. I'm so bent on concentrating on these bunches and keeping them intact that I forgot about Linda." Mom smiled and turned around to face the grape bunches hanging above her face. Her aching body bent under the dusty, bushy vine could handle no more toiling. Turning enough to see that Linda had moved a few feet away, she smiled with relief and tried continuing her work. Through her pains, a hymn spilled out of her mouth.

"Mom, I'm tired. Can we take a break?" Daniel asked, throwing a dirt clod across the trench.

"Sure, let's stop for a while. Julian, run to the station wagon and bring the paper sack and the jug of water. Please, dear." After removing her headscarf, Alice shook it and wiped moisture and dirt off her forehead. Then she placed it around her shoulders, exposing her head to the gentle wind.

They sat under the shady bushes and caught their breath. Julian returned with a wrinkled brown sack and a water jug. Alice took out the tinfoil-wrapped sandwiches and passed them around.

After taking a bite from the fresh sandwich, Daniel commented, "Oh, Mom, the filling is delicious."

"Yes, Mom. It's savory with homemade fried potatoes and scrambled eggs." Marta was grateful her mom was creative with her cooking, especially when ingredients were meager.

"Well, they say hunger makes a good cook. I guess that's true." Alice chuckled with satisfaction that she'd pleased her children.

The difficult work continued throughout the week and on Saturdays, when they worked from sunrise until late afternoon. On these long days, the children became overheated. An occasional light wind blew between and over the furrows, cooling them off for a few minutes. Their dad allowed them to take mini breaks while he and their mother finished picking their bushes clean.

On one particular Saturday, a hot, relentless sun beat down on them. "Whoa, the temperature has gotta be over a hundred degrees," John said as he looked to the sky to check the sun's path. Based on where it stood in its path, he could tell it was eleven in the morning.

By two o'clock, Marta couldn't stand the dust that had worked its way through her clothes and hair, even though a cotton scarf protected her hair. Her legs felt weak and ached from the constant bending. Her back throbbed; she could hardly get up to move to the next bush.

She thought of the next day, Sunday. They would be too tired to attend church service. "Mom, can we sleep in tomorrow?" Marta asked, knowing the answer already.

"No, honey. It's Sunday, remember? Gotta attend church." Alice spoke without admonishing tones. "I'm sure your dad will have a wonderful sermon for us. Besides, it wouldn't be right for pastor's kids not to attend their own dad's service. Would it?"

"Mom, about our income. I want to say thank you for spending it wisely to care for us. I don't begrudge you and Dad. But couldn't we get a small allowance, like maybe twenty-five cents a week?" Marta used tactful words to get her point across.

"You oughta be glad we have food in our cupboards," Julian scolded.

"Quit your fussing. Your mom and I already considered treating you young'uns to ice cream every Sunday. Also, we're planning on buying coats for you children. That'll take some earnings. But if we make enough, I also wanna buy school shoes," John spoke proudly, sure they'd make enough to meet their needs.

Marta's thoughts returned to their work. The sun was

setting. *Soon it'll be time to go home and head for the bathtub. I can't wait.*

"Lord, we're thankful for the work, but we'll be glad when this work is over. Please give us the strength to endure till harvest is over," Alice prayed out loud, throwing her knife into her pail. The children stopped their work and listened. They couldn't agree more with her.

"Let's call it quits!" Dad announced. "Julian, bring the water jug and trash. I'll pick up the knives. Everyone, drop them in this leather bag. Mother, you stack the pails and bring them along. Marta, hold on to Linda." Exhaustedly, they marched in a straight line to the vehicle, leaving the dusty field behind.

At the end of the line, Julian would occasionally pick up a dirt clod and pitch it at Marta's legs. "Stop, that, Julian!" Marta shook the broken clod off the back of her legs and shoes. She hurried to get away from him and walked next to her dad. Upon arriving at the station wagon, she eyed Julian, keeping her distance from him. She pulled off the dirty scarf around her head, exposing black hair wet with perspiration, and her ivory forehead clear of dust. The rest of her face was covered with grime, which extended to her chin and down around her neck. Her forehead was quite a contrast compared to the rest of her face.

While sitting in the back seat of the old rig, she pulled off her shoes. "Ah, this feels cool." She sighed with relief, wiggling her toes. She could now relax. Everyone else piled into the station wagon. "I'm so tired I barely made it here," she said weakly to Linda, who had just sat next to her.

Then Daniel voiced his thoughts. "I'm glad we're together, except for Phil." Fearing receiving a blow from

Julian, Daniel sucked in his lips. He expected his explosive treatment over every word he spoke. He looked over at Julian to check out his fists, but he was busy counting coins in his pocket.

Daniel was glad he'd not heard his remarks. Mom and Dad would not have been able to stop Julian because they were outside at the rear of the station wagon, putting away the work tools. John pulled a writing pad and pencil from a bag, leaned against the back seat, and made some scribbles.

"How many boxes did we make today, John?" Alice looked at the tablet John held. He was tallying boxes they'd filled with grape bunches.

"Well, we made enough to buy groceries for one week and shoes for the youngsters. I tell you, Alice, havin' the children workin' with us is like havin' two extra adults. They're a mighty big help."

"Maybe if this rate keeps up, we'll be able to afford maintenance on the car and get new tires. Don't you think?" Alice spoke apprehensively, afraid of hearing grim news.

"Alice, everything's gonna be all right. Let's git home; it's been a long, weary day."

Sometimes the drive home didn't seem long and unbearable, but today the humid September air made it intolerable. While looking east toward the Sierra Mountains, Marta could see cumulus clouds forming over them. Their flat bases touched the mountaintops, and their tops rose like whipped cream into the blue sky. The setting sun shot amber and red light rays over and through them, mixing the colors into an array of violets, oranges, and crimson. The tinted clouds reminded Marta of the Arizona sunsets.

"Linda, look at the colorful sky. What a beautiful sight!" Marta took Linda's braid apart and raked back black strands with her fingers, releasing fine particles of dust.

"I wish I could grab the colors and bring them home with me," Linda spoke longingly, causing her family to laugh at her sweet thought.

Marta couldn't wait to get into the bathtub filled with cool water. Thinking of removing the grime off was exhilarating.

After getting home, the family prepared to bathe. Marta threw her dusty shoes on the front porch and then removed Linda's shoes and socks. Alice expected the children to follow the bathing schedule she had prepared.

"Mom, as soon as I finish my bath, I wanna take a quick nap. I can help you fix supper after that. Is that OK with you?" Marta exhaled, feeling as if she'd been running a marathon and had just stopped to catch her breath. "My bones ache, and I need to rest."

While removing her dirty shoes, Alice's concentration was on the amount of boxes they'd filled; she didn't hear Marta's comment.

"I'm in the tub first," Julian hollered, running into the bathroom and slamming the door shut, paying no mind to the bathing schedule. His selfishness was apparent. John didn't see or hear him because he'd been working outside.

"Oh, it's another day in the life of Julian," Marta uttered to herself despairingly. She undressed, placed her soil clothes in the corner behind the door, and flopped into bed. Soon, she fell into a deep sleep.

She woke to a warm, bright Sunday morning, her stomach aching with hunger. *What happened after work yesterday?* She could only speculate. Her weariness wouldn't allow her to remember, yet the growling noises coming from her belly told her she was hungry. *How long can we keep doing this cruel labor? Will our health succumb? Lord, help us make it to the end of grape harvest. We need the income it provides.* Tears flowed uncontrollably for Marta, though she didn't make a whimper. Her stiff body ached with excruciating pain.

Chapter 28

The Family Is Accepted

The family came to feel welcomed and secure in the town, but there was a problem with the mail deliveries. John and Marta wondered whether the postmaster, Mr. Brewster, was misplacing Phil's letters—or worse, whether death had come to him. John said nothing about it to the family and would change the subject whenever somebody brought it up. Marta's intuitions, like her dad's, were always operating on high.

One day while checking for mail, Mr. Brewster told Marta that earlier that week, he'd seen an airmail letter from Phil and would put it in her family's mailbox. Marta had been to the post office every day hoping to find the letter but had found the box empty. On this stiflingly hot afternoon, she asked Mr. Brewster about it.

"I'm sorry, Marta. I thought I had seen such a letter. I went through all the mail, but I didn't see it. Must've been mistaken." He pretended he had to go back to work, leaving Marta to wonder what could have happened.

"I'll come back tomorrow and check again. Hopefully, there is such a letter from Phil. Thank you for looking, Mr. Brewster." Disappointed, Marta walked out of the post office. Her family hadn't heard from Phil for a while. It should've been time for another letter to arrive. She solemnly walked over to Mrs. Waters's store. An ice-cold Coke would restore her outlook.

"Hello, Mrs. Waters," Marta said as she entered the small store. Upon walking over to the Coke machine, she noticed a stack of mail sitting behind the candy jars sitting on the counter. "Are you helping the postmaster with the mail, Mrs. Waters?"

Marta reached into the red icebox with giant letters on the front spelling "Coke" and brought a soda pop out of the ice water. After popping it open with the can opener attached to the front of the machine, she walked over to the counter containing the mail. She stood there, one hand wrapped around her Coke and the other in the pocket of her dress, looking unconcerned about anything.

Mrs. Waters, who'd been standing on a ladder stacking canned goods, stepped down and hurried to the mail. "Oh, my, no—this is mine. I need to sort it by vendor names and pay the bills." She picked up the bundle and set it under the counter on one of its shelves, away from the public's view.

Marta had learned a long time ago not to trust anybody nosy like Mrs. Waters. Marta had witnessed many customers who'd been misled by her deceptive questions. Later, they found that Mrs. Waters was misconstruing their words to others and making trouble for them. Marta remembered such incidents during her Coke breaks.

The worst gossip had been hearing how mean an old lady named Mrs. Somerset had been to the town. Marta recalled that conversation.

"Marta, you do not understand how mean Mrs.

Somerset has been with this town. You know, when her husband was alive, she gave the town money to complete many projects, like a new well and steel piping to haul water into town. They provided the sewer system located outside of town and helped build an electrical plant. Can you imagine anybody having so much money? I think they did it to show off their wealth."

"It doesn't sound like she's mean at all." Marta had defended the lady though she didn't know her. She felt Mrs. Waters had no cause to judge her.

"No, you just don't know how suddenly she stopped her generosity," Mrs. Waters had huffed, showing her frustration against the lady.

"Maybe she had a reason?" Marta had tried to sound optimistic about the old lady. She didn't like this kind of talk about anybody.

"No, no, it's true. Even Jake at the other store says the same thing. He said there was no reason for her to stop funding the growth of this town just because her husband died. You know, he left her all his money, and she was already wealthy herself. What is she going to do with so much money, especially at her old age? She don't have relatives around, that I know."

Mrs. Waters turned to grab the duster when the doorbell twinkled, bringing Marta out of her thoughts.

"I'm here to pay my bill and tell you to close it out. I'm not shoppin' here anymore!" The angry shopper raised his voice to Mrs. Waters as Marta sipped her soda.

Then another man and woman entered. "You can't be spreadin' any more lies 'bout us if we don't shop here anymore. We've had enough of your ways. It's one thing to talk 'bout people's problems to others, but using lies to embellish the truth is an entirely different matter."

After pulling out a file drawer containing small credit registers, Mrs. Waters quickly found the couple's register and handed them their bill. The couple slammed some money on the counter, picked up the tab Mrs. Waters had handed them, and stomped out. Then the next couple stepped up to the counter.

Marta realized this store was not a decent place to take a break. One day she'd tell her dad to quit shopping there and open a credit line at Jake's store instead. She'd never heard Jake gossip about anybody. Perhaps Mrs. Waters was embellishing words about his talk about this old lady, Mrs. Somerset.

She wondered if Phil's letter was stuck inside the stack of bills. If she left now without checking, she'd never know the answer. Marta felt she had to check as soon as Mrs. Waters turned away. While slowly drinking her soda, she waited for an opportunity to sneak into the stack.

The doorbell tinkled again. A family of four entered, each carrying an empty grocery basket. "Afternoon, Mrs. Waters," the man next to the woman said while the two children ran to the candy jars.

"We'd like some groceries. Can you help us fill this list?" The man spoke in a deep drawl.

"Let me have the list." Mrs. Waters looked over the list and said, "Oh, the hardware is kept in the back. I'll get those tools for you." She left the room and walked behind a curtained side door.

Marta looked at the counter and then at the family standing by the vegetable baskets. The man intimidated her, but as of that moment, his back was turned against her. *What if he told on me?* Fear crept into Marta. After throwing the empty Coke bottle into the trash can, she started walking out the front door, ignoring the stack of mail. Then she stopped for a second, turned around, and dashed to the back of the counter. While fumbling through the letters, she found it.

"Corporal Philip Rodrigo," read the small inscription on the letter. It was in the middle of the stack. It belonged to her family, and she took it, stashing it into her dress pocket. Marta ran out the door and went straight home.

Upon arriving home, she gave it to her parents, who were already back from work.

"Howdy, Phil!" Dad hollered with glee, holding the letter to the window light. "Gather up, everyone. We're gonna hear what Phil's been doin'! And thank you, Marta, for this wonderful delivery." The children couldn't believe a letter had come in. They sat silently around the table as their dad read it. Phil wrote that he was tired but in good spirits. After the reading, Marta pulled her mother aside.

"Mom, I gotta talk to you. It's private," Marta spoke softly to her mother, who'd started preparing supper.

"What is it?" Alice checked for the kids. They'd already gone out.

"Well, you see, Mrs. Waters is a trouble instigator. She talks awful about people, and I don't think we ought to do business with her any longer." Marta spoke without hesitation.

"Have you witnessed this behavior?" Alice pulled out fresh fish Julian had caught earlier at the pond outside of town.

"Yes, Mom. I think it's best if we keep away from her

and shop somewhere else. I don't want her spreading awful stuff about us. We don't have a foothold in this town yet. Maybe we can shop at the other store while cutting back at Mrs. Waters's. What do you think?"

"Very well. I trust your judgment, but let me handle it with Dad. We might rile him up ourselves, and then he'll storm to her store and give her a piece of his mind. This'll start trouble for us, for sure. We're not prepared financially to leave suddenly or be run out. Let's not mention it anymore. Now set the table, dear."

After supper, John and Alice went outside to discuss the matter in private.

"We have enough money coming in from the fieldwork to get caught up on things, and we'll have enough to keep our church open too," Alice announced one day in late October at the dinner table. "I have so much more hope than before. I mean, look into the cupboard: they're mostly all full of canned goods, and we've been able to purchase four new tires for the station wagon."

"Mom, what about our winter clothes? When can we buy 'em? It's getting cold now," Daniel said, chewing his lima beans slowly as he waited for an answer.

John tried to assure his young son. "Son, we'll get to those when the weather turns cold. Who knows? Winter might get a late start, giving us more time to get situated even better."

"Will you have other work after grape harvest is over?" Marta asked, picking up her glass. She had many questions to ask him about his employment.

"Yes, yes, I'll have more work. Tom at the gravel pit offered me part-time work; he'll hold my position. I like part-time work 'cause that'll give me an opportunity to prepare sermons. Then there'll be the walnut harvest. If I must, I can work that too."

"Can you all believe this? We're still newcomers, but so many townsfolk respect us already. My, things are looking up for us, even in church. Thank God!" Alice spoke good-naturedly. "Does anyone want more tea?" She raised the pitcher and began refilling their glasses.

"I can truly see God's blessings. Just look at the congregation. We have fifteen friendly people, older folks who'll demonstrate respectability to you children. At one time they were migrants themselves, and they arrived in town years earlier looking for work. God helped them adjust too." John appreciated the growth of his church.

"I remember when we met them working in the fields. They didn't bully us with unkind words or judgmental quips because of our background. Well, neither did the townspeople; they also turned out to be caring and generous folks." Alice spoke with pride for their blessings.

Marta said, "Mom, you and Dad made a wise decision when you decided to come to this town. I mean, it contains everything a family could need to sustain itself. They even welcome and encourage new businesses. Maybe someday I'll open a business to help make it a better place for everyone, including migrants like us. Better yet, if I finish my schooling, maybe I can be a teacher." She felt elated to be part of a growing community that held the potential for personal growth.

The family became acquainted with the grocers, Jake and Mrs. Waters; the supervisor at the gravel pit, Tom; the teachers; their landlord, Mr. Sam Fowlerte; and a neighbor or two. The townspeople appreciated them starting a church, giving people more choices to attend according to their beliefs. People appreciated the hard-working family who contributed at town hall meetings.

John and Alice attended these meetings, grateful city hall had allowed them to have the church at a reasonable cost. They joined in with the townspeople whenever there were town-cleaning details, bringing their own tools and the children to chop weeds growing around sidewalks, or roadsides around neighborhoods and picking trash blown in by heavy winds. They helped paint the outside of city hall and any other public building like the community center, which needed a facelift.

The townspeople were happy with Marta's family and continually held them with great regard. Eventually, John and Alice were shopping at Jake's store. John made arrangements for Marta to charge Cokes on the newly opened credit register. *I hope this will stop any negative words against our family from Mrs. Waters. We've got to keep our respectable reputation. We can't afford to have our name muddied.* Marta lived every day thereafter with careful caution. She was vigilant with her words and studied every question poised to her that held a hint of nosiness.

Chapter 29

Somerville Needs a Library

There was one service missing in Somerville, according to Marta: a library. She wished they had a small library, like the one they had back home, in the general store. It wasn't much, but there was a shelved wall next to the canned goods filled with books. She recalled how she and her siblings would go on Saturdays and check out a book or two. Every month, the townspeople had donated books and paid a small fee to the grocer, Mr. Jenkins, for maintaining it.

One day while visiting Henry, Marta asked, "Why doesn't this town have a library? Or is there one I have overlooked?" She sat on a bale of hay reading one of her schoolbooks while Henry prepared to close the shop.

"I don't know. No one has ever mentioned it. Must be no one has given such an amenity a second thought. Maybe they felt we didn't have that need. You know, the school has a little library already." Henry threw the last bale of hay onto the truck's bed. He would drive her home and continue with hay deliveries.

"I know about that one. We check out books every two weeks, but it's only used during school hours. It would be nice to check out books on weekends and in summer, when school is closed. If we had one here, then everyone could have access to books, magazines, and the daily newspaper."

"You're wasting your time wishing for a library. This town can't afford one. You'll have to drive to one of the bigger towns to find one. Besides, people here are too busy making a living to think about libraries."

"I think it's a shame! When I'm older, I'll join the city council so I can make that proposal and make it happen!" Marta pursed her lips, returning to her reading.

"Yeah, with that pouting mouth, anyone might believe you—except me. I think you'll do it when you're an old lady, but not anytime soon. Believe me, the townspeople are just trying to make a living. A library is an extravagance we can't afford. Maybe in about thirty years, if this town doesn't dry up and blow away like the tumbleweeds, we'll be able to afford one." Henry laughed while thinking about tumbleweeds invading the town.

"Henry, speaking of tumbleweeds, when do you expect conifer trees to arrive? Or will we end up using tumbleweeds for Christmas trees?"

Jokingly, Marta smiled and looked up at him. Then she quickly turned her eyes back to her books.

Henry smiled at her sense of humor. "That's not an awful idea. I've heard they used 'em as such around here sometime back." He turned around and finished packing his truck for his delivery. After walking back to his desk, he picked up his Bible.

"Come on, quit your thinkin' and get in the truck. I gotta lock up." After helping Marta get in, Henry made his way around to the driver's side and stopped to smile with appreciation for his young friend. *The young girl's earnestness and care for the town are worthy of being praised. She's gonna make it in this town, all right.* He got in and drove her home.

Chapter 30

Blessings and Trials

*F*og *will soon arrive. How dreadful,* Marta thought. While dashing to the post office, dragging Daniel and Linda along, she noticed the leaves soaring in the wind. She enjoyed the coolness of fall and the orange, red, and brown leaves playing around her legs, chased by the wind. Every tree in town was showing fall colors. While kicking leaves out of her way, she wished she'd experienced this wonder in her old home. It was an exhilarating feeling, breathing in the fresh air scented with dried plums, dry leaves that took on the scent of spices, and wet earth.

After wrapping her scarf around her neck tighter, she turned to Daniel. "Daniel, take Linda home with you. Tell Mom I'm stopping to see Henry. Tell her there was no mail. And hold on to Linda's hand. Now, don't forget to tell her," Marta instructed, hollering into the wind.

The quick change in the season caused Marta to question their future. She knew better than to question God, yet she did. She'd learned that this was a natural reaction for many Christians when placed in unusual situations. Fear overwhelmed her when thinking about their needs, such as thick winter coats. They had never required coats in Arizona, except for her dad and Phil when hiking the high mountains looking for a cypress tree, chopping wood, or hunting for deer. *Perhaps we'll all get new coats soon. Work is supposed to continue in the grape fields for another week or so, but eventually this type of harvest will end. I hope we can find other work.*

Dooming doubts hunted Marta during any trial, small or large, instantly blinding her faith. The deluge of homework, babysitting, helping with house chores, and searching for lost books interfered with her prayer times. Thinking back to some of those trials gave her chills.

The last time Julian had hidden her schoolbooks after arriving home from school was mentally pressing on her mind. She'd cried at the thought of losing them for fear of having to pay for them and for not having them to do her homework. She'd searched everywhere. Her parents were not home, so she couldn't ask them for help. Daniel and Linda helped with the search but had had no success. Marta began cooking supper before her parents got home from work. She hoped the books would turn up later. Her swollen eyes and fast breathing told her parents of her panic when they came inside.

"Marta, was wrong?" Mom had asked her upon entering the kitchen and pasting a kiss on her forehead.

"Mom, I lost my books. I don't know where I left them."

"Lately you're always forgetting things. Girl, what's gotten into you? Quit crying. We'll look for them later. I'm sure we'll find them," Alice said, turning around to go into the bathroom for her bath.

"Marta, are these books yours?" Dad asked, coming in from putting their work tools away.

"Oh, Daddy, you found my books! Where were they?"

"I found them inside the trailer when I was adjusting the tarp. How did they get there?" His expression was one of impatience, yet he spoke kindly.

"I don't know, Daddy. I spent most of the afternoon looking for them."

"Julian put them there!" Daniel hollered from outside the screened back door. He'd been listening to the conversation and had previously kept quiet so as not to rile Julian. With his parents now at home, he wasn't afraid to speak up.

Marta gasped. "What?"

"Julian, come here," Dad demanded. "Did you put these books inside the trailer?"

Julian dared not lie. "Y-yes, sir, I did. I was only playing. I would've given them back."

"Uh-huh. Let's go to the shed." Dad and Julian returned later, with Julian sniffing and wiping his eyes. "Don't you ever play such a mean trick on your sister again. That goes for the young'uns too. Leave them alone. Remember your promise? It looks like you have forgotten it." Dad disappeared into his bedroom.

Julian behaved for a while and left Marta alone. She was glad difficult times with Julian were over. She couldn't face such meanness again, as well as the stress that went with his antics. However, other trials began and ended, and though they'd caused her agony, they'd instilled in her determination, patience, and forgiveness. They'd also served as reminders to trust God and to lean on His guidance and understanding. Marta thought of those times of hardship.

Helping her mother with the wash one Saturday afternoon, Marta sorted the dirty clothes while Alice filled the ringer tub washer with water. She had emptied the last bucket she'd carried from the kitchen sink and poured it into the washer's tub. "Mom, aren't our troubles ever going to stop?" she asked while placing the color clothes into the tub. "As soon as we remedy something, another problem comes up: the car needing repairs, plumbing, or bills."

"Marta, that's how life is. Our problems help us appreciate the answers. I'm grateful you're not spoiled; otherwise, you'd never learn from life's lessons. That might account for why you're so responsible. As for our troubles, those are mine and your dad's worries, not yours. Why don't you consider all the blessings we've received? That'll help strengthen your faith. Remember, the enemy wants to steal your blessings. That includes your faith, hope, and love. Don't let him put doubts in your mind."

Marta took her mother's advice and began thinking of their many blessings. There were the many field labor jobs available to her family; their comfortable rental; her kind teacher, Miss Jones; the kind and helpful townspeople; and a letter from Aunt Ellen telling them Grandmother was better. Grandmother enjoyed sitting on the front porch and overlooking the parsonage. She could speak a few words and could relate her fondness of the parsonage.

Marta thought of the fall garden they'd helped Mom plant in the backyard. She thought of the vegetables they had added: lettuce, leeks, small onions, and garlic. She also thought of the fertilizer Dad and Julian got free from a local dairy. They'd added the manure around the fruit trees, hoping that in the spring, they'd produce healthy blossoms and later bear sweet fruit. They watered the citrus trees often enough so the fruit might grow and be ready for picking in January or February.

She was thankful for the melon packing season, which had provided her parents with jobs when they first got there in the nick of time before their money ran out. That job had afforded them groceries and gas money for the station wagon until other jobs became available. It had been a genuine miracle to find employment shortly after arriving. Marta realized this and gave God credit.

She thought of her friend, Henry. *He's another blessing.* But doubt crept into her mind, causing her to think of losing it all. That night, Marta dreamed they had to move and leave Somerville behind. She couldn't bear another move! She tossed in her sleep, mumbling. *The enemy is coming to steal my blessings and curse me with more trials. God, save me! Please save me.* She woke up and talked herself into remembering God's blessings. *Yes, Lord, You're here to bless us. Thank You!* Marta was filled with a peace as if sent from heaven.

She didn't care what the morrow would bring. She fell into a deep sleep filled with warm, soft clouds. They wrapped themselves around her, soothing her gently. Tomorrow was another day, and God was going to take care of their needs.

Chapter 31

Henry, Her Best Friend

"Marta's got a boyfriend!" Julian laughed upon seeing her new haircut. "That's why you got a new hairstyle. It looks silly!" He laughed louder.

Alice had followed John's advice to perk Marta's appearance. He hoped she'd feel happier and more confident if she had a fresh look. It would undoubtedly detour her timidity. Therefore, Alice had taken funds from their savings for Marta to get a haircut. She'd also allowed for the purchase of silk embroidery thread for updating her faded denim jacket. Seeing her daughter happy meant more to Alice than any amount of money Marta could work for. John would agree with her.

Marta's hairstyle was a short bob, allowing her black hair to fall at chin level. She felt stylish and well-groomed. New bangs lay above her curved, dark brows, gracefully framing her oval face. Marta felt confidant, as if fresh life had been breathed into her soul.

She ignored Julian's snide remarks. Instead of frowning on his misbehavior, she took it as a compliment. Smiling, she began embroidering red, pink, and orange roses on the jacket's front and back shoulders. Her precise work and bright thread colors gave her pleasure. This Saturday was turning into a productive day for her.

It was late afternoon when Marta finished her sewing. After examining it, she stood up to put away her sewing gear. At that moment, she noticed Julian poking his tongue at her and then running out the backdoor, giving it a hard slam. Marta pitied his jealousy. She did not want to see him hurt but wished she were somewhere else. There was nothing she could do to help him.

"Mom, can I go to the post office and then stop and talk to Henry?" she inquired hopefully.

"I see no reason why not. You can show off your new hairdo and jacket."

"Mom, you know I don't enjoy showing off my things. I don't care for attention."

"I'm sorry, Marta. Be sure you're back before supper."

When Marta entered the hay shop, the smell of dry hay and coffee brewing in the office struck her nostrils. Marta saw Henry next to a pile of grain sacks, a clipboard in his hands.

After throwing a sack of grain onto the bed of his old pickup, Henry stopped and faced her. "Afternoon, Marta. What brings you out today?"

"I came looking for shipments of evergreens." She pretended she was searching for conifers but had actually come to visit Henry, though she dared not say so.

"I ain't got anythin' in yet, but it was nice of you to come visit me." Henry turned away, trying not to show his grin.

"Can I help with something?" she mumbled.

"What's that?" Not waiting for an answer, he added,

"Say, how 'bout a Bible study lesson?" Henry changed the subject, hoping she had time to stay awhile. "This lesson sticks to my mind, so it must be for me to share. Do you wanna hear it?"

"Sure, I'll listen, but afterward may I water the plants?"

"Maybe. You just sit here for now." Henry patted a bale of hay. "This message tells of stewards of God, as you and I are. It's the first lesson I learned after I came to the Lord several years ago."

"I'm a steward? Of what?" Marta remarked.

"God's provisions require that each one of us guards those bounties with care. We must be responsible and frugal with them."

"Where did you learn that?"

"Here, let me get my Bible. I'll show you." Henry came back with his Bible and sat beside her. "Here in Luke, the sixteenth chapter." He read a passage and waited for her reaction. "What do you think?"

"Can you please explain it?"

"Well, as stewards, we must care for our blessings. This includes family responsibilities, finances, and talents. But you must also tend to your mind, body, and career."

"What? We're also caretakers of these?" Marta had never heard such teachings.

"Taking care of His blessings requires us to be good stewards of them." Henry pointed to the passage in the book.

"Oh, I see. Dad never explained it so. I never knew this verse applied to everything else in our lives. I enjoy your viewpoint and explanations."

The lesson enlightened Marta to a truth she had been performing without realizing it. Unconsciously, she had been a responsible steward when taking care of her siblings. Armed with this biblical information, she aimed to apply it consciously, and she would strive harder to do more for her family. She was grateful for the Bible study.

"Henry, I'm obliged. I enjoyed the lesson and understand those verses better."

"One more thing: don't forget to pray every day. It's the power that'll allow you to plow through problems."

"Do you mind if I water your plants and check out your plant inventory?"

"Go ahead. There's a new shipment behind the building, so help yourself. I gotta finish my work."

After dashing to the back, Marta saw various containers holding tall and short plants. She glanced through them and didn't see conifer trees. When she strode back into the shop, she saw Henry near a pile of grain sacks. "Will you place an order for conifer trees before Christmas?"

Henry considered her question and then answered, "I might. I'm not sure. You know Jake will do the same. Maybe I won't order them."

While eyeing the shop, Marta spotted how untidied it was. "You have an awful lot to do. Have you thought of hiring somebody?" She picked up a watering can and began watering small potted plants sitting on a shelf against the office.

"Why? Are you looking for work?" He picked up another sack, slung it over his shoulder, and carried it to the truck.

"I'm always looking either for myself or for someone in my family. It doesn't hurt to ask."

"Well, I need a strong, young man to unload shipments. I brought these last night from Tuleville." Henry studied

Marta's appearance. "Say, what's different 'bout you today?"

"I had my hair cut, and I embroidered my jacket." Blushing, she patted her thick dark hair. The bob felt comfortable as it neatly lay around her face.

"Real nice! You are lovely." Henry threw another sack onto the truck. Marta had hardly uttered a thanks when he spoke again. "Do you know Mrs. Somerset? She lives near your home." Henry stopped his work and rested one leg on top of a truck tire. "I understand she's looking for a young lady to help clean her kitchen. You might wanna talk to her soon. Tell her I'm recommending you; she knows me very well." He walked around the vehicle and picked up a bag of alfalfa seed.

Marta watched him with unbelief. Did she hear him, right? Was it her haircut that portrayed her capability of holding down such a job? Or was it the change on her denim jacket that made her appear responsible and capable? "Henry, you're a great friend and minister!" She fumbled her way out of the shop. "I'll try to see her as soon as I can. I gotta go. Goodbye!"

"Don't wait too long," he hollered. "The job won't last!"

She hurried home and found her mother fixing supper. They had not worked in the grapes for two days because the farmer was catching up on extra fruit inventory. Marta's family was using this downtime for chores around the house.

"What's the rush?" It had been a long while since Alice had seen her daughter this happy.

"Ah, nothing, I've been scouting places that might carry evergreen trees for Christmas."

"That's a long way off. You must concentrate on your

schoolwork instead of wasting your afternoons on fruitless ventures," her mom scolded.

Marta wanted to tell her of the job with Mrs. Somerset but feared reproach. She needed to wait for an opportunity to talk to her about it. *Hopefully the old lady won't hire anybody immediately.* Marta would wait for the chance to speak to her parents. *How and when can I approach Mom and Dad for permission? I'll wait for an opening in their conversations.*

Marta concentrated on her parents' needs as they returned to fieldwork, so her conifer tree search ended. She remembered her Bible lesson of being a good steward of God's provisions, and she planned to do her share as this concept taught.

Her plan of notifying her parents of a job prospect with Mrs. Somerset was always on her mind, but finding the right time to do so was going to take patience. Meanwhile, her family was getting grounded back on their routines, especially family time together.

Her dad required they make time for praying together again, which Marta appreciated. She needed a boost with her prayer schedule. But one afternoon, John and Alice got home late from work. It threw their evening routine off course, causing them to hurry and barely finish their evening chores. The children went to bed with their dad reminding them to say their prayers.

That night, Marta woke up bothered. She sat up and thought about this concern. *What could it be? I've neglected to finish something, but what?* After careful consideration, she realized she'd forgotten to recite her prayers as her dad had instructed. She ran halfway through them, soon fell into a deep sleep, and dreamed of Phil. In her dream, he was lost in the snow, but a hero showed up to save him. Henry was there; He'd bring him home.

"Mom, last night I dreamed that Henry went to Korea to bring Phil home. What do you think that means?"

"It sounds as if God is trying to tell you that He's put Henry in our path, probably to bring us more blessings. God has used him a couple of times in our lives, and He can use him again."

Marta thought of the job with Mrs. Somerset. Was Henry the blessing between her and this lady? *Oh, my! What other wondrous ways will Henry continue to bless us?* She couldn't wait.

Chapter 32

Marta Takes on a Job

The early cold weather in late October threatened the family's comfort, and with the small amount of wood they had set aside for the woodstove, John worried about his family's health. After stepping outside to observe the inky sky, he saw lightning in the eastern hills making its way toward the valley. John and Alice had been working steadily harvesting grapes Monday through Saturday, from sunup until late afternoon. The children still helped after school when the weather permitted.

"Alice, don't let this threatening weather take away your hope. We will survive this winter." John hugged Alice, who was standing over the sink and staring toward the east. She saw what John had seen. He stepped out the front door and walked over to the trailer parked next to the house.

Father, stop the storm from heading this way. We need the work, Lord. Amen. John understood the calamity that moisture would cause to their work. Rain would cause the grapes to spoil, causing the family to lose work and precious income. He quietly continued praying as he checked the canvas straps around the trailer.

John went in to wash his hands. Alice handed him a towel and said, "John, fieldwork is almost over. We can't afford to lose one day's work. I hope this rain will hold off awhile."

"Don't worry, honey. Walnut harvest begins in November. If nothin' else comes along, I'll take that job. The weather is gettin' cooler and won't be suitable for the children to work outdoors. Do you think you can finish workin' grape harvest with me till then? That is, if rain don't stop the work." John held her close and kissed the top of her head.

"I can. Don't worry about me." Alice's stomach churned with worry, but she knew what ever happened would be God's will. He always took care of their needs.

That cold evening, there was no conversation as the family felt uneasy. John hadn't spoken a word, letting them know something grievous was on his mind. "I need to talk to everyone. After supper, please stay in your seats. Ladies, please clean the kitchen afterward. Alice, will you tally up our savings later tonight?"

Alice nodded yes and turned just in time to see a flash of lightning across the kitchen curtain. *It can't be too far off,* she thought. The faint light from the overhead bulb was barely enough to light the kitchen.

Sitting quietly, Marta and the children waited for Dad to start the meeting. Julian's face showed fear. *Have I done something wrong?* His pale face told on him. He was still taunting Marta when no one was looking and felt scared he was in trouble if she'd tattled.

"Winter is comin'," Dad began. "With dampness as heavy as it gets here, it'll get freezin' cold and foggy in a month or two. Your mom and I are workin' as much as we can. We've been able to save a little. I wanna thank you, children, for helpin'. I know it's been difficult finishin' your homework at school; I appreciate your sacrifices. From now on, y'all will stay home and continue your home chores after school. I thank God for His many blessings. However, we don't know whether there'll be work during the winter months."

"Dad, we can help after school, when it's warm. Don't worry 'bout us. We'll be all right," Daniel said, trying to calm his dad's fears.

"I appreciate every one of you, son. We've got to continue workin' while there's time and save what we can for the winter months. But I wanna buy each of you a coat before that time." John studied his children's faces, wondering what they were thinking. "Daniel, you're right. I wanna ask if you'd all like to continue working after school in the grape fields. That is, when it's warm."

Marta saw her chance to ask her long-awaited question. "Dad, I can do fieldwork, but I found an opportunity to work indoors. You remember Henry?"

"I know Henry," he stated proudly. "He's a good man." He glanced at Marta to see her reaction, but her face was blank.

"He told me of a Mrs. Somerset, who is searching for help in her kitchen." Marta stared at the savings jar sitting on the shelf above the kitchen window. *How much is in it, and is there enough for the purchase of coats?* "Can I go talk to her? It might be work I can do in the coming cold months."

"Go ahead. But don't get disappointed if you don't get the job. People around here are finicky 'bout newcomers. Also, don't sass her like you do your mother."

"I understand, Dad. I'll get recommendations from people who know me well. Miss Jones, my teacher, said she'd give me a letter of reference."

"Who's Mrs. Somerset?" Daniel asked, looking up from picking the last of his fried potatoes.

"She's a wealthy retired teacher who lives on Rose Street. Her husband had a farm and sold it just before he passed away a few years ago. Mrs. Waters told me so. She's elderly now and needs help with house cleaning chores. I'll go tomorrow after school and talk with her." Marta appreciated the proper opportunity to talk to her parents had shown itself.

"Is Mrs. Somerset that grumpy old woman who's always scolding kids not to pick her flowers? You know, that mean lady who lives at that house with a white picket fence around the corner and across the street? The one we see every day on our way to school?" Julian asked, half scared. Just mentioning her name put fear in him, and he walked on the opposite side of the road if he saw her outside. He felt convinced she could read his obnoxious thoughts, prompting him to steer away from her home.

"Yes, I've heard she expects perfection from everyone who works for her. That's why she can't keep anyone." While listening to their conversation, Alice appeared worried but said no more.

"I can hold up to her standards and do even better," Marta declared, remembering Mrs. Somerset's white house. She could never bypass it without admiring its appearance, which of late had been frequently on her mind.

The front porch of her home was inviting with two wooden rocking chairs resting against the front wall.

Arraying the porch floor was a row of geranium flower pots sitting at its edge. The red-tiled roof matched the red roses lining the inside of the fenced yard. There were three tall pine trees on one side of the lush lawn. The two brick chimneys, seen from the roadside, spoke of wealth.

"Thanks, Dad, for your permission. What's the meeting for?"

"I want to ask if y'all can hold out longer without coats. I'm wondering if you'll use your sweaters during this cold spell till I get more saved. They're expecting rain. After that, the fogs will roll into the valley. I pray the heavy cold and rain will stay away for a while."

"Daddy, we'll be OK. My sweater is thick; it'll keep me warm till I get a new coat," Linda said, assuring her dad.

"Don't worry, Dad. We'll be all right," Marta interjected, sounding confident.

"Hopefully in a week or two, we'll have made enough money to do that. I didn't want y'all to feel forgotten. And if it rains on a school day, I'll leave the station wagon with Mother. She'll drive you to school, and I'll hitch a ride to work."

With the meeting adjourned, Alice and her daughters cleaned the kitchen. Julian and Daniel went to their bedroom to do homework.

"I can't wait to talk to Mrs. Somerset," Marta told Linda as they got ready for bed. After kicking off her slippers, she heard the boys finishing word problems with what sounded like cheerful bliss.

Before visiting the Somerset home the next afternoon, Marta gave her siblings instructions to finish their homework. Upon her return, they'd help her get supper ready. On her way to the home, she worried about what she would do if she didn't get the job. She couldn't stand fieldwork anymore.

Marta arrived at the lady's home and stopped at the gate. As she admired the exquisite home with its verdant yard, she thought how it appeared like a bleached-out mausoleum, such a type she'd seen in a women's catalog. She slowly pushed through the wooden, slatted gate open to reveal a freshly mowed lawn. Marta inhaled the scent of cut grass. Never had she seen so much grass, packed neatly and edged around the roses and pine trees.

The beauty before her took her breath away. A cement sidewalk leading up to the porch steps separated the yard into two parts. While strolling along, she admired the scented flowers lining the walkway. They were nearing their flowering limit for the year. The scent from the tree roses standing against the picket fence with red geraniums sprawled beneath them was sweet. Small white mounds of sweet alyssum stood in front of the geraniums. As Marta came up to the steps, she heard someone speak.

"If you're a saleslady, I don't need anything." A corpulent older woman sitting in one of the rockers behind a porch column spoke sharply.

After stepping softly to the top of the steps to see who was speaking to her, Marta blurted, "No, no, ma'am. I am not a saleslady. Henry, at the hay store, told me you were looking for someone to clean your kitchen. I came to check if you were still interested in hiring somebody." She stood straight and spoke with confidence, not minding the intimidating attitude of the woman.

Meanwhile, Marta studied her appearance. Her gray hair appeared shoveled under a knitted black hat. A frayed black shawl draped round her bosom had slipped to the side of one of her shoulders. Black leather shoes, with a two-inch square heel, appeared in need of polishing. Her thick beige stockings ran crooked up her legs. By her appearance, Marta would have thought the woman was an old beggar. But this was not the case.

The elderly lady also eyed Marta's appearance and thought, *Her hair is quite short, brushed back and pulled behind her ears. Looks nice. Small turquoise earrings, thin sweater faded from many washings shows longtime wear. Hmm. It hangs on the girl like a sack and an oversized cotton skirt.* The woman appreciated the scattering of small flowers spread over the skirt's faded yellow backdrop. *Her stretched gray socks, white at one time, almost match her worn tennis shoes, but they're clean enough.* The woman continued to critique Marta's appearance, but her expressionless face revealed nothing. "I don't know who you are, miss. Never seen you before!" The opposing, apathetic woman pulled the black shawl up around her broad shoulders. With massive wrinkled fingers, she held the ends at her large bosom.

Marta continued to study the woman's appearance. *The knitted cap appears too small for her copious head but seems sufficient to keep out the cold. Those wisps of gray hair spilling around her massive face aren't attractive. And why does her large, wrinkled neck twist and bob with each word she speaks?* "Perhaps you've seen me come by here on my way to school? I walk with my two brothers and little sister. We moved in at the edge of town—Mr. Sam Fowlerte's place."

"Oh, yes. You're the family who hauled that nasty pile

of trash out of that back yard. Sam told me about you people. He's mighty glad you moved in there."

"Yes, ma'am, we did. We have a lovely garden growing there now. It's filled with fall vegetables …"

"I hear you, I hear you. Now, tell me why I should hire you. How old are you anyway? Fifteen?"

"No, ma'am, I'm seventeen. I'm a good house cleaner." Marta's soft eyes continued studying the woman's facial features. There was an awkward silence. Marta didn't know what to say as the lady continued scrutinizing her, making her feel uneasy. The woman appeared dispassionate and cold-hearted.

"Where did you get that skirt? I ain't seen that pattern since my fiftieth wedding anniversary. Why, that was twenty years ago!"

Marta blushed, knowing very well what she was saying. "It belonged to my grandmother. This is an outfit she gave me last year, before her stroke." Marta ran her hands against the sides of the skirt, hoping to disseminate any wrinkles that she might have overlooked when pressing.

"Sorry to hear that. Who else knows of you besides Mr. Fowlerte and Henry?" The woman twisted in her rocker and stretched her head forward, hoping to get a better view of the young girl.

"I can pick up a letter of reference from my teacher, and from Tom at the gravel pit.

"Um." The woman seemed perplexed. She turned her head to stare up the street, ignoring Marta. Then she turned toward her again. "Very well. Bring me that letter; I might consider you then. But don't get your hopes high, you hear me?" The woman snarled and then turned to look up the street again as if Marta had disappeared.

"Thank you, ma'am. I appreciate this so much." Marta turned and started down the steps when the lady spoke again.

"Call me Mrs. Somerset. I want to know your grades too, so make sure you let your teacher know."

"Yes, ma'am, I will." Elated, Marta bounced out of the lovely yard and ran the rest of the way home, a refreshing wind brushing back her silky hair.

A day later, Marta was knocking at Mrs. Somerset's home holding her teacher's letter of reference.

"Come in," the woman hollered. "Oh, it's you," she said upon seeing Marta walk in. "Shut the door behind you, child. It's cold out there. Come over here."

Marta entered a dark foyer and then followed the sound of her voice. Through the light of a large picture window in the dining room, she could make out Mrs. Somerset. The old lady sat at the end of a long, oval dining table covered with a white lace tablecloth. In front of her lay her Bible, a photo album, and her eyeglasses.

Marta's eyes adjusted to the dimness. Silence surrounded her as she waited for the next command. She looked behind her and admired the lovely foyer. A large, round cherrywood table stood in the middle, and an enormous porcelain vase holding fresh red roses sat on top. Underneath the table, an oriental rug in crimson, ivory, royal blue, and sunny yellow covered the dark wooden floor. Across the foyer was a parlor, complete with Victorian furnishings.

"Come over here and let me have a look at you," The woman curled her fingers up and down, motioning for Marta to move closer.

"Good afternoon, ma'am. I brought the reference letter you requested."

"Just a moment. Let me grab my glasses." The woman reached for her glasses, which sat next to a large black Bible sitting in front of her. "Here, come take a seat near me." She pointed to a silk-covered chair. Marta noticed her large frame sat in a captain's chair with her back against a large china hutch filled with fine porcelain dishes, the finest she had ever seen.

Marta made her way to the chair specified. With a deliberate hand movement, she handed her the letter. The lady grabbed it out of her hands and carefully read it.

"This is a good recommendation. I've known your teacher since she was a child. I was her teacher for many years, and I know she has common sense." Mrs. Somerset placed the letter and her reading glasses on the table, and then she took in Marta's appearance.

Are those the same clothes she was wearing the other day? They look like 'em but smell clean. Oh, that's a lovely pattern on her shawl. Don't like its brown color though. Probably so grime won't show on it. She's in need of clothing. The old woman's eyes missed nothing. She appreciated the fact that Marta smelled of lye soap. *She'll do,* she thought, but she didn't state so to Marta.

Suddenly she began talking, "Mind you, you'll be cleaning my kitchen every day, Monday through Friday. I expect you to dry the dishes after washing them. I want the floor swept and mopped, and the stovetop cleaned. You'll have two hours to finish every day. Is that understood?"

"Yes, ma'am, I understand." Marta felt relieved the work was familiar to her.

"You might as well know now that you'll get paid

monthly at fifty cents an hour. Do you have any problems with that?"

"No, ma'am, I don't."

"Very well. When can you start?" Mrs. Somerset didn't give her enough time to answer before asking another question. "Can you start tomorrow?"

Marta sat still, keeping her emotions of joy from showing. "Yes, ma'am, I can do that. I'll come after school. Will that do?"

"Yes, that'll do. If you can't manage the work, let me know. I won't need two weeks' notice from you if you decide to quit."

"I understand that! I hope not to disappoint you, ma'am." Marta parted her lips in a smile, showing her straight white teeth. She got up to leave and picked up her letter.

"I'll keep that, young lady. I'll call you Martha. You don't mind, do you?"

"No, ma'am, I don't." Marta didn't want to protest now that she had the job. *Maybe later when I get courage over the old lady's ways, I might protest.*

"Very well. Run along. I'll see you Monday. Does school still get out at three twenty?"

"Yes, ma'am, it does."

"Fine! That'll give you ten minutes to get here. I'll show you then what to do. Best you get an apron if you don't own one already."

Marta said, "Good afternoon," and walked out of the warm home and into the breezy afternoon, rejoicing the meeting was over. The old lady could almost intimidate her, but Marta had faced worst fears and had overcome them. She wrapped her shawl tighter and stepped into the yard, thankful she didn't have to work in the fields any longer.

She enjoyed the crisp, cool air of late October, not realizing how any amount of rain would give rise to fog. It would swallow up the town with its long, white fingers curving around the buildings. It would coil up and over the dust-covered homes and around the farmworkers working out in the chilly, damp fields and the pruning trees, or discing under the rotten vegetables or hay stubs. Fog knew no boundaries when it moved stealthily throughout the valley.

A nippy wind seemed to warn that it could be unforgiving. Marta paid no attention and walked home. Her mind was on the money she'd make before December 24. At fifty cents an hour, she hoped to have more than enough to purchase a conifer and perhaps some things they needed. Then she recalled a paycheck coming at the end of October. *What can I do with that small paycheck? I could save it till it adds up for something expensive.*

Though Marta felt a little guilty knowing that her mother needed her at home after school, she knew they were all making sacrifices to uphold the family in any way possible. *Perhaps I'll give this first paycheck to my parents. I'll be pulling my weight financially that way.* She beamed with gratitude for Mrs. Somerset.

Marta got home with daylight still on the horizon, and she entered to find the children finishing their homework. She had finished hers at school, so she began taking out pots, pans, and bowls to fix supper. She quietly mixed ingredients to make biscuits.

Working diligently to please her mother, Marta thought

she shouldn't disobey or upset her now. She wanted her mom to be proud of her. She now had a real job, working indoors. Marta recalled the conversation that had taken place earlier between them.

She had used certain words to justify her insistence on seeking work outside fieldwork. "Mom, it'll be fine. I'll do my homework at school, so I'll use that extra time to take on a job and be home early enough to cook supper. Besides, we'll use any extra money to purchase a Christmas tree and presents for the children. They've earned it for all their hard work." *At least I'm not thinking only of myself.*

"Marta, it's noble of you, but I need you here caring for them and getting supper ready for the family, especially on those days when they can't go with us. We're nearing the end of the grape harvest season and need to catch as much work as possible. The rains have been holding off. We have to keep working," Alice reminded her.

Marta had protested, "I'll make more money in an hour working for Mrs. Somerset than in the fields. Besides, this job is permanent, unlike fieldwork. I can keep the job as long as Mrs. Somerset needs me. As for supper, if Julian doesn't go work with you, he can start it until I come in. I'll finish cooking then." Marta bowed her head, ashamed she'd talked to her mother in that tone.

"Marta, I appreciate your austerity, but honey, you'll overwork yourself."

"I'll get my rest on Saturday. I won't get a Coke at the store or see Henry. I promise!" Tears had welled up in Marta's eyes. She knew her family needed that extra income, but how could she convince her mom she'd be OK?

Alice had sat down to think and then clasped her

hands to pray. Remembering her mother's faith, Marta had tried to comprehend such tenacity.

Marta had stopped praying. *When had this happened?* She had remembered Henry reminding her. Her mind had then gotten back on justifying her job with her mother.

"Very well, Marta," Alice had continued. "But if you get overwhelmed with the extra work, let me know." Mom had hugged her, assuring her she was proud of her. Marta had her permission, even if she didn't say so in so many words.

After knocking on Mrs. Somerset's front door, Marta stood catching her breath, her heart thumping with excitement and her apron hanging over one arm as she arrived for her first day. The apprehension she felt was overwhelming, but it was too late to turn around and forget the job. A roaring engine went by; it was Henry. Marta glanced up just in time to see him wave. Marta waved back and wondered when the lady would open up. After she knocked again, she heard, "Come in!"

Marta opened the heavy door, fearing the unexpected. After entering the dim foyer, she squinted, trying to adjust her eyes to the dimness. She stood still and looked around for Mrs. Somerset. A musty smell stung her nose.

"Come over here, child," Mrs. Somerset said in a raspy voice.

Marta turned to face the voice coming from the dining room, where she saw her employer standing next to the china hutch by the kitchen doorway.

"The kitchen is this way, Martha." She held the door open for Marta to enter the kitchen. "The broom closet is in that corner; you'll find the cleaning detergent there too." Mrs. Somerset pointed to a door in a corner.

While admiring the ample room with its checkered red and white linoleum floor, Marta noticed how lavish it compared against her family's small kitchen. Her eyes landed on the sink, which was piled high with dirty dishes. *How many days' worth are in there?* She noticed the cobwebs in the ceiling's corners. *When was the last time this room was cleaned?* The lady had walked out without further instructions. Marta walked toward the sink and began her work.

After washing the fine china cups and saucers with care, she prepared to scrub the crust off the plates. The delicate beauty she held in her hands captivated her attention. She was careful not to drop them. Though she felt tempted to glance around the well-designed room with its large stove with four regulating heat knobs and the latest frost-free refrigerator, she remained tuned in to the dishes.

"I finished, Mrs. Somerset! I'll be going home now. Is there anything else I can do for you?" Marta waited for an answer while the old lady entered the kitchen and began her examination of Marta's work.

"Very nice," she said as she walked around, taking in the sparkling white stove top and floor. "Thank you for remembering to clean the stove. It needed a good cleaning. My, but it looks new again. Oh, the floor is bright and shiny again. I didn't think a young, frail-looking girl like you could do such a big job."

Marta didn't understand this comment but said nothing. She removed her apron and stepped into the dining room.

Noticing Marta's stare was on the china hutch, Mr.

Somerset exclaimed, "Lovely, aren't they? My husband gave them to me for our fiftieth anniversary. They came from Europe."

"Yes, they're gorgeous. I've never seen such sparkle or anything with gold trim." The sheer joy of seeing such beauty filled Marta with unexplainable happiness, causing her eyes to well up.

Mrs. Somerset noticed the tears but said nothing. "I will mark your work hours on my kitchen calendar, Martha." Her tone was not as raspy or as grumpy as before.

Marta was glad for this change. *What could have changed her attitude toward me?* She speculated, *Perhaps it was my high marks noted on my letter of reference, or maybe my neat appearance. It might even have been the fact that I worked fast and carefully.*

Whatever the reason, Marta was pleased. She hoped to keep the job for years to come. Perhaps she'd even work more hours after graduation. *Oh, graduation,* she thought. *I must work hard to keep my grades up. They're my saving grace with Mrs. Somerset. Can I keep them up with all the work I do?*

Chapter 33

Marta's First Paycheck

"I can't believe my paycheck is so large!" Marta placed her check on her chest as she entered the kitchen and found her mother preparing supper.

"Calm down, Marta," Alice admonished while placing lard into an iron skillet. "Please hand me the potatoes in that bowl, would ya? Marta, are you listening? We need to get supper cooked—everyone is hungry. Did you work late?"

"No. I waited for Mrs. Somerset to tally up my hours and write out my check. Here, look at it. It's my end of October check. I got paid for three weeks only, but now with November, I'll get a complete month's worth of work. Can you imagine how large that check will be?"

Alice glanced at her daughter's check as Marta held it up for her to see. "She overpaid you by eight hours," Alice replied, doing quick math in her head. She stirred the potatoes while Marta placed her check under the cookie jar, washed her hands, and then carefully added drenched chicken into another skillet.

"Well, I believe she paid me for the extra work I did."

"Oh, what was that?"

"I cleaned out her cupboards and kept the front and back porches swept."

"She paid you extra for doing that?"

"Yes, Mom. She's grateful and generous and not that grumpy, greedy woman people talk about." Marta empathized with Mrs. Somerset. It was beyond her understanding why anyone would talk ill of her, making her feel unwelcome in her town. *Why would they say such awful things and shun her?* Marta turned the fried chicken over and stood silently, her thoughts running through her mind.

"Who's been telling you such terrible things? That's shameful." Alice found that incredible to believe. Some church members had added Mrs. Somerset's name to the prayer box, asking blessings for her and her generosity toward the church. "It doesn't sound like her. Marta, I don't know who's been filling your head with such awful ideas, but I want you to stay away from them."

"Mom, remember? I told you Mrs. Waters had. But I don't think she meant it in any mean way. She likes her and sends an errand boy with her groceries to her home every Friday. It's the same groceries; the list never changes. Mrs. Waters finds it odd and says it's 'cause she's tight with her money, but it's nice of her to send the delivery boy."

"Mrs. Somerset can spend her money in any way that suits her. As for groceries, maybe that's all she needs. And as for nice things, Mrs. Waters gets paid for it. Why they speak awful things about her is beyond me. Do you remember how Grandmother became after Grandfather died? She quit cooking and went into a depression." Alice pulled out the biscuits from the oven and had Julian fix a pitcher of tea.

Overhearing the conversation, Julian added, "Mom, I heard that after her husband died, the town turned against her because she quit funding the town's projects, such as paving more sidewalks and oiling the dirt roads. They say she could've afforded it. Instead, she hid away in her home and lost contact with everyone in town—except Henry."

"That sounds like nonsense, Julian. What Mrs. Somerset does is her prerogative, which brings me to defend her. She's been giving offerings to the church. That's a mighty kind act! No one asked her to do that. It came from her heart."

"Is that what the errand boy from the store brings into the church before we begin service every Sunday?" Julian asked.

Marta had only caught half of the conversation. Her mind was filled with paycheck thoughts.

"Yes, Julian, but this is confidential. I don't want to hear around town, how you're spreading her life's story to everyone you meet. Do you understand?"

"I understand," Julian retorted.

"Marta, do you understand too?"

"Yes, Mom. I do." Marta wasn't sure what she was supposed to have understood with her mind being on her paycheck. "Mom, she's a decent and kind lady who means no harm to anyone. She showed me friendship and respect. Do you know how much that means to me?"

"I'm sure that's true. I believe your love and appreciation for her is mutual." Alice saw her prayers for her daughter answered. How the rest would play out, only God knew. The outcome would be good; Alice had no doubts about it.

The cool, cloudy days of November were an obvious reminder that winter had set in the valley. Marta had given every penny of her October paycheck to her parents, who planned on buying coats for the children. With the next paycheck, she planned for Christmas needs. The thoughts of all the purchases she could make made her giddy with delight.

Marta was excited about her kind and wise boss, who confided in her. Marta did extra work to please the dear lady. She remembered the conversation about the townspeople's disagreements with Mrs. Somerset. Marta understood why Mrs. Somerset scowled when sitting on her porch, not to mention the loneliness she felt from the loss of her husband.

Mrs. Somerset would not let the townspeople have the last word on her feelings. She'd sit on her front porch, letting all the pedestrians see for themselves that she was in good health and needed nothing from them. Marta pitied her more but understood that a proud person such as Mrs. Somerset didn't need pity, nor did she welcome it.

After wrapping Linda and Daniel in their warm, new coats, Marta made sure gloves and hats were on before going to school. "Everyone ready? Let's go before we're late." Marta waited for the children to go out before locking the door. Her parents were now at work picking walnuts. She had made sure the gas stove was off and the woodstove's door was shut tightly.

"Come on, let's hurry." Marta stepped down the porch steps where Linda was waiting and held her hand. Their street didn't have sidewalks, but the scattered bits of short weeds were glazed with ice. Once they got to the corner, the sidewalks began. While leading Linda through the icy sidewalk that lead toward school, Marta watched for safety hazards. The school was half a mile away. When they got there, the first thing they did was go into their classrooms and stand on the grate inserted into the green tiled floor, where bursts of warm air thawed the cold off their feet and legs.

This was such a relief for Marta and Linda because the dresses they wore were not long enough to cover their legs. "Why can't girls wear pants? They're much warmer, and these short socks don't keep the chill off our legs, Mom," Marta had said earlier that week. Considering this problem, Marta resolved to purchase cotton tights for her and Linda with her next paycheck. *I'm sure I'll have an extralarge paycheck. I can't wait!*

Mrs. Somerset Falls III

Marta was faithful in her duties for Mrs. Somerset and found the job easy to perform. Every day after school, she walked to her home and performed her chores in amenable ways. She was always careful to leave everything neat and clean in its usual place. Mrs. Somerset was an astute person; nothing went without her notice.

Upon entering Mrs. Somerset's home one day, Marta heard, "You're late!" The lady sat at the end of the dining table having a cup of coffee and cookies, knitting materials laid on her lap. Her craggy face showed no emotions.

"I'm sorry, ma'am. I had to take my sister home. You see—"

Mrs. Somerset cut her short. "Never mind. Just start in the kitchen, will you? I found extra dishes you forgot to wash yesterday, so I put them in the sink. You must soak them for a while before they'll come clean." Her heavy frame sat nestled in the captain's chair as aged, heavy fingers picked up her yarn and needles and began knitting.

"I'm sorry, I don't know how I could've overlooked them." Normally, Marta would have griped about the complaint, but her attitude was improving. She saw it as her fault and was willing to accept the mistake.

"I must cut back your hours for today, 'cause I know your folks won't want you staying late to make up for your tardiness."

"Very well, thank you." Marta didn't protest but was glad she would not be forced to stay late. There were chores at home she needed to get done before her parents returned.

"You'd better get started—talking won't get it done!"

Mrs. Somerset had a disconcerting habit of saying what was on her mind. But Marta inferred nothing out of it because Mrs. Somerset wasn't serious with her aloofness or vehement-sounding voice. What counted was her true kindness, and Marta realized that.

"Oh, Martha," Mrs. Somerset spoke in a kinder tone.

"Yes, ma'am?" Marta replied, stopping before entering the kitchen.

"Thanks for washing the kitchen towels. I didn't know you knew how to run one of those newfangled washers." Mrs. Somerset didn't look up to see the expression on Marta's face.

If she had, she'd have seen it was one of gratitude. *Using modern equipment in Home Ed back home paid off. It shows I'm not ignorant. I was worth hiring*, Marta thought proudly. She felt she had landed the job by her own talents, strengths, and people who'd recommended her.

She overlooked the woman's snide remark and took it as a compliment. "You're welcome," she said, smiling. Upon entering the kitchen, she heard a gagging sound coming from Mrs. Somerset's direction.

Without wasting a moment, Marta ran to check on her. Mrs. Somerset's red face was a fearful sight. Marta knew she was choking on an object. *Probably a piece of cookie.* Marta knew very little first aid but had done a maneuver on her sister, Linda, when she was choking on a cookie last year. It had saved her life.

Marta made a fist with her right hand and gently pounded her back. With her other hand, she pressed her stomach in, then released it. She continued until the old lady spat out a large piece of cookie. Her breathing returned along with her sallow skin color. The gagging and coughing spell was over. "Are you all right, Mrs. Somerset?" Marta picked up a napkin and wiped her mouth and chin with gentle strokes.

"Child, I am so thankful you were here. You knew what to do for me." Mrs. Somerset reached for Marta's hand. She wanted to hold it, her way of saying thanks.

"Are you OK, so I can return to my chores?" Marta noticed the tiny smile on the woman's face as she nodded in affirmation. She was glad her old friend was breathing again.

After walking into the kitchen, Marta began filling both sides of the sink with hot water. She washed, dried, and put the dishes away without banging them, and she finished the rest of her chores with an occasional check on Mrs. Somerset. Her caring attitude was clear. After being satisfied the old lady would be all right, Marta prepared to leave.

"I'm finished, Mrs. Somerset. I'll be going if you're sure you're feeling better. Or is there something else I can do for you before I leave?" Marta removed her apron and noticed Mrs. Somerset had finished her afternoon snack. "Can I get you another cup of coffee before I go?"

"No, child, thank you. Do you have a phone number I can have to call you in case I have an emergency?"

Marta kept a straight face, not showing any attitude with rolling eyes or a smirking lip corner upon hearing the question. The phone was only for her parents' use and for emergencies arising while they were out. Rather than snapping back with this answer, Marta answered politely. "Yes, I'll give you my home phone number. Please call me if you need anything; I live only a block away."

"Thank you for helping me today. Sounds like my

bronchitis is getting worse. It always does during the wintry weather."

"Do you take medicine for it?" Marta looked around the dining room for medication.

"Well, I take medicine, but I've run out of that. I need to have it refilled."

Marta saw the opportunity to help her friend. "I can pick up your prescription, if you'll have your doctor call the pharmacy. I'll pick it up after school. Is that OK with you?" She expected to hear another snide remark, but there was none. She stood still waiting for an answer, and suddenly the woman spoke.

"Why, that's very kind of you, Martha. It's not part of your chores, but I'll give you extra on top of your wages for running such errands for me."

"That's unnecessary, Mrs. Somerset. Call your doctor and tell him to make it a rush order too, so the druggist can have it ready for me to pick up." Marta thought for a moment. *The purple, deep-set eyes explain her sleepless nights; her bronchitis is the reason for it.*

"My, you are a little bossy. It's a noble type of bossy though." Mrs. Somerset chuckled, her voice sounding squeaky and tired. "I didn't think you had that trait in you, child." Mrs. Somerset continued laughing, showing her yellowed, wasted teeth.

"Your laughter is sincere, Mrs. Somerset."

"Yes, I'm satisfied having you work for me, dear. It's been awhile since I was this happy."

Marta felt ashamed, because there had been a time or two she thought she was a mean, snooty old lady. Upon noticing her deep stare, Marta glanced away, fearing she might guess her thoughts.

The ill-conceived judgment Marta held for the old lady had melted away. Any condescending or rude remarks Mrs. Somerset might have made were forgiven. Marta knew the dear lady suffered from loneliness, which caused her depression and perhaps agitated her bronchitis. *The death of her husband must have been detrimental to her health and social life.*

Mrs. Somerset's disposition was similar to Marta's in that they were both stubborn. She appreciated and depended on Marta. Seeing her as a daughter and loyal companion was important to her. She appreciated the girl's honesty, loyalty, and hardworking ethics.

Marta had also changed her attitude, but only for her employee. She felt sorry for the lady and wished she could do more for her. For now, she would support her in any way she could, because she understood depression and how devastating it could be. In her case, however, she had her parents' support to help her overcome it. They'd also helped lift her out of her times of fears and doubts. Marta stopped her thoughts as she heard Mrs. Somerset speaking.

"Yes, like I said, you're a noble kind of bossy."

"No, ma'am. It's not quite that way; it's just that I have to be a little bossy for my brothers and sister. When a situation arises, I don't consider myself and how my actions might appear to others. I consider those who need me first. It's an old habit with me." Marta wasn't bragging, in her opinion; she was being honest.

"Well, I think it's a mighty decent trait," Mrs. Somerset repeated, picking up her knitting again. "Don't forget to pick up my medicine tomorrow after school. I'll call my doctor in the morning. Thanks for your help."

Smiling tenderly, Marta said, "Good night," and went out the front door. She sprinted down the porch steps, a thin veil of gray moisture stung her face. It had rained a few days ago, and the valley had wasted no time in bringing on the enemy to the farm laborer. The opaque landscaped appeared mysterious and foreign to her, but Marta's mind would rather focus on the blessings she would give Mrs. Somerset.

She had finally done something Mrs. Somerset appreciated. Marta knew not to take it for granted. There was no assurance her attitude would remain docile. Meanwhile, Marta thought of tomorrow, elated. She'd do something extra generous for her—something that possibly nobody else in that town had ever done for her before!

After stopping outside the gate, she listened for oncoming vehicles and, when hearing none, hurried across. The chilly dampness penetrated her skin. Marta wrapped her scarf tighter around her neck, but it did little to warm her face. She was glad her new wool coat kept most of the chill off her body.

Marta made it home in time to help Julian finish cooking supper. He didn't speak to her when she entered the kitchen, so she kept quiet. He'd fried potatoes and onions, opened cans of peas, and drenched the chicken. Marta needed to fry it. *Julian is changing for the better. Hopefully he'll keep going at this pace.* Marta was proud of him.

After supper, she sat in front of the woodstove, her body clad in a heavy robe and her feet embedded in her house slippers. While sipping hot cinnamon tea, she thought of Mrs. Somerset and her health. *How long has it been since she's had company over who were aware of her illness? Does she have any relatives who come by to check on her and keep her company in her old age?* Marta had not thought of such questions before and felt neglectful of her friend. She made a plan to learn more about her using tactful means. It was time for her to pray again. Her new friend's name was to be first on her prayer list.

Chapter 34

Mrs. Somerset: A Friend and Confidant

The grumpy old lady had truly changed her attitude toward Marta. She'd become kinder to her. "Martha, thank you for picking up my prescription."

"It's no problem. And please don't pay me for running this errand. I'm honored doing this for you."

"You're such a blessing to me in more ways than I can tell you. Please visit me anytime, dear."

"I will, thank you." Marta spoke without fear. She had found another friend who was friendly and pleasant. She didn't mind her frankness because the old lady was honest and meant well.

"Child, you remind me of myself in my younger years. I was obstinate, yet considerate too. Eventually, I used these traits to better my home and community. I also appreciate your coming to work early and going home late—more than you know. You ought to know I have noticed the extra things you do for me. They mean a lot to me."

"I worry for you. It's not the money I'm after but your well-being. Is there anybody who comes by to check on you?"

"No, I have nobody out here. No one in town either,

except Henry. He comes by to pay his rent on the acreage he uses to raise alfalfa, and he brings me a basket of fruit every time."

"What extra things do you mean?" Marta couldn't see where she was doing more for Mrs. Somerset.

"Well, you take out the trash, clean out the pantry shelves and refrigerator, and sweep the front and back porches. The canned goods are in alphabetical order, and you've taken more upon yourself without expecting extra pay. That's noble of you."

"Oh, it's nothing. I've got time to do it."

Marta's reply impressed Mrs. Somerset. "You're humble and hardworking, child. I've only seen those traits in myself and Henry."

Mrs. Somerset always spilled tears when seeing the niceties Marta performed for her without expecting compensation. One cold afternoon before Marta left, she went into her closet and pulled out many of her fine clothes that were too small for her.

"Martha, can you or your family use these clothes?" Mrs. Somerset asked in a humble tone.

Marta stopped wrapping her scarf and looked up to see Mrs. Somerset had brought out three large paper bags filled with clothes. "There are also two coats I received for Christmas three years ago. They were gifts from family back east. They're beautiful, but the styles are not to my taste. Besides, the colors are not fitting for an old lady like me." Mrs. Somerset pulled out a wool coat in bright red. "Here, try this on. I wanna see you in it."

"Oh, my! Are you sure you wanna give them away?" Blushing, Marta giggled with delight as she pulled on the coat. "Oh, it's beautiful. But I don't want you to feel obligated to me!"

Mrs. Somerset hugged the girl. "Thank you for all you've done for me. You're a sweet girl." Tears welled up in her tired eyes. She wished she could do more for the young girl.

Chapter 35

Mrs. Somerset's Fear of Death

Mrs. Somerset stared pensively out the dining room window. Marta had just brought her some hot tea and sugar cookies she'd baked at her house on Saturday. The woman said, "It's not rational to be afraid of death, Marta, but I am. I have outlived my husband, and I survived off of funds I received from selling some farmland here in the valley and in San Francisco."

Marta stood still and politely listened, offering no advice. Normally she was very talkative and opinionated, but she felt this was not the time for chatter. Mrs. Somerset continued in her rambling.

"I'm a puzzle to myself. I don't know what I have accomplished for myself, much less for the town, or its residents. I wish I had time to do grand things for them, but I feel my time is running out, and I'm getting too tired to do much. Martha, do you think I have wasted my time on nothing?"

Mrs. Somerset didn't wait for Marta to answer but continued speaking her thoughts out loud. "The absence of my husband in my life left me with complete emptiness. I became a hermit in my own home. Looking it over now,

I regret it. I have wandered from the friendship of the townspeople. Death is a frightening thought, you know; I don't want it to come near me. Why am I afraid of it? You're too young to know the answer, but perhaps your father knows. He's a wonderful preacher—that's what I hear. There is an answer; pray I receive it before I pass, so that I may die in peace." Tears flowed down her heavy cheeks, a sight Marta had not seen before.

"Mrs. Somerset, I recommend you quit thinking of such issues. Besides, you believe in God's Son, Jesus. You have nothing to fear knowing that. I see your Bible in front of you every time I come here; you must read it. Let's change the subject and talk about happy things, like Christmas. There's no point in talking badly. You'll get yourself worried and saddened and maybe bother you're breathing. I've heard how you helped this town plenty. There's no need to think of yourself in those terms, or to think less of yourself."

"Martha, the fact is since you've been helping me and showing me your kindness and love for me, I have come tried to come to terms with death, though it's been a hard concept to accept. I pray I haven't failed God. Though I fear it, I'm more tired of waiting for death to come. I've enjoyed your friendship greatly, but child, one day you'll go on with your life. If I'm still alive then, who will come and be as cheerful, kind, and thoughtful as you've been to me?"

I'd like to tell her I suffer from depression, but that might discourage her hope in my strengths. It's been through prayer that I've fought it off. Come to think of it, I don't do enough like I used to do. But it was God who brought me joy, renewed hope, and a job through her.

It wasn't by my talents and strengths that got me this job. And she's been my anchor in getting me back to my prayer life.

"Mrs. Somerset, I want you to know that God loves you too. If ever you want to come to our church, please call me. I'll drive the station wagon down here and take you." Marta hugged her sincerely. "Now, let's talk Christmas. What will you be doing then?" Marta hoped to get her mind off her fears of death. *But will the dear lady feel like talking of something cheerful?*

Chapter 36

Mrs. Somerset's Meaning of Christmas

"I know what I'd want to do—something I haven't done since my childhood days." Mrs. Somerset spoke excitedly, almost tipping her cup of tea onto her cookie plate. Meanwhile, Marta put on her apron and wondered what could be so exciting to her friend.

"I want a tumbleweed for my Christmas tree. How would you like to help me search for one that's just right?"

"What's that?" Marta asked, thinking she had misunderstood.

"I want a green tumbleweed, fresh from the fields."

Not showing her shock, Marta answered, "If that's what you want, that's what you'll have. I know a weed field filled with them." She hugged her dear friend and received a warm hug back. It was heartfelt, mutual love.

"I quit celebrating Christmas after my husband died. It's been lonely without him. I didn't feel up to reveling by myself because it's a lot of hullabaloo. Yet it's pleasurable with him and company," the woman said pensively. There was a longing in her eyes with which Marta empathized. She felt sorry for the lady and wished she'd known her longer.

A tumbleweed Christmas tree.

"Yes, one more Christmas in my lovely home. I'm not feeling up to it this year either, but with your help, I'll manage. I want this house cheerful looking again, with bright lights twinkling, my mother's ornaments hanging, and the dining table laid with many delicious treats. Wouldn't that be grand?" The old woman's eyes lit up with excitement; it was a sight Marta hadn't seen before today.

"Mrs. Somerset, you get your plans together. I'll be happy to help." Marta said with a smile. The glee she felt for her friend was astronomical.

"I enjoy my solitude, but I want one more go at it."

As silence came upon Mrs. Somerset, Marta thought of her chores. "Perhaps I had better get to work."

"No, not yet. Have a seat. I want to ask you a question that's got me full of curiosity. Why do you work so hard? You know you only have to do the things I've requested of you. Are you looking to get a raise?"

Marta clasped her hands together and set them on her lap. Without hesitating she answered, "I didn't think I was working hard. I do these chores at home. It seems natural to do them the same way here, otherwise I'd be doing half-baked work."

"I'm sorry, what sort of work is that? I've never heard of that expression." Mrs. Somerset set down her cup and ate the last of her cookie. With compassion, she looked into Marta's soft, sad eyes and sensed something was wrong.

"Well, half-baked means my work isn't finished properly because of my lack of planning. I must plan my duties in order so they are completed properly." Marta hoped she was explaining it well. "Regarding money, I need only so much and not any more. I have a few needs, so it won't take much to settle those. I'm grateful to God for helping me procure things."

Marta paused and looked at the floor before adding, "There is one thing I want." She was ashamed she had to mention her most heartfelt desire.

"Speak up, Marta. I can't hear you."

"I'm sorry. There is something I want. It's an evergreen tree. I wish to save enough to buy one this year." Marta released the tight hold on her hands, which were damp with perspiration.

"Is having a conifer for Christmas that important to you? If so, why?"

Marta didn't hesitate in answering the question. "A tree is important to me because it has special representations, giving me hope for my family. On Christmas Eve, my dad and brother Phil harvested a cypress from the nearby mountains back home. We'd decorate it and then sit around it singing Christmas carols and Christian hymns. Then we'd share old memories and refreshments. Before retiring to bed, we'd read the nativity story and pray. We were together. It's not the same today. Phil is in Korea, and my grandmother is no longer with us; she's staying with our aunt on account of her stroke."

"It sounds as if you were all extremely happy."

"Yes, we were. We had our faith. It was a simple lifestyle but satisfying, even with the homemade gifts we received. The tree is a symbol of my hope, joy, and unity with my family." Marta smiled while looking at the Bible on the table.

The bliss on Marta's face was clear. *There is nothing hypocritical about her*, Mrs. Somerset thought. *I can see she's sincere by her demeanor and tone of voice.* Though satisfied with the young woman's answer, it concerned her that Marta placed the holiday's meaning in evergreens. *Has she forgotten its significance?*

"Martha, I was childless, but I see you as the daughter I wish I had birthed. If you don't mind, may I give you words of wisdom from an old woman's perspective?"

"Go ahead." Marta sat up, making herself comfortable and ready to hear her advice.

Mrs. Somerset cleared her throat before speaking. "When I was growing up, we were quite poor and didn't have a tree. My family focused on the meaning behind Christmas. It was the time to remember God's love for us by sending his Son, Jesus, who brought salvation to humankind. You mentioned the nativity seen earlier. Well, I do know about Him. But sometimes we need someone to remind us of God's love for us, and that we celebrate His Son's birth on that day. Don't we?"

Marta thought she had inferred this point but had somehow overlooked mentioning these facts. She assumed Mrs. Somerset understood she knew of Jesus too. Then Marta realized what she was saying.

Mrs. Somerset picked up her teacup, but before taking a sip, she said, "It's true that conifers are a symbolic representation of these ideas. But we need to remember that Christmas is a time to celebrate the Christ Child's birth. He is the reason we have this marvelous season of celebration and time of remembrance of everlasting life." She stopped talking and sipped her tea.

"I know what you mean, but I focus on the fun parts of it—the refreshment preparations, pulling out stored decorations, and sitting around it and enjoying each other's company."

"My parents did the same as your dad and brother, but

before they began that practice, because we were too poor to go up into the mountains and haul one home, we used the weed kind." Mrs. Somerset stared blankly out the window.

"Oh, I'm sorry!" Marta felt ashamed knowing how blessed they had been. "But eventually you had a conifer?"

"Yes, yes! We had one every year, after Dad's business flourished. But before that we always had a small, round bush."

"But … how, where?" Marta couldn't get the words out of her mouth.

"My daddy would take us out to a meadow near our home. We'd look over the tumbleweeds before choosing."

"Tumbleweeds?" Marta heard herself ask out loud.

"Yes, tumbleweeds. We'd haul home the tallest we could find. Daddy and my brother prepared it outside while we girls fixed snacks. I remember those days fondly! I loved seeing our tumbleweed decorated. Mother prepared popcorn, and we children strung it for a garland. Then we'd hang it around the 'tree.' It was lovely."

"I'd heard of them being used in Arizona. It was part of the tradition in certain areas." Marta felt humbled and ashamed for thinking only of herself.

Mrs. Somerset placed her cup on the table and cleared her throat before speaking. "My mother had ornaments she'd brought back from England when she was a child. They were from the time of the Victorians. There were tin figures shaped as fruits. There was something else she called Christmas crackers."

"I've never heard of such ornaments," Marta said excitedly.

"They were lovely!" Mrs. Somerset remarked with memorable fondness.

"Originally, they came in crimson and gold. There were also some in silver and cream tissue, with sweets and wise verses wrapped inside them. Though the treats and verses were long gone, Mother kept the lovely wraps and restuffed them with homemade candy on Christmas Eve."

"How simple and beautiful it sounds," Marta marveled.

"Yes, it was. Christmas is what we make of it. It's where your faith takes you. Rather, it's a journey of faith. No one can take your faith away—you're the only one who can make it stop! It is what is in your heart that matters."

Marta thought of her comments for a moment and felt she'd had enough faith but had never examined how much was in her heart.

"Child, are you all right?" Mrs. Somerset noticed the change on Marta's face, and then she picked up her conversation again, glad Marta was understanding. "Sometimes memories can be the best, as long as we don't let self-pity build up in us. That is a cruel taskmaster. I feel sad only when I miss my husband." In her melancholy, Mrs. Somerset spoke as if to herself. She yawned, hoping it'd ease the pain out of her tone. "Tell me, Martha, what else do you want besides a tree? Is there something enormous you wish you could do for this town? If you could, what would it be?"

"I don't have to think about that because I've already given it a lot of thought. I'd like to have a library in Somerville. I have grown to love this town and wish it to be the best town around. As soon as I graduate in June, I wanna start that project. There are several ideas that might work. I'll see when I get to that bridge."

"That's a mighty big effort for such a young girl. Who can help you with that?"

"Henry will. He's been kind to me and has become my best friend."

"Remember these words as best you can, child: if you start from a bad place, then you'll end in a bad way, but if you start from a good place, you'll end in a good way. Starting to build your position in this town with the library is a good place."

Hearing this statement perplexed Marta, but she knew that one day she'd understand its meaning.

"Why don't we call it quits for today? Go on home and get some rest. Whatever work remains can wait until tomorrow." The old woman yawned again and got up from her comfortable chair.

Marta wanted to complain. She stared toward the kitchen door, wondering about the work that awaited her, but she dared not defy Mrs. Somerset.

"And one more thing, I hope you get your wish and find the right tree for your family." She didn't say it but was happy to have had the fortune of meeting Marta. She hoped she'd soothed the young girl's fear of not having a conifer for Christmas. "Good night, child. I'll see you tomorrow after school."

After buttoning her coat, Marta opened the front door. She then stopped as if forgetting something and turned toward the dear lady. "Mrs. Somerset, thank you for sharing your memories of Christmas with me. I'm glad to hear I'm not the only one who's had Christmas tree concerns." With a calm look, she smiled at her friend and stepped out into the stinging, icy wind. *What sort of tree will we have on Christmas Eve?*

Chapter 37

Marta Dreams of a Tumbleweed Christmas

"I can't believe people used tumbleweeds for Christmas trees here in the valley! That's what Mrs. Somerset said. Mom, remember people used them back home too?"

"Yes, I do. My parents used them. I'd almost forgotten about them till you mentioned it." Her mother pulled a casserole out of the oven and set it on the table. The family immediately started piling steamed spinach and biscuits onto their plates.

"But, Mother, she's so rich. It doesn't seem possible this could have happened to her family. Do you think she was serious?"

"Oh, yes, she was serious. Maybe they weren't always wealthy. It doesn't matter what we use. The important thing is that we are all together as a family and that we haven't forgotten why we celebrate Christmas." Alice spoke softly. The glow of the oil lamp was barely able to light the table and its contents. The electric lights were shut off so they might save a few coins on the electric bill.

Outside, frigid wind blew across the house, causing loose boards to squeak. The family ate in quiet solitude until Marta brought up the subject of the tumbleweeds again.

"Marta, Mrs. Somerset never forgot the true meanin' of Christmas, and so can you. If it's a tumbleweed we must use for our tree, then it'll be so. We must remember that we are celebrating Jesus's birthday. That's the point to this holiday," Alice reminded her.

"Let's finish supper and get you all to bed," Dad interrupted. "It's been a long, bitter day in those walnut fields."

That night Marta went to bed with thoughts of tumbleweed trees rolling in her mind. She couldn't shake the thought. In her restless sleep, she dreamed of fields filled with tumbleweeds—tall and short, wide and thin, fresh and dried-up. They were all around her.

The dream began this way. "You won't be disappointed, children. We'll have a grand Christmas!" Mom blurted while pulling a gray cap over her hair, which tied back into a bun.

"We'll find a dandy one!" Dad exclaimed. "Children, get ready to go for a walk. Mama, see to it they get on their coats. The fog might have settled on the damp weed field. I'll get my work gloves and ax." He went out the back door and left the children to get ready.

They had never seen their dad so happy. Marta had just put on her red checkered coat, a hand-me-down from Mrs. Somerset, when she heard Dad in the front yard hollering, "Let's go!"

The family marched to the field, the fog sitting high above the wild weeds. The blue-gray light of late afternoon penetrated the thick mist, appearing as doomsday light. While standing at the edge of the field, they could see green and brown tumbleweeds. The brown ones had dried during the summer and had rolled in or been carried by hot, dry summer winds. Then they saw Dad move into them. He looked all around slowly and deliberately, ax in hand.

"OK, y'all stay there. If you see one you like, let me know. I'll go chop it down." He spoke as if it were a tree. The children trusted his wisdom and waited patiently.

Marta appeared bewildered and almost petrified at seeing the looks on their faces. *Do they comprehend the ordeal at hand? Maybe we shouldn't have let them see the "tree" until decorated and looking like an actual Christmas tree,* she thought woefully. Nevertheless, she had to trust her parents. They knew what they were doing.

"I see a nice one over there, Dad!" Julian hollered. "See it? It's in the middle of those small green ones to my left." He pointed to its direction.

"I do, Julian," Dad bellowed as he walked over to a large, round tumbleweed. It was half as tall as he, with a lovely blue-green hue. Dad chopped it down and tied a rope to the tiny trunk. Then he dragged it toward the family. "All right, I got it. Let's go home, clean it up, and decorate it!" Dad beamed with pride as he pulled the round object behind him. "Stay clear of it—it has prickly ends," he shouted into the white haze now settling on the wet ground.

When they were home, Mom said, "OK, children, pull out the decoration's box. They're in the hall closet. I'll give this tumbleweed a good dusting." She moved with excitement in her steps.

"Mom, it doesn't have a trunk. How are we going to get it to stay in the pail?" Linda asked worriedly.

"Wait, everyone. Linda's right. Let me cut a few small branches around its bottom, and then it'll be ready," Dad said, pulling out his pocket knife. After removing the lower branches, he waited for Mom to remove the kerosene lamp off the corner table in the living room.

"John, you and Julian can place it on there." Mom and the girls stood back, giving their dad and Julian space. Then there were oohs and aahs as the family watched its tip almost reach the ceiling, amazed it looked like a Christmas tree. Marta could understand why Mrs. Somerset missed them.

"Here, John. Place this tin star on top. Do you remember making it for me when we first married?" She hugged him firmly, displaying her appreciation for him. "Boys, place the glass balls on it, would you? Girls, let's go make popcorn and hot chocolate. Julian, when you're finished with the ornaments, please sweep up the floor." Their mother moved into the kitchen, followed by the girls.

Before long, with the popcorn popped and the hot chocolate poured into the old, mismatched mugs, they sat down to string popcorn.

"What do you think you'll get for Christmas?" Julian asked Linda.

"Oh, I'll get a doll. Remember I gave mine to Grandma when she got sick?" Linda picked up some popcorn and ate it methodically.

Marta hoped Linda would get a doll, but then again, it had been a struggle for her parents to stretch every dollar. They were hoping to save money for a down payment on a home, with perhaps a few to send Grandma, so they had said. Marta figured to expect meager gifts for Christmas. Then she thought of Mrs. Somerset's last words.

"Mom, may I repeat something Mrs. Somerset said to me about Christmas season?"

"Go ahead, say it." Alice put the popcorn pan in the sink and waited for Marta to speak.

"Jesus is the reason for the season. We should look forward to remembering Him and the everlasting life He brought to us. We're reminded of this by the evergreens we use. He brought everlasting life to everyone. It's a time of peace and goodwill to all people.

"I believe that," Linda replied.

"Me too," Daniel added.

"Well, I guess I do too!" Julian scraped the floor with his shoe as if something was sticking to the heel.

As they were finishing stringing popcorn, something unexpected happened. The door burst open, and in walked Phil. He was carrying a large green duffle bag over his shoulder. A green military cap sat over his smartly cropped hair, and a bushy black beard covered his youthful face. At first look, the children figured it was a Californian Santa Claus. Bewildered and spooked, they sat motionless, eyes wide at the stranger.

In an instant, the man hollered, "It's me, Phil! Don't any of you remember me?" The family froze. The great shock left them speechless.

"Phil!" Dad finally exclaimed. "Boy, you came home! What a gift we're getting!" He rushed to hug him.

Marta and the family woke up out of their amazement and ran to greet the young soldier. They were beyond ecstatic. His presence meant the world to them. The first thing Phil saw was the tumbleweed trimmed with colorful glass balls and the tin star he remembered.

"Oh, hey, that's a splendid idea. Why, it's beautiful!" He didn't laugh or poke fun at their makeshift tree.

Marta hugged him the most for not saying any derogatory remarks about it.

Their mother rushed to hold him. "Seeing you in person is the best present any of us could ever have received!" She cried and then laughed, hugging her son repeatedly. "Would you like some hot chocolate and sugar or persimmon cookies? You being gone for a year and a half, I don't know what you've become accustomed to." Marta

"Thank you. I haven't had homemade cookies since last I was home with y'all." He took one of each and ate heartily, almost swallowing the treats before chewing them.

While the family asked Phil questions, Marta admired the tumbleweed.

"What are you thinking about, Marta?" he asked, seeing her yearning eyes on the Christmas tree.

"I was wondering who would've thought these roving weeds would be good for anything this wondrous."

Marta woke up feeling content for dreaming the dream. She was excited about the prospect of finding a lovely tumbleweed bush for Christmas. There would be two of them, one for her family and one for Mrs. Somerset. *Who knows? They might be prettier than conifer trees. They will make memorable Christmases.* She couldn't wait to find the perfect weeds—but would she find them?

Chapter 38

Phil, Coming Home

Will the Military Affairs Committee approve furlough requests for the soldiers? Phil wondered.

This committee had been given slight notice for leave requests, therefore limiting their time to study the proposal. Phil prayed for a way to get home for Christmas. He'd been there for over a year and, like the other soldiers, was drained of all energies.

Hopelessness continually crept in, but Phil kept it at bay through prayer. He'd spent too many days out in the cold, living in tents and only occasionally getting a hot meal. He was homesick, more than he could have imagined.

"How many brothers and sisters do you have back home?" Phil heard a young man ask while washing his mess kit.

"I have four, two sisters and two brothers."

"I have two brothers myself. They're younger than I am. I worry about them an awful lot. Mom's raising them by herself. I send my paycheck to her. I hope she's been getting it." The young man sounded depressed and tired.

"Yeah, I know what you mean. I worry most for my

sister Marta. She's seventeen and has to help care for the younger ones. One of them, Julian, is troublesome. He causes her and the young'uns trouble. I worry he's too much for her to handle."

"Can't your parents control him?"

"They don't know about his meanness; he sweet-talks them all the time. When he strikes the children, he does it behind my parents' backs and then threatens to beat the kids more if they cry or tattle. Mom and Dad believe he's innocent." Phil thought of Marta and how well she took care of Daniel and Linda. He was glad for her wisdom and boldness to stand up against Julian. But compared to his present condition, Julian was a minor concern. "I have placed the family in God's hands though. Things will work out for them."

The bitter cold stung his face as he got ready for bed, weapon ready for instant combat. He took out his Bible and read Psalms. In his situation, it filled him with hope and joy.

Phil wrote one last letter to his family before blowing out the kerosene light. He slept uneasily as usual, dreaming he had gone home for the holidays.

He dreamed he went home the hard way. The dream showed how he got caught in gunfire while defending a ridge up north. Snow had fallen around them, and a full moon revealed human movement in the valley below. His unit could not be sure who they were.

They planned to allow them to come up halfway before calling out for identification. Meanwhile, the men were to be quiet and lie still. The wait seemed an eternity until they heard a foreign language and laughter moving up the hill. They waited a little longer.

It was the enemy! The soldiers opened fire. Enemy gunfire struck many of the Americans, including Phil, who'd been shot in the leg. Still, he continued firing. The skirmish lasted for a few hours; it was dawn by then. Triage took place, and the injured were evacuated to a safe zone.

I guess this means I'm going home? Phil thought of his injury. He needed confirmation of what the future held and looked worriedly at the doctor by his bedside.

"Yes, young man. This means you'll be going home." The young doctor seemed to have read his mind. "You're very lucky; you'll be leaving this afternoon. We've had men waiting to leave for a month. Some needed severe operations. We've managed and are doing a great job of keeping them on the mend." The doctor hoped to ease Phil's mind.

"Doc, thank the good Lord—and smart people like yourself," Phil said appreciatively.

"Yes, I can say amen to that too. We've been able to save many lives, and now they get to go home and finish recovering. You'll be going along with them. I'll send someone in here to get some information from you." The doctor patted Phil on the shoulder and walked away.

Phil was so thankful his family had given him their new address in California. He could give that to the officer in charge of medivac evacuations going to America.

Afternoon could not come too soon. Phil had his duffle bag brought to him. "The plane taking you home will leave within an hour. Somebody will be by to take you there," the orderly advised him.

When he was wheeled into the plane, Phil cried with

joy at the prospect of seeing his family once again. Once on board, his tired body took a long, peaceful nap.

When he woke up, he found they were airborne. He looked around and saw many other injured servicemen. *How long will it be until I see my family?* He could hardly wait to get home.

Chapter 39

Julian Has Remorse

"With Marta's misfortune, she probably won't get a check for November!" Julian mocked, not stopping to make a move on the game board he and Daniel were playing.

Linda, sitting next to them, listened. She liked the game of checkers but didn't care for Julian's rude words.

Daniel tried ignoring him and tried concentrating on the game, but it was difficult. The remark infuriated him. "I know better than to say such a mean thing. Why can't you leave her alone? She's not hurting you. She's working for all of us." Daniel loved his older sister and didn't enjoy seeing her hurt.

"Yeah, leave Marta alone, you bully!" Linda snapped. "You're always picking on her. I wish you weren't our brother."

Marta overheard the conversation between the children, and she got up from the sofa and went into the kitchen. "Julian, that's enough out of you. I am getting a paycheck, so you mind your own business. I got one for October, didn't I? And didn't I give that money to Mom and Dad so they'd buy you a coat? You might appreciate that."

"If I were bigger, I'd hit you, Julian." Daniel made a fist and aimed it at him.

"Oh, yeah? Y'all think I'm nothing but a peon around here. It's always, 'Julian, bring in the firewood. Julian, watch your little brother and sister. Julian, go pay these bills.' I mean, it never ends with someone giving me orders. I wish Phil was back so he'd take back his chores." Julian sulked, crossing his arms on the table and laying his head on them.

"Let's stop quarreling. Daniel, I never want to hear you wanna fight anyone. Let's not lose our tempers over Julian's immature ways. I'm restraining myself too. Julian, you know we all carry our fair share of work around here. You're not the only one working."

Julian sat up but hushed his mouth. The words Linda had spoken hurt the most. "Well. Linda, I am your brother, and I always will be." Julian loved his little sister and was sorry he'd hurt her feelings, but he wouldn't say so because it hurt his pride. Instead, he pushed the game board away from him and bowed his head.

"Listen, everyone. I can see Julian is sorry. Let's apologize to each other and get to bed. The town meeting should've ended. Mom and Dad will be back shortly."

Marta got the children to bed and then got herself ready. While standing in front of the bathroom mirror, she brushed back her hair. Julian's mean words would not keep her awake. *Everything will turn out well. I'll go back to work after the weekend, and before too long, I'll have another paycheck from Mrs. Somerset.*

On Sunday, the family was in church. Alice was on the piano, warming up. The children sat in the front pew, their usual place, and waited for the service to begin. The box boy from the store came in, walked up to Alice, and handed her an envelope.

"Mrs. Somerset asked me to request prayer for her. She's not feeling well today." After delivering his message, he walked out somberly.

Marta heard him and got up to speak with her mother. "Mom, may I go check on Mrs. Somerset as soon as the service ends?"

Alice saw the earnestness in her daughter's eyes. "Please do, and let us know how she's doing."

"Marta, do you mind if I come with you? I'd like to help if I can." Julian had gotten up from his seat and had been listening to the ladies. He seemed moved by something.

Wondering what was up with him, Marta decided to trust him. "Sure, you can come along. You're gonna behave, right?"

"I will. I promise." He lifted his right hand and went back to his seat.

His generosity was unusual, but Marta wanted to trust him, to believe he was changing for the better. He also needed to trust her. She realized this and had pity for him. Soon she would see what was the matter with him. *The visit will do him good, but I doubt he'll go through with it.* Marta was right. At the last minute, he bailed out. *I'm glad he changed his mind; he's too much of a risk to bring along. Why did he want to tag along, anyway?* Marta hoped he had no evil intentions behind his show of care.

Chapter 40

Marta's November Paycheck

"Marta, be prepared to get another short paycheck for November," John warned his daughter.

"Why is that, Dad? Mrs. Somerset hasn't mentioned that to me," Marta said, feeling faint.

"You might be off on Thanksgiving Day. My boss warned me to be prepared not to work during that time. He said that's how employers bless their employees. It's a tradition here in the valley."

"Mrs. Somerset might not know that!"

"I'm just warning you in case it happens to you. Don't count too much on your check being full pay."

"I hope it is, 'cause I wanna give you money to buy a new fixture for the living room ceiling light. I'd like it to be well lit in there so I can do my homework in the evenings."

It was November 25 when Marta entered Mrs. Somerset's home. "Mrs. Somerset, I'm here!" Marta hollered into the dark, musty house. The shades were drawn in the foyer, the parlor, and the dining room.

"Over here, Martha. I'm over here." Mrs. Somerset sat in her usual place at the dining table. The lit overhead light revealing it to be an Austrian chandelier, an ornament Marta had seen only in magazines.

"How are you feeling today?" Marta inquired, sweeping cookie crumbs off the table with her hand.

"Doing much better, thank you. How's your family? Are they getting ready for Thanksgiving?"

"Yes, they are. It'll be a small dinner, but we're thankful after all."

"Here, Martha. Take this envelope and give it to your parents. It's my Thanksgiving present to them."

"Oh, Mrs. Somerset, you don't have to do that."

"But I want to. It will bless me. Here, take it and put it away." Mrs. Somerset handed Marta the envelope.

"Thank you for your generosity. You've been very kind to us. I'll get started in the kitchen. Oh, would you like to come over for Thanksgiving?" Marta stopped before entering the kitchen.

"No, child. I enjoy my solitude in my home with my memories."

"Do you mind if I bring you a Thanksgiving dinner plate?"

"I'll enjoy that. Thank you for your thoughtfulness, child. I need to tell you now: I'll be giving you the holiday off to spend with your family."

"Oh, I don't mind working, Mrs. Somerset." Marta didn't want her pay shortened. She was hoping to get a large check for November. She had stopped being pushy with her parents and siblings and didn't want to be pushy with Mrs. Somerset.

"Oh, I insist, child. You need to be with your family on that day. I'll pay you for that day."

"But, Mrs. Somerset, that's too much money for doing

nothing. For me to take it and not have earned it isn't right."
Marta wasn't expecting this gift. Her parents had taught her
this ethic. They'd learned they had to earn their living, and
getting money for not working wasn't part of their ethics.

"Child, it's OK. Otherwise, what am I going to do with
my money when I die? It's better to share it while I can."

Marta thought of her words. "That's nice of you. I
appreciate it. Thank you." She turned and entered the
kitchen with its scents of mint dish soap and pine-scented
floor cleaner, the envelope tucked in her pocket. The
kitchen was still fresh smelling from the cleaning she'd
done on Friday.

November payday was one week away. Marta trembled
with mounting excitement at having such a large paycheck
to herself. She rejoiced at the thought of purchasing store-
bought presents for everyone in her family and for Mrs.
Somerset. Soon, she'd start examining the local shops for
items her family needed but hadn't been able to afford,
including buying an evergreen, which would soon arrive
at Jake's store.

Though she was elated in her good fortune, sudden
doubtful thoughts burst her joy. *What if the tree shipments
don't arrive on time? If the mountain snow is thick, the
trucks won't make it through. And what about my paycheck?
Julian might be right—I might not get a paycheck. But what
could go wrong?* Stress got the best of her. She went into the
bathroom to pray. *I'll rely on you, O Lord, for help. Leaning
on You will calm my fears. You wouldn't let these things
happen! It can't be Your will. Don't let it be. Amen.*

Chapter 41

Marta's Hope and Vision

"Julian, quit taunting Marta about her paycheck," Alice admonished her son. "I've heard enough. I'll cross you off my Christmas gift list if you don't stop it!"

Marta sat in her room, listening to the conversation. She'd get her check on time and make Christmas purchases. She'd check Jake's store as soon as possible for conifer shipments. With Christmas so near, she opted for anything her family could afford. She consoled herself with God's provisions, because she'd found her happy place. *God assigns an outcome to every matter. Whether it's what we desire or not, it's for our own good and future blessings,* Marta thought.

She would see Mrs. Somerset on Monday, the first of December, hoping to work for her through most of the month and the rest of her senior year. Having a long-term job gave Marta more hope than she'd had since their arrival to Somerville.

Marta planned on taking tea bags to Mrs. Somerset in hopes she would enjoy the brand. It was the last box her mother had brought with them from Arizona. It was a special blend of local Arizona herbs.

The weekend would be short, as were all weekends before Christmas. Marta placed the box in her purse on Friday evening so as not to forget it on Monday. On Sunday, her family sat quietly in church waiting for the service to begin. When the church members arrived, Marta planned on moving to the bench behind her where she'd finish her school reading. It was a diversion she'd handle with care.

Graduation means my future. A straw bag Marta had brought along was large enough to conceal her schoolbook. Since she'd been working for Mrs. Somerset, she'd been doing her school work during her dad's sermons. *Graduation will come soon enough; it'll be too late then to catch up on achieving passing grades.*

Her hope for her future gave her new visions, thanks to Mrs. Somerset's kindness and wise counseling. It also seemed to have cleared up her depression, which allowed her to remember her prayers and chores daily.

The church members seemed to be running late, so Marta sat next to her siblings, waiting for the diversion to begin. Meanwhile, she thought of the hard work her family and friends had done on the church.

Removing the stale carpet was hard work, but we exposed beautiful walnut planked flooring. And the broken benches received a few nails and a coat of varnish. Thank God for the elder who tuned the piano, and thank you, Julian, for staining and varnishing the pulpit. How nice the inside looks with new plaster and paint, and the outside too.

Marta was also thankful for the hedge plants, which were anonymously donated. Henry and Jake donated tree roses and had taken time from their work to help plant them. Tom spread crushed gravel in the parking lot. The church looked brand-new, attracting many new members.

Marta was excited for Monday, payday, the day she would also gift Mrs. Somerset with the tea.

After church, Marta and Linda went window-shopping. Marta carefully browsed through shops open on Main Street. She had a general idea of her family's needs. She found a lovely, twenty-inch doll at Jake's. It was the last one left, sitting behind some infant wear boxes. Its plastic blue eyes caught Marta's attention, and the shiny, curly brown hair reminded Marta of her grandmother's locks before they grayed. Linda couldn't reach to see, so Marta kept quiet about it. She would return after payday and purchase it for her. It would be the first of many purchases for her family's gifts.

Later, she would purchase wool hats for her mother and dad. A football for Daniel and Julian to share would be next. After realizing Julian wouldn't share, she decided she'd get him a basketball. This would eliminate any arguments.

"Oh, Mom," Marta marveled at Sunday dinner, "it's the most wonderful thing to have hope and a vision. I'm different now, and I feel I got out of a deep mire. I'm excited all the time now; whether things work out or not, God has me in His plans. It takes all worry out of me." Laughing pleasingly, Marta looked up to see her bewildered family watching her.

Alice was glad her daughter was changing for the better. Even this afternoon, after returning from window-shopping, Marta started fixing dinner without complaints.

"Oh, I can't forget. Tomorrow is Monday, when I'll go see Mrs. Somerset. I'm going to give her that last box of tea, Mom, if that's all right with you." Marta took a bite of chicken she'd fried herself. She was more than satisfied with herself.

"That's fine by me. She's blessed the whole family and deserves more than a box of tea." Alice was proud of her daughter. The transformation she'd gone through was an absolute miracle. *What's next for her? Only God knows.*

Chapter 42

Surprise at the Drug Store

"Hurry, get out of the bathroom, Linda. We will be late for school. It's foggy this morning," Marta ordered her younger sister.

After opening the cupboard door with the goal list, she crossed out everything that needed doing for the morning and had now been completed. In the afternoon after school, she'd get Mrs. Somerset's prescription.

Making sure the permission slip was in her purse along with the box of tea, she gathered up her siblings, who were wrapped in their winter clothing and waiting for her.

"Afternoon, Marta. What can I do for you?" Mr. McMaster asked with a somber face, putting away prescription bottles he had just filled.

She wondered what the matter was. He *seems distant and aloof.* "Well …" She stopped talking. In alarm, she moseyed to the counter. "I came to pick up Mrs. Somerset's prescription. Here's a note from her giving me permission." Marta dared not pry into his business. *It could be personal.* She stared out the glass door, wondering about the abundance of pedestrians and cars honking outside.

Mr. McMaster looked up from reading the note with startled eyes. He realized she didn't understand what was going on in town. "Marta, you haven't heard?" He wondered the best way to tell her. He began with, "I was loyal to Penelope Somerset." He paused, unable to complete his sentence.

"What do you mean, 'was'? What's happened to her?" Marta wanted to run to Mrs. Somerset's house to find out what was wrong, but taking the prescription to her was of prime importance. She turned to the door again and noticed the street was still busy with people and slow-moving cars, one following another. This was unusual for the normally quiet town. "What's going on, Mr. McMaster? I've never seen so many people milling outside, and such traffic!" Marta pulled her scarf around her neck when the door opened with a bang, a gust of frigid air hitting her face.

Henry rushed in. "James, I need to use the phone. You know it's for that emergency!" His voice sounded frantic as he moved past Marta, not noticing her or even saying hello.

She had never seen Henry looking so frightened as he dialed the phone, his face insipidly pale. She dared not ask what was happening. She scooted away from the stir of people entering the shop and realized something awful had happened.

"Mr. McMaster," she said in a scared voice. "What's happening?"

Her eyes filled up with tears. "You need to go home right away. Stay home awhile." He turned his body around to face the prescription shelves, hiding his grief from the public.

Marta trembled with fear. The mingling voices of the crowd were filled with dismay, anger, and fear, which told her something was terribly wrong. While standing in a corner of the store, she waited for Henry to get off the phone. She stared at the crowd and sensed their panic and confusion.

When Henry quit talking, Marta made her way to him. "What's happening?" Marta could only think to hug her friend, whose weeping alarmed her. She didn't know he could hurt so much and pulled him in closer. It was a somber moment for everyone. She realized not to pester him with conversation but to give him his space.

After awhile, above the crying in the shop, she heard someone say, "I can't believe Mrs. Somerset died. They say it was asthma. No one knows. They found her hobbling up the street gasping for air."

"It was awful," someone else said. "Just a terrible way to go. It had to have been painful!"

Marta dropped to her knees, placing her face in her hands. "No!" she hollered above the noise. "Mrs. Somerset can't be dead!"

By now, Henry was talking to someone next to him. Upon seeing Marta's grief, he knelt and held her. "It's true: Penelope Somerset passed away a few minutes ago. The ambulance took her to the hospital in Tuleville about five minutes ago. It was holding traffic back—that's why the street was packed with cars." He continued embracing the young girl, wishing their friend hadn't passed. *Dear Lord, help Marta, my best friend. She needs You more than ever in her sorrow. But why did You take her, Lord, before Christmas?*

Chapter 43

Marta's Paycheck Is Gone

Marta ran home crying. Her friend and employer, Mrs. Somerset, had passed away. There was no way to ask for her paycheck. She dared not ask anyone how to go about getting it. She'd rather lose her paycheck than show insensitivity.

Upon arriving home sobbing great tears of grief, Marta heard her mother speak. "Marta, you've heard the bad news, then? We heard about it at work. They released us early. Honey, I'm sorry for your loss." Alice couldn't console her heartbroken daughter. She hugged her and let her cry all she could.

"Oh, Mom," was all Marta could say, and then she sobbed some more.

"I know you came to love her dearly. But think of it this way: she isn't suffering anymore. She's at peace with God." Alice didn't know what else to say to her grieving daughter, so she held her until Marta moved into the bathroom to finish crying.

That night, Marta went to bed without supper. She couldn't eat; her aching heart felt torn in pieces, and her stomach ached deeply. She slept uneasily. While tossing and turning in her bed, she dreamed of her friend leaving on a long journey, but before going, she handed Marta a small Christmas tree and said, "Enjoy it for me!" Marta saw her leaving her beautiful home, the town, and the foggy valley as she climbed gleaming stairs reaching the clouds of a peaceful summer.

Though Marta was penniless, she waved to her friend as she went farther up. She was now out of her pain and smiling down at Marta. Seeing her this happy was more important than the material things that had been foremost of importance, like the conifer tree and gifts for everyone in her family

Marta woke up feeling sad, lonely, and grief-stricken to the point she didn't want to leave the house. She remembered her dream and realized she felt that same way: material things were not as important as her friendship with Mrs. Somerset.

Alice worried for her daughter, though she'd ended her bouts of depression. She gave her permission to stay home from school in hopes this would keep the severity of symptoms grief could create to a minimum. Unbeknownst to her and the family, Henry had reminded the town council of Mrs. Somerset's generosity in her younger days. He had convinced them to proclaim the week a time of mourning the old lady. The businesses and school closed on the day of her funeral.

The day after Mrs. Somerset's funeral, Marta walked by her house. The white picket fence surrounding the lovely yard was just as beautiful as when she first came by to apply for a job. Marta stood a long while like the townspeople who had also come to mourn her, bewailing the loss of their dear friend.

Marta wished she could go inside the precious home and have one last look. After buttoning the buttons on her coat, she stood bracing the frosty December morning. Memories of her old friend flooded her mind. Tears filled her eyes, and the overflow ran down her frigid cheeks. Then she remembered the lovely furnishings inside the charming home; the Victorian furniture, the lavish kitchen, and the china hutch with the gorgeous, imported, porcelain china, which all spoke of her friend's fine taste. *Perhaps I'll find out to whom she willed it,* she thought. *I can then ask if I can come in for one last look, for memory's sake.*

Marta turned and walked in the field's direction at the end of her street. Upon arriving there, she stood and looked through a thin veil of fog that had settled on the weeds. She looked over the enormous amount of tumbleweeds. *How lovely they are, green and brown, tall and short. Well, God, You have this. I'm not worrying about Christmas trees anymore, come what may. Father, I'll accept whatever You have in store for me and my family.*

She remembered Mrs. Somerset's last words to her: "There's no hypocrisy in you, Martha. I like that about you."

Father, let me not be hypocritical, but thankful, truly thankful for everything. I love You, Lord! Marta walked home in a somber attitude, thankful for the time she had spent with Mrs. Somerset and for the wisdom her friend had imparted to her. She was the catalyst causing a change in Marta's attitude and viewpoints of Christmas. The woman had forced Mart to wake up to reality, accept it for what it was, and desire to live with its blessings or shortcomings in contentment. It wasn't being materialistic that mattered; it was family, God, and what one left behind as one's legacy for others to enjoy.

Marta walked home, meditating. Her mother met her at the gate. "Hi, honey. I saw you pass by here earlier and thought I'd come out and meet you."

"Thanks, Mom. I went for a walk to think about Mrs. Somerset. She loved her town and its people. But what a time to die. I'll miss her, but I will accept whatever else God allows, and that includes our Christmas. He knows best, right, Mom?" Marta held her mother's waist as they walked up to the house. "Mom, this is not the end of my life. I still have you, Daddy, and the children to think about. May God help me! He will, won't He?"

"Yes, dear. He has everything under control." Alice tightened her hold on her daughter's waist as they stepped up the porch steps. *Everything is going to be all right. It has to be, right, Lord?* she prayed silently.

Chapter 44

Christmas Surprise

This December, Christmas was to be nonexistent for Marta's family. She hadn't heard her parents discuss holiday plans. She would not give in—not now, after trying so hard for so long to plan their Christmas season. "God is the God of the midnight hour," her mother always said. Marta would use her faith and believe in a miracle. She had behaved herself, been obedient to her parents, been kind to the townspeople, and helped with the house chores while her parents worked in the fields. She had no fears of wrongdoings and felt she should practice her faith. It was there for the taking, if she'd only believe.

Mrs. Somerset's passing had put them and the townspeople in a grave predicament. No one was in the mood for celebrating, yet for the sake of the children, they'd do their best. The town put up red and green wreaths on the streetlight poles, stores decorated with pine boughs and red bows, and homes had their wreaths hanging on the outside of their doors. Somebody had gone to Tuleville and brought back several fresh pines because none were to be found in Somerville. But those were soon sold out.

Though Alice and Marta were not in the mood either,

they worked at getting in the season's spirit and began decorating their home. John and Alice continued making homemade gifts and wrapping them in butcher paper. Though their hearts were not in their work, they didn't stop. The melancholy echoed from home to home the best it could, considering the sad circumstance.

"Mom, we're all better off for having known Mrs. Somerset. She was a wonderful person. It's because of her that I changed my disposition and my outlook toward the residents." Marta took a handkerchief to her eyes. "She was kind to them even when they ostracized her. Did you know she paid Tom to spread gravel on some of the dirt roads? And she made him promise not to tell who was paying him for the work. Some residents got out to help spread the gravel. This made me realize these people are as ordinary as those back home. They too are caring, yet selfish to a point; curious, yet standoffish hateful, yet amiable to those who are fair; and loving, yet fearful of the stranger. I realized they're humans, and I'm not better than they are. It's by God's good grace that we are good. May God forgive me my blindness."

Alice had never heard her daughter speak such truths. *When had this occurred?* she wondered. *God works in mysterious ways.*

On December 24 after breakfast, John gathered up the family for a meeting. "As y'all know, we are goin' to be needin' a Christmas tree. Well, last night a brilliant idea occurred to me. We'll go to the field at the end of our street and choose a lovely tumbleweed for our Christmas tree, one that we can agree will fit in our home." He smiled at the children as if this was one of his most brilliant ideas.

"A tumbleweed?" the children murmured.

"Children," Mom answered, "it'll look splendid! I pulled out the Christmas box. Our ornaments are in there, including the string of electric Christmas lights Aunt Ellen gave us last year. You'll find the paper stars you cut out from last year too. I'll pop the corn, and we'll string it for garland." With euphoric enthusiasm, Alice moved with urgency into the kitchen.

"Mom, I don't want to be rude, but there's no electricity in the living room. The string of lights won't work in here. I don't know if they even work. We've never had 'em on because we didn't have electricity back home." For some reason, Julian had been polite to everyone. They'd all noticed his civil attitude. But he was right: the electricity in the living room was off.

"That's fine. We'll still place them on the weed, make it look prettier." Alice smiled and patted his hair, something she rarely did.

Marta couldn't break her dad's heart and openly frown at his idea. Besides, this meant there was no money for buying a conifer. But she went along with it. "Sure, that's a grand idea!" She looked at her siblings, smiling harmoniously.

She noticed the disdain on their faces, but upon seeing agreement on her face, they also smiled and appeared to appreciate Dad's idea. As second eldest and the most responsible child in the family, she had to do her share of instilling hope.

That evening, the young family prepared for the Christmas Eve dinner. While Mom and Marta prepared the evening meal, the children strung popcorn. Dad and

Julian walked to the empty weed field, found a large green tumbleweed, and dragged it home.

Upon entering their home, they smelled apple cider brewing with cinnamon sticks, persimmon and sugar cookies, roasted chestnuts, and hot coffee. A small turkey and hominy pork stew scents mingled with the other enticing aromas. It smelled like their old home.

After cleaning and preparing the weed, John stuck it in a pail filled with sand and set it on the corner table. The children rushed to decorate the spiky green bush with popcorn garlands; glass globes of red, blue, and white; and the string of electric lights.

The evening celebrations had just begun when Henry knocked on the door. "Merry Christmas, folks," he declared, walking past the door Julian held for him. In his arms he held presents for everyone and a store-bought fruitcake. The family and acquaintance sat in the small living room enjoying each other's company. When Marta entered carrying a large tray, Henry got up to take it from her, set it on the coffee table, and said, "Marta, please have a seat here." He patted the space next to him.

The dim light of the kerosene lamp sitting on the wall shelf created a serene mood, with the colorful tumbleweed casting its aura of hope into the comfortable room. It was peaceful and filled with joy, making them satisfied with the humbleness of their home. Pleased with sincere gratitude, Marta took a cup of cinnamon tea and passed it to Henry, who declined it graciously.

"Julian, please put another log in the woodstove," Alice said cheerfully, feeling contentment with the outcome of their Christmas celebration. The family ached to have Phil and Grandmother join them for the festivities. Yet

Alice accepted their absence without complaints. Noticing Henry was not helping himself to tea, she asked, "Henry, can I get you a cup of coffee instead?" She got up to get the coffee.

He didn't answer, his mind being heavy with sorrow. "I'm sorry 'bout the conifers, Marta," he said disappointedly. "Jake was goin' to order 'em this year. I didn't see any sense of both of us ordering 'em. It's a small town, and I thought of how last year's trees dried up and had to be thrown away. I lost money on 'em and didn't wanna repeat that mistake again. I'm sorry, but I never thought Jake would forget to send in his order. I heard Tom went to Tuleville and brought a few to sell at his shop, but those sold out within the afternoon." With regret, he bowed his head. He couldn't look into Marta's sad eyes and see her devastation after her many weeks of searching for a conifer.

"Henry, don't you fret yourself. We have this lovely tumbleweed tree before us. We're happy with it. It's not the tree that makes it special but our family, friends, and the real reason behind the season, Jesus. Besides, I didn't have money to purchase a conifer tree." Marta smiled at him and patted his arm.

Henry smiled back, his face blushing. "I'm proud to call you friends!" he exclaimed, looking around at the people he had come to love.

"Well likewise, son," John said. John sat in his rocker next to Henry, and he shook Henry's hand. Suddenly, as if he'd changed his mind, he pulled him in for a hug. He hadn't finished speaking his thoughts when there was a knock at the door.

"Who might that be at this hour, and with this thick

fog?" John asked, walking to peek out the window. "Why, it's a stranger I've never seen in town before." He looked with alarm at his family as he opened the door. They heard a man introduce himself as Mr. David Hopper, Mrs. Somerset's lawyer from San Francisco.

"Mrs. Somerset's lawyer, here? But why on Christmas Eve?" The surprise on Marta's face showed she was dumbfounded. *What can this mean? It can only be more bad news. Why can't they wait until next year?* Marta wiped moisture off her forehead with the palm of her hand. Was it the warmth of the room that heated her head to this extreme? She began to shake with fear. *No, I will not be afraid. God has this matter in His care. There's a reasonable excuse as to why this man is here. I've started my life in this town in a good place, and surely my life will end in a good way.*

Chapter 45

Mrs. Somerset's Last Blessing

The sterile man waited for John to speak. "May I help you?" John asked the stranger holding onto his hat as the blustery wind blew past him and into the warm home.

"Yes. Are you Marta Rodrigo's father?" the man in the dark suit asked.

"I am. Marta, come here," John commanded while opening the door wider to the stranger. "Won't you come in?"

The stranger walked into the small living room and noticed the tumbleweed tree decorated with unusual decorations. He'd never seen popcorn garland or paper stars hanging on a bush. He kept his thoughts from showing on his face and waited for Marta.

She can't be in trouble! John stood wondering what this stranger wanted with his daughter. John knew Marta was a dutiful daughter, but having a lawyer in his home asking for her was a daunting occurrence.

Paleness covered John's face as the fear for his daughter bled his strength. He was a man of integrity and expected the same from his family. He couldn't imagine what this visit meant. "Marta, did you hear me? Come here!" He spoke in a harsh tone, indicated he wasn't pleased with the gentleman's presence during this time of celebration.

Marta timidly approached the man, who extended his right hand toward her to shake it and reintroduced himself to her. "Please excuse me for this late inconvenience. However, I'm following my client's wishes that I see you before Christmas. I couldn't make it any sooner. I'm sorry it had to be on Christmas Eve."

Marta stood stunned, waiting for further instructions from her dad.

"Where are my manners? Would you like to have a seat?" John offered.

"Thank you. It would be convenient if we could sit at the table. We need time to ourselves. That includes Marta and her mother. Would that be possible?" The man pointed to the kitchen.

"Yes, that'll be fine. Julian, take care of Daniel and Linda. Keep them in the living room until we're finished."

"Can I help?" offered Henry, standing up.

"I think the children will behave themselves, but thank you anyhow," Dad declared as he walked the lawyer into the kitchen and offered him a chair next to Marta.

"As you all know, Mrs. Somerset passed away. She completed her will in November, shortly before she passed, and made sure I knew where Marta Rodrigo lived. You're the young lady who made a big difference in her life."

"I didn't think I was doing anything special, only what I would've done for anybody," Marta muttered, fearful of the man dressed in a fashionable gray, wool suit and a burgundy tie protruding from his white collar. His dark, shiny hair was slicked back with pomade, and dark-rimmed glasses took up most of his face.

He pulled out some papers from his briefcase and set them on the table. "Here is Mrs. Somerset's will. She has bequeathed some things to you and your family and instructed me to do a reading of it before you. Because you are underage, I need your parents to be present, but also because they're included in her will." Mr. Hopper began reading the will under the glare of the kitchen's light bulb.

After a long while, the reading was over. Marta and her parents sat quietly, astonished and unable to ask questions or think how this would affect them.

"Why, I don't understand. She hardly knew me and our family!" Marta said after a few minutes.

"Did she leave an answer why she wanted to bless us like this?" John asked bewildered.

"I can tell you she meant to bless a family who'd brought her back to the truth and had given her happiness in her last days."

"But how?" Marta couldn't imagine having done anything extraordinarily nice for her. She'd only shown the kindness and patience her dad had taught as the fruits of the Holy Spirit. She expected nothing from her dear, old friend.

"I can tell you she appreciated you not turning against her. You accepted her as she was, unlike some town residents who caused her to become a recluse. They didn't realize she wasn't shunning them but was in deep sorrow for the loss of her husband. They misjudged her and turned away from her friendship."

Alice pulled up her apron to her face and cried, not understanding either, but understood God did. Nothing He did astonished her, but this was an unexpected and enormous blessing of receiving Mrs. Somerset's wealth.

What they'd heard sounded incredible, too remote of an idea to accept. They would not be in need of money anytime soon. Alice couldn't comprehend why. Then she thought of Mrs. Somerset's generous tithes to the church and the visits she and John had secretly made to her home, ministering to her needs.

Meanwhile, the children and Henry were silent, except for some metal clanking sounds coming from the living room. Marta poked her head in after hearing the sounds and checked on the children. They were quiet, and she wondered what they were doing but said nothing. She saw Henry standing on a stool working on the ceiling light. *My,* she thought, *God is full of surprises for us tonight.*

"Now, if you, Mr. and Mrs. Rodrigo, accept the conditions stipulated in this will, you may sign these papers. Marta, you will sign after them here, please."

Marta held back her tears. She felt she had not lost a friend but gained an eternal benefactor whose last desire was to bless her young friend for the rest of her life. Through Mrs. Somerset, Marta had learned not to judge those who came through as overbearing and formidable, because underneath there could very well be a person with kind intentions. And though the dear lady hid her true characteristics from Marta, she had divulged them at the end through her kindness to her family and the will.

Marta came to realize that she didn't need to fear people's attitudes, realizing that like her friend, who'd been hiding behind a facade of formidable courage, cold hardness, and what appeared to be total indifference, there would be others just like her. Yet all along, what the dear lady was hiding was her suffering and longing to be with her husband.

Over the years, Mrs. Somerset had shared her wealth with the town to make it suitable and convenient. Her goal was to make it more suitable for the next generation, even for newcomers. *She cared. I'm so ashamed of myself. Dear Lord, forgive me,* Marta repented. *I let people influence me on my views of her, but You helped me fight through them. You let me show Your love to her, even in my times of distress. Thank You, Lord. I see Your hand upon this town.*

Mr. Hopper spoke, bringing Marta out of her reflections. "Here are the keys to her home and automobile. Mrs. Somerset expected you and your family to live in her home and continue God's work in this community. The home will always be in your name, Marta, but as long as you have your parents and siblings, you'll be expected to let them live in it until your siblings marry and move on. Your parents can move into the cottage behind the house when they're ready, or when you start your own family."

Marta wanted to cry out loud. She wanted to speak face to face with God and tell Him what a miserable person she'd been. She wanted to apologize personally. *Father, forgive me for ever having thought wrongly of Mrs. Somerset. Don't let her have died with regret for not having spent Christmas with me.*

"The acreage is yours too, Marta," the lawyer said again, bringing Marta out of her reflections. "You can rent it out to a Mr. Henry Barnes, if he so desires. He can continue to grow alfalfa or use it for whatever purposes suit him, as long as he has your permission."

She wondered whether Henry had heard but could only hear Linda talking.

"The trust fund she left you is at the local bank, under

your name. You can make withdraws with your parent's permission. I'll release it to you when you turn twenty-one and have completed your high school education. As you heard, there's also an account set apart for your parents and the church at the bank."

"We didn't know Mrs. Somerset was so wealthy. God rest her soul," Alice said humbly.

"She was a bighearted person," John stated. "I knew that when she started tithing the church."

"I didn't realize she was tithing so much," Marta announced.

"No, it's true. That's how we could afford supplies to repair the church. Every one of her dollars went to that project. Also, she rededicated her life to the Lord."

John blinked back the tears. He thought about how God had answered their prayers in such mysterious ways.

"Oh, here's one last thing. She left you this note," Mr. Hopper said, handing Marta a pink piece of paper. Then after putting some papers into his briefcase, he got up, put on his coat and hat, shook their hands, and turned to leave. Marta read the note.

Marta,

Use these bountiful blessings for the Lord's work. There's enough money for you to one day raise a large library in your town, Somerville. Thank you for bringing me back to Christ. Your belief was in your kindness and generosity. You had faith all along.

Your friend,
Penelope Somerset

Marta recalled one last conversation with Mrs. Somerset. "Marta, I think this year I'll have a tumbleweed Christmas, just like my family had when I was a youngster. You'll help me pick one from that field near your house, won't you?"

Marta would miss her friendship more than she would enjoy the inheritance. After standing up from the table, she walked toward the tumbleweed tree now lit up with small, colorful lights. "Thank you. I dedicate you to, my dear friend." She patted it as if it understood.

Chapter 46

Marta's Merry Christmas

Where did this bright light come from? The electrified living room was a wonder. "What happened here?" Marta wiped away tears and placed the copy of her will in a token box sitting on a shelf next to the stove pipe. "Henry, did you fix that light fixture?"

"Good job, son," John announced. "I haven't had time to fix it."

Alice held a tray of persimmon and sugar cookies, and she joined the happy group. The house, filled with wonders and blessings for the night, was more than they had expected for Christmas Eve.

Marta looked at her family tightly fit in the small room. It was their home for now, a place she'd long for, but it was missing Phil and Grandmother.

"Henry fixed the light fixture while you were in your meeting! It made the wall sockets work too," Linda said as she laughed with glee.

"I think we'll be having television nights from now on," Julian said with dignity.

"Look how bright the hanging ornaments appear now!" Daniel raised the palms of his hands and placed them on his head as if cheering the display before him. "And look at those lights on the tumbleweed!" He chuckled. "None of us saw this blessing coming! Thank you, Henry."

Over the joyous noise, they heard another knock at the front door. Julian got up to answer it. The porch light revealed a short, wrinkled-face woman with a long nose. A dark oversized coat hung down to the woman's ankles, and a dark heavy shawl hid her gray hair. Behind her stood a tall, gaunt man.

"Phil! Grandma!" Julian hollered, recognizing his relatives. "Come on in! Hey, Mom! Dad!" He hugged their grandmother before she had passed the threshold.

John, standing behind him, couldn't seem to move or close his mouth at the shock of seeing his mother.

"John! Stop gaping and invite us in. It's freezing out here!" Grandmother said in a raspy but loving voice.

"Oh, my!" he cried. "Alice, come look who's here! Folks, get in out of that wet fog!" He gently helped his mother enter and hugged her. Then he noticed the young man behind her leaning on crutches in an army uniform. "Phil, son, don't stand in the cold. This home is yours too. Come, get out of that nasty weather!"

"Phil! Grandmother!" Daniel and Linda cried, running to greet the couple.

"Phil?" Marta asked in disbelief. How could it be? The family hadn't heard he was coming home on a furlough for Christmas. *God managed this miracle too!* It took her a minute to realize what the rest had realized.

The overhanging military coat and hollowed cheeks told her Phil had lost a lot of weight. He was three inches taller and used crutches to stand. Grandmother appeared to have healed from her stroke, though she was shorter and more wrinkled than Marta recalled. She was speaking better than Marta remembered and was walking on her own strength.

"Take it easy, young'uns," Phil said with a burst of hearty laughter to the younger children. He turned and looked at Marta, who stood against a wall; her shock at seeing them freezing her feet.

Alice came running out of the kitchen with arms stretched out. "Mother, you're here!" she said to her mother-in-law. "And Phil, you're as handsome as ever—a bit underweight but looking great!" She held them both and sobbed loudly.

Phil's attention turned back to Marta. He was beyond belief at how mature and ladylike she appeared. She was older and prettier than he'd expected.

Still stunned at the sight before her, Marta could only stare into Phil's brown eyes. *Has God answered all my prayers?*

While she stood frozen, Julian turned to Phil. He hugged him again, tighter than before, almost squeezing him. He cried into his shoulder. "Phil, I'm sorry I've misbehaved. I don't know what got into me."

"Whoa, boy, it's all right! I've forgiven you." Phil patted him on the back, not knowing what this was all about.

"I feel so ashamed of myself for having been so spiteful. I resented your leaving. I'm sorry. But I've changed. I'm glad you're back." Julian held so much remorse that if he apologized a million times, it wouldn't be enough for him. Then in a shaky voice, he said, "Phil, can I get you a chair and something to drink?" He hurried to get him a chair and some coffee without waiting for a response.

Phil saw Julian as he'd never seen him before. "What's

wrong with him, Marta? He's not that arrogant, brash, ill-mannered sneak I used to know. I don't think he can apologize enough for his misbehavior either." Phil limped closer toward Marta and waited for her to recover from her shock.

Finally, she cried, "Phil!" and hugged him as a sister ought to hug her brother.

"So, what's wrong with Julian—or should I say, what is right with him?" Phil waited for a reply.

Marta released him. "I'm not sure. He seems to be full of regret for his wretched actions. He's humbled, sorrowful, and filled with remorse. I don't get him," she replied, wondering herself. *Has Julian changed for the better? Forever? I didn't see this change coming!* She was in dismay over his remorse. "What's this regret about, Julian?" she asked in disbelief.

"Marta, I've behaved wickedly to you and the family. I'm so sorry. We've had a hard go of it all, but God came through for us, mostly for you. I'm glad things worked out as they did. He answered all our prayers!" He spoke humbly, with some words getting caught in his throat.

Phil overheard the conversation. *It sounds like a lot has gone on while I was gone.* He placed his crutches against the wall and took the chair. "Well, sister, I'm so glad to see you and the family. You've managed Julian, haven't you? Does that mean I won't have to worry 'bout him anymore? I'll be home from now on—no more army for me!" Phil was happy to hear the voices of his siblings and looked forward to resuming his duties as assistant pastor. His faith had never wavered. He looked at Marta and saw a young woman who was capable of holding her own fights.

Marta heard and saw sincerity in Julian's apology. "There's no elusiveness in his conduct tonight. I believe he means what he's saying," Marta whispered to Phil.

"Well, it looks like he's seen his ways and the brevity of his misconduct." Inwardly, Phil praised the Lord for this miracle. "And he's so cordial. I believe he has changed, but I hope this new conduct isn't temporary."

"I can tell you, Phil, I've forgiven him. I'm giving him the benefit of the doubt though."

Julian went into the kitchen to bring out some more cups.

"I can imagine what you went through with him. Must have been tough." Phil took a sugar cookie and bit into it. "Mmm, my favorite."

"I can tell you he's not as callous and deceitful as before. He'd help me with chores even when he didn't feel like doing them. He never backed out and helped with the family's maintenance. He might've grumbled and taken his time getting things done, but even so, he was there beside me, ready to help."

"I'm proud of him." Phil stated. "And he never winced or complained as he'd done so often before, huh?" Phil sipped his coffee. "That's quite a change for him."

"No, he didn't, and he's lost his flair for petulant outbursts!" Marta could hardly believe she'd said that.

Henry stood quietly by the tumbleweed tree, hands in his pockets, observing the joy on his friends' faces. Seeing their happiness was the best gift he'd ever received.

"Henry." Marta extended her hand to him, grabbed his elbow, and pulled him closer to her. "I want to introduce my brother, Phil." With pride, she rocked on her heels as the two young men shook hands.

They began a conversation, and Marta went into the kitchen to bring out more snacks and drinks. The family, grateful for the blessings before them, talked for a long while exchanging stories and enjoying snacks. Marta introduced Henry to Grandmother and felt an instant bond between them. In their revelry, they had forgotten their Christmas Eve supper.

Then they heard Linda say, "Hey, everyone, let's eat so we can open presents afterward. I got a doll; I heard something squeak when I lifted the big box." The whimsical child ran to the table, picked up silverware wrapped in red cotton napkins, and passed them to everyone.

Marta praised the Lord silently. *God has restored our family, home, church, and companionship with each other. We have many friends in our new town. His blessings have not been elusive, and the enemy did not gain a foothold on us. As Genesis 50:20 states, "But as for you, you meant evil against me; but God meant it for good, in order to bring it about as it is this day, to save many people alive."*

The End

About the Author

Beth Torres Johnson is a minister and retired high school teacher and has also served as chaplain, home and hospital teacher, and substitute teacher. Her work roles have led her to interact with students ages five to eighteen years old. She has also assisted her husband, Reese, of forty-four years, with missionary work.